# Matagam Pagwa #1

## Defender Down
## and
## Bleak Realities

## Colin F. Carter

Susan Kuelbs, Editor

Fathom Publishing Company
Anchorage, Alaska

ISBN 978-1-954896-04-8 Paperback
ISBN 978-1-954896-05-5 e-book

Cover illustration Argeo Jobim

Printed in United States of America

fathompublishing.com
Fathom Publishing Company
P.O. Box 200448
Anchorage, Alaska 99520-0448
Telephone/Fax 907-272-3305

# Dedication

To the residents of Atlin, British Columbia
and
their Atlin Supportive Living Society.

# Acknowledgments

The author wishes to thank the following people
    for their time,
    for their patience,
    for their encouragement,
    for their constructive criticism,
    most off all for their much needed support:

    Susan & Jerry Kuelbs, Douglas, Alaska, and Atlin, BC.

    Richard & Diane Stephens, Atlin, BC.

Without these four individuals, the author would have given up twenty years ago or more.

Thank you for the much needed kicks!

And thank you for getting hold of Connie at Fathom Publishing in Anchorage, Alaska.

Colin F. Carter
Spring 2023

# Atlin Supportive Living Society

Atlin Supportive Living Society (ASLS) was formed in 2001. It is a volunteer driven, multifaceted, non-profit, registered charitable society operating in Atlin, British Columbia. It is managed by a board of six directors and twelve active core members. The organization is headquartered and operates most of its services from the former Anglican Rectory, known as "The Pew."

ASLS currently provides care, support, and advocacy for Atlin senior citizens in need, ensuring a better quality of life and the ability to remain in their own homes and community for as long as possible. Atlin is a small, tight knit community of four hundred with a prevailing aging demographic. Since its creation, virtually all community members have involvement with the Society in one way or another, either benefiting from services or donating services. ASLS has an eclectic group of members: ranging from nurses, teachers, home care workers, cooks, cleaners, journeyman carpenters, equipment operators, book keepers, accountant, drivers, underground miners, placer miners, business people, big game outfitters, contractors and lay people. Everyone is welcome.

Over the years, ASLS has successfully built strong working relationships and community partnerships to assist with the mandate of advocacy for Atlin seniors. Such members include the Atlin business community, Atlin Community Improvement District, Taku River Tlingit First Nation, Social Health, Atlin Health Centre, Atlin Community Recreation Centre, BC Ambulance, BC Northern Health Authority, Northern Health Home and Community Care in Terrace, and RCMP (morgue services). ASLS was instrumental in ensuring that a new health center was built for the community of Atlin.

As an NGO, Atlin Supportive Living Society combines funding support from community donations and governments to carry on its work. By pairing this funding with our volunteer network, ASLS stretches every dollar of funding raised for maximum benefit to the community. The support from the community allows us to provide: Meals on Wheels, Foot Clinics, Palliative Care, Morgue Services, Bathing Services,

Advocacy Work, and other needed services. Support comes, every year, through community fundraising and community volunteering. By working in cooperation with governments and with the support of the Atlin Community, ASLS is able to fulfill its mandate of "caring for the community."

The Society has been growing and diversifying its services since ASLS began twenty-three years ago. In the first five years, ASLS operated Meals on Wheels, home care, and palliative care services. These services relied solely on community support in the beginning.

In the following five years, the Society built on these services and began developing a working relationship with BC Northern Health Authority. This resulted in the expansion of ASLS services to the community through the development of our medical equipment loan cupboard. It was during this period that ASLS encouraged government policy makers, by speaking with Provincial and Territorial governments, to develop a Memorandum of Understanding so that Atlin seniors could access long-term care facilities in Whitehorse. This support from British Columbia and Yukon continues to this day. Since 2008 until the present, the Society has continued to provide an array of services and it has advocated for support of medical travel expenses for residents of Atlin who need to access health care outside of the Territory or in southern British Columbia.

Like most organizations in the North, ASLS has developed over the years to meet the needs of its community. People are the focus. "Caring for our Community" is the goal.

Atlin Supportive Living Society cared for Colin during his final months in Atlin. Colin was very supportive of the Society. It was his wish that the net proceeds from the sales of his books be donated to Atlin Supportive Living Society.

Members of Atlin Supportive Living Society
Atlin, British Columbia, Canada
2024

# Table of Contents

# Introduction

We met Colin Carter at the Pine Tree Services Gas Station while on a visit to Atlin many years ago. He pumped our gas. We became friends. We had heard he liked to write stories and asked if he would share one with us.

The stories became a book. Colin would stop by in the evenings for tea and book discussions. He shared his stories with many friends in town, looking for feedback. During one such discussion, a suggestion was tossed out that it would be interesting to find out what happened to Matagam Pagwa, one of Colin's characters. Colin was off and running, or a better word would be writing. Thus, this series of books beginning with *Defender Down*.

Two years ago, Colin asked me to help prepare a book for publishing. I firmly declined, explaining I had absolutely no experience. To myself, I wondered how that would work for Colin, living in a small cabin without phone or Internet services and mail service only three days a week. I couldn't imagine how this could be done in today's publishing world.

Colin persisted, writing another book, and another, in what would become a series. Finally, I agreed to help him write a cover letter to send with a manuscript to a publisher in Alaska. Fathom Publishing Company was recommended by the Atlin library helpers and had published a book about Atlin by a former resident. Connie agreed to look at the manuscript and give Colin feedback. I shipped the manuscript north to Connie as Colin was headed into Whitehorse for his first tests and treatment for cancer.

That winter between treatments in Whitehorse and trips to Vancouver for surgery, Colin wrote and worked with Connie. The cancer was not going well. Colin kept writing. Word on the street from the medic who visited Colin daily was "as long as he is writing, he is strong."

Colin finished his series. He set about putting his life in order, preparing a will, and giving away all his belongs. He left us the Matagam Pagwa Series to "do with as we wished."

Preparing a manuscript for publication is an incredible amount of work. It has taken all winter and would not have happened without Connie's guidance and help. She has been a rock of strength and encouragement. Colin, your final gift to us was a worthy experience. Writing is a powerful tool for the soul. Thank you for showing us that.

*Defender Down* and *Bleak Realities* are ready for the press. Net proceeds from the Matagam Pagwa Series sales will be donated to Atlin Supportive Living Program. This program is run by local volunteers who care for elderly and sick residents in their homes, providing clinics, meals on wheels, and social get-togethers during the winter months. They took wonderful care of Colin during that long last winter.

Susan Kuelbs
Atlin, British Columbia
August 2024

# Defender Down

# Planet and Character List

## Solar Systems
Tevely Solar System
> Home Planet Volough
> Planet Avanac

Silhouette Solar System
> Planets Yovex and Xevoy

## Volough

### Fleet Headquarters
Fleet Admiral Comm., Minister of Defense Bert White
Rear Admiral Oilskin "Three-in-One"

### Battleship *Defender*
Capt. Allen Zeff
EXO Russell Maxx
Comm. Officer Lt. Alice Dawa
Chief Engineer Lt. Connie Frohm
Dr. Ann O'Casey
Flight Deck Chief Aaron Llelu
Flight Tech. Lucy Tyyne
Fighter Pilot Ray Oseeka
Mess Cook Fross
Galley Staff Member Sandra Buffet
Deck Mate/Crew Member Martha Vulla
Fighter Pilots Mary, Sam, Beth

### Battleship *Raven*
Acting Fleet Admiral Capt. Richard Dobbs
Comm. Officer Lt. Pamela Morris

### Battleship *Rapture*
Acting Commander Rear Admiral Oilskin "Three-in-One"
EXO Stephanie Bozzar
Commander Squadron Leader Lt. Bart Cassel
Comm. Officer Lieutenant Zoyia

### Battleship *Vanquish*

### Battleship *Dreadnought*

## Yovex
Jenna Simon
Ben Simon, Jenna's husband
Jenna's father

# Prologue

In the Tevely solar system near the planet of Volvough, the inter-galaxy battle between Zolleck and the Catherian forces had been raging for three days. The debris and fuselages of forty-eight assorted full-size battleships, smaller battle cruisers and carriers, along with hundreds of fractured fighters littered the Tevely solar system. Although the Zolleck Acting Fleet Admiral Capt. Richard Dobbs of the battleship *Raven* was badly outnumbered, the Zolleck fleet was holding its own with his tactics and his people's resolve.

Each time Capt. Dobbs had his Comm. Officer Lt. Pam Morris request support from Rear Admiral Oilskin at headquarters, the response was always given with the same curt demeaning attitude, "You tell Dobbs he has his orders and you quit giving me his shabby excuses."

"Sir, with all due respect, Captain Dobbs has repeatedly asked me to make it clear to you that—"

"Listen. If you don't stop bothering me, I'll have you up on insubordination charges. Now tell Dobbs to get the damn job done."

When Rear Admiral Oilskin cut the radio link with Lt. Morris, Capt. Dobbs asked, "What did Three-In-One say this time?"

"He says he'll have me up on insubordination charges. The man's tone and attitude are totally demeaning."

"Someday someone's going to airlock that bastard. Pam, if he ever comes within arm's length of you, tell me. And that's an order."

* * *

Two days later, *Defender, Raven, Rapture* and *Venture* were among the eight Zolleck ships that survived the battle and landed on the planet Volvough. It was eleven days later before the battleships and carriers with a supply convoy arrived to relive what was left of Capt. Dobbs' force. The *Dreadnought* and *Vanquish* arrived with the Minister of Defense, Fleet Admiral Commander Bert White. The next day, the crews of the eight ships were assembled on the tarmac so the Fleet Admiral Commander could congratulate them and award medals to the eight captains.

After the ceremony, Bert White asked Capt. Allen Zeff of *Defender* to speak to him in his quarters on *Vanquish.* "Son, you're the youngest captain in the fleet with the youngest group of senior officers. I admire the way you got them to bond together. It's a sign of a natural leader."

"Thank you, sir, but please realize each of my senior officers are strong individuals with the potential of advancement."

"Zeff, I reviewed and scrutinized their records and you are right about them with two exceptions. Your mess cook, Fross, and your EXO, Commander Russell Maxx."

"I agree Fross has his limitations. As for Commander Maxx, he's opinionated and stands his ground, but he does listen to reason and will back my orders."

"Well put. You read people and know how to motivate them. That's one of the reasons I want to put your name forward to replace me as Minister of Defense."

"Captain Dobbs of the *Raven* is the one who was in command. Should his name be put forward?"

"Dobbs is a fine captain with a loyal crew, but he doesn't have the leadership skills you exhibit. He stands too much on orders."

"May I ask where will you be?"

"Within a year, hopefully, I'll be given an air lock funeral. Zeff, that's how long the medical specialists have given me. So far, the war is going well, and I could have your EXO promoted with you as your personal aide."

"What would Oilskin have to say?"

"Zeff, I've heard numerous unsettling rumors of how Oilskin disciplines his subordinates. Yet no one has come forward to officially press charges. Plus, the fact is he has some strange ideas on how to reform the military. You and your EXO will have to curry some political backing or end up being sheep to the slaughter. I'm scheduled to leave in three hours, so I need your answer."

"I'd want time to talk with my EXO."

"My health problems are classified. If the Catherian ever found out, they might see it as a time of confusion and try to take advantage of any changes in command. Whatever you decide, what has been said here, stays here. Now what's your answer?"

"Without talking with Maxx, sorry, sir, I decline."

Capt. Allen Zeff left the Minister of Defense, not fully realizing the long-term negative effects his answer would have on the Zolleck military. It was eight months after the meeting that Fleet Admiral Commander Bert White's funeral was held. Oilskin was promoted to the position of Minister of Defense. He soon started to hear all the hushed rumors discussing how his predecessor Bert White had offered the position to Zeff of *Defender* first and the man had turned down the promotion.

With the war continuing, the changes Oilskin instituted in the Zolleck military changed the tide of the war to the advantage of the Catherian forces. At the beginning of the fourth year of Oilskin's appointment as the Minister of Defense, he was replaced and demoted down to a desk-bound rear admiral. His last official order as Minister of Defense was to have *Defender* with its Capt. Zeff relegated as chaperone to the hospital ship *Noble*. Oilskin's hope was that the small battle cruiser would meet its end going in and out of raging battle zones.

When Zeff received his ship's new orders and saw who had signed off on them, he knew Oilskin had made one last attempt to put his ship and crew directly in harm's way. With the war going more and more in the Catherian's favor, Zolleck hospital ships were called into the worst situations to evacuate the wounded. The chair-bound Oilskin ordered *Noble* into the areas of the worst-case scenarios with *Defender* chaperoning.

# Chapter 1 Hard Landing

Capt. Zeff woke up in his quarters and showered, then dressed. He was about to head to the mess for breakfast when a ship-wide alert sounded. That changed his goal from having a leisurely start to his day to a hurried pace to the bridge. When he stepped onto the bridge, Comm. Officer Lt. Alice Dawa was listening to the ship-to-ship comm. She reported, "Captain, three full-size Catherian battleships came over top of that massive asteroid belt we passed and launched their fighters targeting *Noble*."

The EXO Commander Russell Maxx had already called the flight deck to get his fighters wheels up to protect the hospital ship that *Defender* was chaperoning. Within minutes, *Defender*'s forty-eight fighters were in position to protect *Noble*. *Defender*'s automated weapons array was online and ready. Zeff watched the screen and gave the orders for his mid-size battle cruiser to target the lead enemy ship. As his ship went head on with the Catherian's full-size ship, *Defender* suffered numerous damaging heavy hits.

Lt. Connie Frohm, the chief engineer, called up to the bridge, "Captain, we're getting pounded. We've lost long-range scanners and the shields are down to fifty-six percent. That last thump caused our main engines to stammer."

"Frohm, just keep us flying. Zeff out."

Dawa informed Zeff, "The captain of *Noble* is holding on the comm, sir."

As Zeff continued watching the screen, he told Dawa to put him through. Before a word had been spoken, *Noble* exploded into a fiery display of red, yellow, and blue colors. At the same time, the EXO reported, "We've lost forty-four fighters and the other two carriers are turning toward us. It's time to run, Zeff."

As the EXO passed the word for the fighters to run, Zeff

gave the same order to Navigation Officer Second Lt. Wayne Wicks.

The damage to *Defender* was so severe that the enemy commander felt the ship would die its own slow death and become a ghost ship floating aimlessly in space. He gave the order for his fighters to return to their carriers and to go wheels down. His primary agenda was to join up with the rest of the Catherian fleet. In the mind of the commander, pursuing a crippled mid-sized battle cruiser was a waste of fuel and a needless risk. After forty minutes of not being pursued, *Defender*'s remaining four fighters went wheels down in one of its hangers.

Zeff sat in his set room with EXO Maxx as they listened to Frohm's report. "The weapons array is offline. The ship's scanning system is down to ten thousand miles. The main engines are cavitating to the point that if we don't cut speed, we'll lose them totally. I seriously suggest we cut speed to half or one-third."

Zeff asked, "What else?"

"Given time, optimistically I can get the shields back to eighty percent. We need an H-type planet to land on. The alternative will be going wheels down on a frozen moon."

"We'll have to take what's closest, Zeff out."

After Frohm's report, he called Wicks into his set room. He had the computer bring up the closest solar systems. "All but one is out of reach."

The three of them looked at the Silhouette System in silence. Finally, Max stated, "Yovex, not a chance in hell. We aren't that desperate."

Wicks stated the reality. "We'd all be collecting our pensions before we got to the next safe system. That's if we didn't run out of fuel and food and lived that long."

Zeff considered Wicks' off-handed remark and put off making a decision. "Tomorrow at eight-hundred, we meet here and discuss any other options."

Dawa had sent a distress signal at the time of the initial attack and another one reporting the ship's damages and Yovex as their nearest H-type planet. Zeff knew with the way the war was going back home, it could be weeks before a ship would be sent to aid them. Wicks went back to his duties on the bridge and Maxx went down to the hanger to meet with his four pilots.

Zeff met with Dr. Ann O'Casey on the med deck to hear her prognosis of the fifteen injured. When the doctor went back to attending the wounded, Zeff took the time to visit with each of them. To him, his crew was family.

After Zeff left Dr. O'Casey, he went to see the four surviving pilots. They talked for twenty minutes before Frohm called him on the comm reporting the state of the engines. Zeff called Maxx to meet him in the engine room. When they got there, Frohm walked them through pointing to the most serious problems. Zeff noted the damage and credited her people for catching the issues.

Maxx asked bluntly, "Frohm, how long will the main engines hold?"

"No telling. Good news is the port and starboard impulse engines are intact."

"Will they be enough to give us mobility through a planet's atmosphere?"

"The real question is how much control we will have?"

Zeff interjected, "Do your best. What about the shields?"

"Give us a couple of days to deal with the engines and then I'll work on them. With luck, I should be able to get them back to eighty percent."

"Try to get some sleep tonight. In the morning at eight-hundred, I want you and Wicks in the set room. Maxx, that goes for Dawa as well." After checking his watch, he added, "I'm meeting O'Casey in the mess. Remember zero-eight-hundred in the morning."

When Zeff got up to the mess, he sat down across from Ann as she commented, "Fross has got his place pretty much straightened away."

Zeff checked the menu board. "Spaghetti and meatballs, that's all?"

"Fross hasn't changed. Zeff, tonight we'll have to talk."

"I know."

After Zeff and Ann finished eating, they went to his quarters where she brought up the subject. "*Noble* had the operating theatre I need here. Zeff, it's just a matter of time."

"Out of the fifteen?"

Ann's eyes moistened as she replied, "Odds are twelve."

Zeff listened compassionately as she talked about the injuries the twelve had and the fact that they probably wouldn't make it. Then he suggested they get some rest.

At 0600 hours, Ann was awakened by the medical alert alarm in their quarters. She used her comm to contact the duty nurse. Zeff and Ann quickly dressed.

She hurried down to the med deck. When she got there, the nurse informed her that a deck hand had passed. Before giving the nurse a hand preparing the body, she called Zeff on his comm link. He in turn asked Maxx to meet him at number two air lock.

At 0630 hours, Zeff made the ship-wide announcement of the death deck mate Martha Vulla. Her ceremony would be held at number two airlock at 0700 hours.

The off-duty crew assembled to hear EXO Maxx give the eulogy. On Zeff's nod, Flight Deck Chief Aaron Llelu pushed the button to open the airlock. The mood was solemn with the knowledge that eleven more of the crew would probably meet the same fate. Dr O'Casey suggested they gather in the mess to remember the good-natured personality of Martha Vulla.

At 0830 hours, Zeff met in his set room with his key officers. When they all were seated, he informed them that he had made the decision to head for Yovex in the Silhouette Solar System.

Maxx was the first to respond. "That's the planet where the legend of the ghost ships began. Five years ago, we came across one and boarded it. It's not a sight I want to repeat seeing."

"I examined some of the bodies and found no wounds or evidence of illnesses. Reluctantly, I reported the cause of death as hypothermia," Ann recalled.

Frohm added, "All the systems were offline. It was as though the ship had lost power to all systems and the crew froze to death. I wanted to couple *Defender*'s electrical system to the ghost ship and try thawing it out. If I could have powered up the systems, we might have found out what went wrong."

"And then jettisoning two hundred and five bodies out the air locks after they thawed out and stunk up the whole ship up. Ann and I mulled over the negative effect of this on our crew. Sorry, Frohm, that's why I had to refuse your request." Zeff stated.

Wicks spoke reluctantly, "I'll be on the bridge checking our flight time to Yovex."

Frohm stood and stated, "I'll be in engineering holding things together."

Dawa shrugged, "I'll send another report stating our course and destination."

Ann looked at Zeff. "I don't see any other options."

"I'll give the crew the heads up and try to quell their anxieties." Maxx said.

"Maxx, set up some bridge and cribbage tournaments. Keep the crew occupied so they won't be overthinking things."

"I'll have them doing physical workouts in the empty hangers. Complaining about me will help keep their minds off what's going on."

# Chapter 2 Three Suns on Screen

Over the following six weeks, the crew assembled for eleven more deaths. Each one was a solemn reflection of the crew's future. After forty-nine days of very slow progress, *Defender* entered the Silhouette Solar System and Yovex's upper atmosphere.

Zeff held an update meeting with his key officers where Engineer Frohm stated her opinion. "Odds are the main engines will calf and the shields will buckle. When the time comes, I'll stay in engineering trying to hold things together."

Dr. O'Casey gave her medical evaluation. "Most of the crew is physically healthy enough if we need to use the escape pods. Some others, their emotional state is fragile."

"With the way the war is going back home, our fleets are being stretched to their limits. It could be months before we get any help." Dawa gave her estimation.

Zeff looked at Maxx to give the order to abandon the ship. The four pilots took to their fighters while most of the rest of the crew left in escape pods. Without the full power needed to maneuver, *Defender* plumbed through the atmosphere like it was being pulled to the planet as a metal object to a magnet. As *Defender*'s shields failed, it resembled a semi-controlled asteroid.

Wicks was on the bridge doing his best to control *Defender* from a total free-fall decent. The screen view confirmed that three suns circled the planet. Earlier the crew suspected the ship's visual systems were in error. There was no doubt about the suns now.

Frohm was at her post in engineering trying to keep the secondary engines and shields online. Before the impending impact, Zeff called Connie Frohm, Ann O'Casey, and Alice Dawa to report to the bridge. The six of them buckled in and braced for the impact. The ship pounded onto the ground and skidded along the surface before careening to a sudden violent stop.

As they sat nearly motionless in anticipation of what would come next, Zeff asked, "Everyone alright?" After they answered the affirmative, he unbuckled, stood up and looked around at the disorder which was once the bridge of his mid-sized battle cruiser. He asked Maxx, "Did the crew get off?"

"As far as I know."

The others got their feet under them and surveyed the damage. Ann stated, "We're the only ones crazy enough to ride this thing down. We should all be dead or committed."

Maxx stated, "Right now committed doesn't sound that bad."

"Instrument readings say the air and gravity is within the norms. Let's get off this wreck and take a look around," Connie reported.

The word "wreck" resonated in Zeff's mind and his expression showed it.

Ann tried to get him to think positive. "The crew got off and we're alive."

One of the lifts was online and they took it down to the hanger deck where the main small arms lockers were located. Each of them strapped a 9mm compact sidearm on their thigh and grabbed an under-barrel grenade launcher rifle. Not knowing what life forms to expect, Zeff wanted to be ready. After they pried opened one of the doors and got their feet on the ground, they looked perplexingly at the dense forest.

Wicks stated, "The bark is red, the leaves are orange, and they're all planted about forty feet apart."

"Except for where we hit the ground and skidded to a stop," Connie stated.

Next, they gazed at the escarpment that faced them a mile in front of the ship's resting place. Alice stated, "From up there we'd be able to see where the others landed."

Maxx responded, "If we'd hit that, we'd all be dead."

Wicks quipped, "What a headstone: Here lie six people too stupid to abandon ship."

Ann quietly questioned, "I wonder what's in the soil that causes the bark to be red and the leaves to be orange?"

Zeff ignored the others' remarks as he stood staring at his battered cruiser. "We're not getting off this planet in that. Alice, how long until we're rescued?"

"Six weeks minimum?" Zeff stared at her and she replied, "As far as I know, none of our ships have ever been stupid enough to venture into this system, never mind landing on Yovex."

Zeff gave the orders. "Maxx and Alice, find a place near the escarpment to set up camp. Connie and Wicks, check the impulse engines and the ship's systems. Find out what works. Ann and I will get the survival gear off the ship."

Maxx questioned, "Why not stay with the ship? The crew's bound to head this way."

"As well as whoever inhabits this planet. Our approach wasn't exactly stealthy, and I want to watch who comes to investigate from a safe distance."

As the others left, Zeff asked Ann, "What are you looking at?"

"Three suns? I haven't ever seen a planet with three suns."

"The main screen showed three suns as we were coming down. I thought it was a mistake or an illusion on my part." Wicks stated.

Zeff observed the phenomenon, "It's not hot enough for three suns. We'll go up to the bridge to see if I can get the main computer working and find out what, if anything, it recorded on the way down."

On the bridge, Zeff did some rewiring to get the backup system up before the main computer came back online. It showed what information had been gathered before going offline. Yovex equatorial diameter was twelve times greater than their home planet's diameter. At their latitude with three suns, a day would be thirty hours with twenty hours of day light. The temperature should be forty degrees warmer than the gauges showed.

After reading the data, Ann stated, "Thirty-hour days?"

"Forty degrees warmer, it's not. Something's wrong."

"Zeff, we'd better get the survival gear and the provisions

ready." The two of them assembled everything on the ground and then went down to engineering.

Wicks reported, "We got the fires out, at least she won't burn up."

Connie stated, "The main engine is toast, but the impulse engines are intact."

Ann interjected, "I'm going to check things on the med deck. Depending how the others landed, we might need it."

Zeff went with Ann and when they got to the med deck, she said with limited optimism, "We won't be doing any open-heart surgery or transplants. But it could be worse."

They spent three hours tidying up and making the small operating theater usable. Then Zeff used his comm to tell Connie and Wicks to meet them outside.

As the four of them stood with their boots on the ground, Connie commented, "More systems are working than I expected, and we didn't end up as a ghost ship."

"At least down here, we have a chance'" Wicks added.

Zeff called Maxx on his comm, "Where are you two?"

"About a thousand yards out."

When Alice and Maxx walked in from amongst the trees, she detailed, "The escarpment looks as though it had been mined. The portal we checked opens up to a maze of drifts honeycombing all over. Years ago, someone's did a lot of mining into the base of that escarpment. There are all old workings."

Maxx added, "From one point, there's an unobstructed view of *Defender*'s starboard side.

The six of them loaded up as much as they could carry and made the hike to the base of the escarpment. When they got inside the drifts, Alice pointed to two, "The guys in that one and us girls in this one."

Ann stated, "Zeff and I will take the cavern in the third drift."

Maxx and Wicks took the cavern in the drift Alice had assigned. Then Alice and Connie shared the cavern of the second drift.

Wicks stated, "They won't be as private as our quarters on the ship."

Maxx stated, "Or in a grave."

Zeff asked Ann to settle in while he, Maxx, and Wicks went out to the vantage point to view the ship. It was a place with good cover with a clear sight line to glass along the starboard side of *Defender*. Zeff turned with his binoculars to look behind them at the escarpment. He saw Alice was correct about it offering a good vantage point to watch for the rest of the crew. His priority was to watch the ship to see when the local inhabitants would come to investigate. He knew there was nothing he could do to locate the crew who left his ship in the fighters and escape pods.

Zeff left Wicks on watch while he and Maxx went back through the opening to scrutinize the drifts. Their hope was the workings would offer clues to the mining technology used and the intelligence of the indigenous inhabitants.

# Chapter 3 Tree Tugs

For five days after *Defender* crashed on Yovex, Zeff's crew took turns watching the wreckage of their ship. For each of them, the expectations that the local inhabitants would investigate the crash was always foremost in their minds. They figured at least the crash would have been reported to some sort of local authorities.

On the sixth afternoon, Ann called Zeff on her comm, "You've got to see this."

Zeff alerted the other four to join them. When they got to Ann's position, they hunkered down to watch the activity around *Defender* with their rifle scopes and binoculars.

Wicks commented, "They look human."

Ann pointed as she explained, "They rode in slowly on those things about thirty-five feet above the ground, stopping occasionally before setting down by our ship."

Alice commented, "It'd be nice to hear what they're saying. What language they speak and if they're friendly."

Ann told the others, "To me it looks like they've measured the bounce and skid marks of our crash and are calculating the damages."

Connie remarked, "I wonder what gives their skin that light crimson color?"

Zeff let the question slide. He noted they appeared to be unarmed and decided to make contact by asking Ann to go with him.

Maxx suggested he would circle left with Alice while Wicks and Connie circled right to cover Zeff and Ann. They got a ten-minute head start to get in position before Zeff and Ann moved out.

When they were a hundred yards from the ship, Ann and Zeff stopped behind one of the large deciduous trees. Ann asked Zeff, "What are you planning to say?"

"One is female – I was hoping you might ..."

"Hoping that women bond naturally where men are more confrontational?"

"Something like that?"

"Fine. You stay on my six and follow my lead."

Ann bent down, picked up some dry branches and broke them to alert the inhabitants to their presence. The two locals looked in their direction and the female said, "Please show yourself."

Zeff commented quietly to Ann, "At least they speak our language."

Ann moved from behind the tree with Zeff slightly behind her and to one side. She spoke to reassure them, "We come with peaceful intentions."

"That's your idea of peaceful?" The male pointed.

Ann glanced at her rifle and sidearm. She put the rifle on the ground and then unstrapped her thigh holster and placed it alongside the rifle. Then she turned to see if Zeff had followed her lead.

Next, she stated, "I'm Doctor Ann O'Casey, the Chief Medical Officer of that ship. Friends call me Ann."

"And the one with you?"

"Allen Zeff, captain of the ship. Friends call him Zeff."

The female asked, "The four hiding, shall they show themselves?"

Ann told the others to come into view and introduce themselves.

"I'm Communications Officer Lieutenant Alice Dawa."

"EXO Commander Russell Maxx."

"Chief Engineer First Lieutenant Connie Frohm."

"Navigations Officer Second Lieutenant Wayne Wicks."

Ann asked, "We've told you our names, how about you telling us yours?"

The female made the introductions, "I'm Jenna Simon and my husband, Ben."

Ben asked Ann, "In your society, are all males subservient to their females?"

Ann laughed before replying. "Not at all, Ben. Zeff thought it would be less threatening if I spoke first."

"That's promising. A male with the good sense to know when to put a female first."

Zeff suggested, "Would you two be opposed to going inside and sitting while we talk?"

Ann caught a side glance of Jenna and suggested, "Jenna, I'm sure we'd all be more comfortable."

Jenna and Ben spoke quietly together before he agreed by saying, "As long as you leave your weapons on the ground where they are."

Ann suggested that Zeff and Maxx with Wicks give Ben a tour of *Defender*, while she with Alice and Connie went up to the mess. Again, Jenna and Ben spoke quietly before accepting the invitations.

Once in the mess, Ann offered Jenna a chair while Alice inspected the food locker and Connie checked the equipment. Ann asked Jenna, "So what do you and Ben do?"

"We tend our trees. Your ship has crashed on our property."

"I'm honestly sorry for all the damage."

"You're fortunate that your craft crashed and skidded along the line where we had already harvested two rows of trees. The damaged ones will be harvested and put to good use. Ben will hire some help to see to it."

"I take it that you usually work with Ben. May I ask why it took so long for you two to investigate the crash?"

Unconsciously, Jenna glanced down. "We had appointments in the city."

Ann smiled, "How many months along?"

"Six. Do I show that much?"

"Your clothes hide it well. When Ben looks at you, I see the concerns of a first-time father."

Connie's ears perked up. "First-time father. How long do you carry?"

"Eight months. And your species?"

"Nine months."

Alice asked, "A boy or a girl?"

Jenna grinned, "We're hoping for a healthy girl."

With Jenna's answer, Alice and Connie decided to explain the friendly tradition of baby showers.

* * *

As the men walked through the bent and cluttered passageways of *Defender*, Zeff asked Ben, "Why hasn't your military come to investigate?"

"We don't have a military and the law states that what falls on private land is the property of the landowner unless he reports it as a threat to national sovereignty."

"So, by your laws, you own my ship?"

Wicks asked, "What would you do with it? It won't fly."

Ben avoided answering the question directly. Rather, he stated his suspicions, "No doubt you've reported your situation and position. So at some point, another vessel will arrive to rescue you. Hopefully, you'll leave peacefully."

Maxx commented, "You're taking this very nonchalantly."

"Yours isn't the first ship to crash or attack our planet. Some pick up their survivors and leave peacefully without incident."

"And if they don't?" Zeff questioned.

"I'm sure you've noticed our planet appears to have three solar suns, two are actually reflective globes. If the globes alter their angles and positions and magnify the sun's rays, you can imagine the effect the heat would have on a ship's systems."

Maxx mumbled aloud. "All systems would burn out and go offline. The ship would stop functioning and the crew would freeze to death."

In a low tone, Wicks stated, "Ghost ships drifting in space, they're legendary. We came across one five years ago. The crew's bodies were frozen. Are you people the cause?"

Ben replied with some regret. "Some species are warlike and don't respond to peaceful logic. Each of those times, defensive actions respond to limit the number of our casualties and to minimize our damages. We're a peaceful race longing to be left alone to our own way of life."

Zeff questioned, "Four fighters and eight escape pods left my ship, what will happen to them? I'm concerned about my crew."

"If they land on government property, they'll be held as aliens until they're peacefully identified and it is determined they are not a threat to our planet.

"And if they are considered a threat?"

"There's a detention area far to the southeast where aliens are held and given work to earn their keep."

That was not a possibility that Zeff wanted to discuss in front of Ben. Instead, he suggested they head up to the mess to see what the women were doing.

When they got up to the mess, Ann pulled Jeff aside and explained, "Ben and Jenna earn a living from those trees. We've promised Jenna we'd help them clean up the mess. It's the least we can do, correct, Zeff?"

"It would seem reasonable and so far, they seem friendly."

"So in the morning, we meet here at zero-eight-hundred."

Maxx commented, "What do we know about trees?"

Alice stated, "We'll learn."

When Connie glanced over at Wicks, he said, "Those trees are awfully big – but we'll learn."

"Good attitude, Wayne."

After Jenna and Ben left, the six of them went back to the escarpment.

Zeff asked Ann, "You seemed pretty determined. What's really going on?"

"Jenna's pregnant and we do owe them."

* * *

At 0730 hours, Jenna and Ben were waiting with tree tugs at Defender's crash site. When Zeff with his crew showed up at 0745 hours, Ben showed the men how to use the tree tugs while Jenna showed the women. To begin with, both groups hovered at fifteen feet above the ground and used a force field to levitate twelve-foot lengths of trees onto the detachable skidder trailers for transport.

Once Zeff and the others mastered operating the tree tugs, Ben and Jenna took them to where *Defender* first hit the ground. The six of them watched as Ben and Jenna offered a prayer of thanks to their Creator for the sacrifice and rebirth of the tree.

Then Ben detailed the procedures for harvesting the tree. "First, you sever the stump and root and replant it. The rotting stump will create a natural food source to nourish its seedlings. Next, you'll limb the branches using laser saws. I warn you, the trees are often entangled and can spring or roll when being limbed. So be careful."

Wicks asked, "Who originally planted the trees and organized the spacing?"

Jenna replied, "Our ancestors. Each generation is responsible for the forest and the health of the trees. The two smaller subspecies between the rows provide needed nutrition. Ann, Alice and Connie will gather the branches to be taken to the chipper. After they're mulched, the end product will be used to cover the stump and surrounding area for insulation over the winter. Ben will direct the men cutting the tree into twelve-foot lengths for transport to the processor. They will be cut to various board dimensions and put through a plainer."

Alice commented, "The mahogany color of the wood must bring a good price."

Ben stated, "Jenna sets the price and usually it's lower than the market value."

After the six of them listened to the overall plan, Ben used a laser saw to free a tree from its stump. Using a tug, Jenna repositioned the stump into the divot. Ben gave the men lessons using the laser saws and showed them how to safely cut the limbs. He restated the warning about branches being trapped and that when cut, they could spring back and cause injuries.

Then he showed them the proper technique for cutting the tree into lengths. When the first tree was limbed, Jenna used a tug to demonstrate picking up the branches and moving them into the floating skidder behind her tug. While Ann, Alice, and Connie picked up branches, Jenna watched and directed them over the tug's comm. When the four skidders were loaded, she took them to the chipper and dumped her load as an example. Then Jenna supervised the others. After four trips, Jenna felt confident the women knew how to work safely. She allowed them to continue while she left.

Ninety minutes after Jenna left, she called the mulching crew on the comm and asked them to go back to the first damaged tree. When they got back there, Jenna's tug was parked with her skidder loaded with a mid-day meal. As both crews were eating, Ben took Jenna aside, "You know things would go quicker if I hired experienced harvesters."

"Ben, they're doing their best and they volunteered in an act of kindness. Ann's a doctor and that's someone we don't have if you were seriously injured while harvesting."

"You know I trust your instincts. It is with an experienced crew that you could take things easier. I worry about you and our baby that you're carrying."

"I promised Ann I won't over exert myself. I make you the same promise."

At the end of the day, the effects of the physical labor showed on Zeff's crew. Jenna drew a map to a lake and told them to use their tugs for transport.

Ben explained to Zeff, "On the right, half a mile down the main passageway of your drift, you'll find a passage one hundred yards long. At the end, there's a ladder that will take you to the top of the escarpment. It's a nice place to relax in the evenings to watch the moons. Grab the rung at shoulder height before stepping on it."

"Because?"

"Because it's automated. As soon as it feels your weight, it will go to the top. It's quick so tell the ladies to hold on and keep both feet on a rung of the ladder."

"What's it used for?"

"It's used as a ladder. The Book of Chronicles says when Matagam Pagwa's people brought us here they parked their ships on the escarpment. There are ladders in all the drifts. That's how they all went up and down."

"Mat-a-gam Pag-wa?"

Ben hesitated before answering. "He and his people were searching in an area of space called the Milky Way. They wanted an unpopulated H-type planet to live on to create a new and peaceful way of life. When they scanned the planet called Mars, it was discovered the ozone layer was decaying and our species would be lost. The book says Matagam's ships made multiple trips to bring us and the seedlings of the trees here. Then they stayed for a number of years to make sure our forefathers adapted. His people made the solar defense and designed and built the tree tugs."

"So why didn't they stay?"

"They were running from a very distant area of space that was overrun by war and greed. If they had stayed and their enemies had found them, our people would have been caught in the middle. They saw Yovex as a sanctuary for our forefathers with an abundance of fuel."

"Fuel?"

"Our planet is rich in cesium and yatterblum, a solid fuel base."

Zeff thought about the three suns, the tree tugs and the drifts in the escarpment. "They must have been here for years."

"The book isn't big on specifics. There were thousands of Matagam's refugees from different planets and galaxies."

Then Ben went quiet, thinking he had explained too much. Ann saw his expression and interjected, "Before we leave for the lake, we need to go back to the drifts and get towels and clean clothes."

Maxx uttered, "It's good, clean perspiration from a hard day's work."

When they got to the lake, everyone washed off the dried perspiration and dirt. Four of them sat on the shore and talked about the day's experience. Zeff and Ann sat alone and talked about the story Ben told of Matagam Pagwa's people.

Zeff stated, "To me the whole idea of finding an uninhabited H-Type planet to establish a peacefully civilization is a sad illusion of a lost idealist."

"Maybe the man was overly optimistic but at least he had a vision and tried. And he helped civilizations like Jenna and Ben's along the way."

When Zeff questioned the reason why Matagam Pagwa's people left, Ann reminded him, "They didn't want to put others in danger."

When the six of them went back to their drifts, Maxx made a point of saying how good Jenna's food was.

Alice made her own point, "Maybe if you ask, she'll make dinner for you."

Over dinner, Zeff explained about the ladder to the top of

the escarpment. After eating, they took a trek to find it to see how it worked. When they got on top of the escarpment, they found the view was spectacular. To the north, they could see over the trees. Using binoculars, they could see the dome of a volcano in the distance to the south. As the evening began to darken, Zeff told them to head back down and get some rest.

# Chapter 4 Flight Deck Chief Aaron Llelu

In the morning when they met with Ben and Jenna, she explained Saturdays were taken as a day of rest. The idea of three more days of work and then a day of rest sat well with all of them.

Over next the three days, Zeff's crew grew more confident with the equipment. The work progressed slowly, but Ben and Jenna saw strong work ethics, good attitudes, and a willingness to learn. For the crew of *Defender*, the first Saturday was spent at the lake soaking their aching muscles and resting.

During the second week, they began to get used to the physical routine and yet the second Saturday did not come too soon. The first part of the day was spent at the lake soaking and relaxing. As a group, they began to rekindle their friendships and relationships.

Later, Zeff and Ann went back to the portal and rode the ladder to the top of the escarpment. They stretched out to relax and enjoy the warmth of the three suns. While Zeff was sleeping, Ann heard Maxx calling him on his comm link. She asked, "Is it important, Maxx?"

"Where are you two?"

"On top of the escarpment."

"I'm outside the drifts and you'd better get down here now."

The talking woke Zeff, and he asked, "What's the problem, Maxx?"

"I've got Flight Deck Chief Aaron Llelu with me."

"We'll be right down." Zeff looked at Ann and quietly stated, "Finally."

When they got down to the mouth of the drifts, Flight Deck Chief Aaron Llelu saluted. Zeff returned the salute and shook his hand while asking, "Where have you been and where are the others?"

"Fifty miles due west of the volcano. Sixteen headed south, me and fifteen others headed north. The rest stayed with the pods."

"And the pilots?"

"No idea, sir."

Maxx interjected to explain that the fifteen who came with Llelu were at the lake. They had been given a briefing on the inhabitants and what they had been doing with their days.

Llelu questioned with respect, "Tree farmers, sir?"

"It's good honest work."

Ann interjected, "We haven't been in this good of shape since we graduated from academy. It will be beneficial to the rest of you."

"Respectfully, Doc, we've just finished a hundred fifty-mile hike."

"It took you long enough. You should've done it in five days, six at most."

There was no argument from Llelu.

"Great idea, Ann!" Maxx spoke up. "There are eight men and eight women. The women can help with the chipper while the guys trim the branches and help cut the trees to length."

"Only if Ben and Jenna agree." Zeff stated.

"Zeff, you and Maxx take Llelu to meet them," Ann suggested. As they got on the tree tugs, she called out to Zeff, "Wait! I'm going with you. I want to talk to Jenna."

When they arrived at the house, Zeff and Maxx introduced Llelu to Ben. Ann went inside to talk with Jenna, so she could state the purpose of the men's visit and then explain her purpose. "Jenna your time is getting close. As a friend and doctor, I'd feel better if you agreed to me giving you an examination. Just to make sure there aren't any complications."

"Now?"

"Tomorrow on *Defender*."

"I'm not sure what Ben would think."

"The city's a long way away and if there was a problem, I could be of assistance if I understood your physiology."

"While the men are talking, we'll make tea. When they come in, I'll ask Ben."

* * *

Outside, Zeff explained the idea of the men learning to help with the trees and the women working the chipper. Ben thought long and hard before responding, "We would lose a few day's production, but we'd make it up in the long run. Do you really think your people would be willing?"

"Zeff's their captain and I'm their EXO. They'll go along with it," Maxx stated in a firm tone.

Ben glanced at Maxx, then looked at Llelu, before declining, "I think it's better if we leave things as they are."

"Why?"

"Zeff, if your people come as you did as friends wanting to help, yes. But if they come only because they've been ordered to? I appreciate the offer, but no."

Llelu spoke with respect, "I understand what you're saying about being ordered, but I'd like to come tomorrow. The EXO can train me, and I'll try not to slow things down too much."

Ben offered Llelu his hand. "Your help would be appreciated. Now let's go inside and see what Jenna's made for tea.

Some of those root tarts, I hope," Maxx blurted out.

"Jenna made four dozen this morning."

"Good, those things are great. I'd like her to teach Alice how to make them."

When they got inside Jenna and Ann had the tea on the table. Ben introduced Llelu then mentioned the tarts.

Jenna asked Ben, "How about giving a hand?"

In the kitchen, she asked him how he felt about Ann giving her an examination. He replied with concern, "If you wouldn't mind, I'd sleep easier. For our first child, I want things to go well."

"Thanks, dear, tomorrow I'll meet Ann at their ship."

"Would you mind me coming?"

"What about the trees?"

"Zeff can handle the cutting crew. The mulching can wait."

"You make me happy. Let's take the tarts out to make Maxx happy."

When they went into the living room, Jenna asked Ann to give her a hand in the kitchen. Ben set the plate of root tarts on the coffee table in front of Maxx and made him an offer, "There are three dozen more in the kitchen. If you want to take some home, you'll have to earn them."

"What do I have to do?"

"Take Llelu to the tug shed and check him out on how to ride one safely."

Maxx smiled as he grabbed four tarts and handed Llelu two, "Get off your six. You're going to learn how to handle a tree tug."

As they walked to the shed, Llelu ate one of the tarts. "These things are really good."

"Jenna cooks as well as she bakes. All of her mid-day meals are worth a day's work. Don't tell Alice I said that."

After an hour of instructions, Maxx and Llelu went back to the house where Ben asked, "Have you trained your friend to ride a tree tug without hurting himself?"

"I told him I wasn't his mother and I wouldn't be cleaning up any blood."

Zeff cut in, "If Llelu's ready, we'll take the tugs and skidders back to the lake. We'll pick up the rest of the crew and take them to one of the drifts to get them settled in. Maxx, you'll brief them and see how many are interested in working."

"I'll make it plain. No food for the lazy."

After Zeff and Ben looked at Maxx, he reworded, "Okay, I'll cordially invite them to participate."

After they picked up Llelu's group and got back to the drifts, Maxx assigned the drifts as sleeping quarters. Then he had them assemble outside for a briefing. Even though Connie, Alice and Wicks had explained things to them at the lake, Maxx went over everything again. He made the point clear that Ben and Jenna were to be seen as friends. After detailing what was involved in cleaning up the trees, he asked who was interested.

The group was more interested in being rescued. A flight technician asked when they could expect to be getting off the planet. Maxx told them that no ETA had been confirmed but the reality could be months. There was some negative muttering and Maxx spoke in a firm tone. "Shut it. We're here and we'll make the best of it. Understood?"

Llelu spoke with a more inviting tone, "I've met Ben and Jenna, they're really nice. They can use our help and judging by her tarts and what Maxx says, she's a real good cook." He paused and asked Maxx sarcastically, "Did you eat all the tarts, or did you save some for the rest of us?"

"I was saving them for people who deserved them."

"Ben wouldn't appreciate that."

"Fine, they can each have one."

While Maxx opened the wooden box he was holding and handed each of them one, Llelu continued to explain, "Those tugs and the skidders you rode on here are what you'll be using. I think if we're careful, they could be fun to use."

Flight Tech. Lucy Tyyne politely questioned, "Frohm said Jenna was pregnant?"

"It will be a great day for Ben when Jenna delivers."

"It will be a greater day for her when she delivers."

Maxx glanced at Lucy, "Yeah, I guess you're right. Now who's in?"

Lucy was the first to answer, "If she's pregnant, I'm in."

Fross, the head mess chef, spoke challengingly, "What's her being pregnant got to do with anything?"

"Fross, pick three others to make the meals and they better come up to Jenna's standards or you'll be wearing them!" Maxx retorted.

Fross knew the EXO was serious and picked three as his mess staff. Maxx asked Wicks to take them to *Defender* to get food from the locker. Then he looked at the rest of them.

"There are no free rides. Those who want to stay here in the morning, you'll be given jobs to do. Those with strong backbones assemble here at zero-seven-hundred. I suggest you settle in and wait for Fross to get back and cook tonight's meal. Llelu, you're with me."

Maxx informed Zeff, "I gave the others tonight to think about it. At zero-seven-hundred, those coming are to be assembled outside our drifts. And I was nice about it." When

Ann glanced at Llelu, he added, "I had to remind the EXO about the root tarts."

She looked at the box Maxx was holding and asked, "Are there any left?"

"I thought you'd want me to save them for after dinner."

"Right after dinner."

* * *

After dinner, Lucy and three other women and four men asked to talk with Maxx.

Lucy stated, "Sir, there's still three hours of daylight. Would you check us out on the tugs?"

Maxx stared at her and then glanced at the rest to make sure they were serious. "Go get Wicks and Llelu and meet me by the tugs."

Until dark, Maxx, Wicks with Llelu taught the eight of them how to safely operate the tree tugs.

In the morning, Zeff came out and found eleven crew members ready to learn how to harvest trees. "Carrots, not a stick."

Maxx stated, "Root tarts, not carrots."

By 0800 hours, they were on site and Zeff divided them into two groups. Maxx was to train the cutting crew while Zeff would train the rest of them how to limb the downed and hanging trees safely.

* * *

Ben and Jenna were prompt arriving at *Defender* for her examination. While they were in the exam room with Ann and Alice, Connie was in engineering making sure everything would run properly. While there, she poked around other systems to see what else she could get back online.

Ann used the ultrasound to produce images to familiarize herself and Alice with Jenna's internal biology. Then Ann warned Jenna, "I want to show you the images. The only thing is you'll learn the sex of the baby."

After Jenna and Ben looked at the images, Ann stated, "Everything seems to be normal."

Ben commented in the slightest tone of disappointment, "A boy?"

"The next one will be a girl. This way she'll have an older brother to look after her," Jenna reassured him.

Alice told them, "In our society, most men would be happy to have a son. When he's old enough, he'll be able to help with the trees."

Ben explained, "Sixty percent of newborns are males. Hiring help is not a problem. A daughter who's brought up with the proper ethics and values is one to be treasured. I was blessed when Jenna agreed to marry me."

"Ann, you don't see anything that concerns you?" Jenna held Ben's hand while asking.

"The baby's and your heartbeats are regular and strong. I'd like to take some blood samples to run tests to check for infections. In addition, we'll find out if our knowledge of fetal health has any bearing on your people's fetal health."

After the blood was taken, Jenna told Ben it was time to get back to work. When they left, Alice and Ann ran the blood tests. Neither of them could determine what the extra marker they found was. Ann decided to ask Jenna about it when they were alone.

* * *

After leaving *Defender*, Ben stopped to help Zeff and Maxx with the cutting crew as Jenna continued home. A half-hour before the midday meal, Jenna called Ben to gather the crews for lunch. As they came to get their meal, Jenna thanked each one for helping. Lucy gave Jenna a hand with the food, and then she sat down next her.

"If I may ask, how are you feeling and what did Ann say?'"

The two of them talked as friends through the lunch break. When Maxx told everyone it was time to get back to work, Jenna asked Lucy if she would come into the house and give her a hand cleaning up. Lucy went over to the EXO and asked, "Maxx, Jenna asked if I could give her a hand cleaning up."

"Don't let her do any heavy lifting."

"Maybe I can get Jenna to teach me how to make those root tarts."

"Those and spew stew. If you do that, I'll talk to Zeff about promoting you."

At the end of the day, Ben thanked both crews for what they had accomplished. Llelu stated that the work had given him a feeling of accomplishment. After that, Maxx and Wicks took the crews to the lake to soak their sore muscles.

Zeff headed back to the portal to see Ann and Alice about Jenna's examination. Connie checked in to explain she had gotten *Defender*'s short-range communications systems working. "If a ship does come close enough, with luck, I should be able to contact them."

Over supper, there were very positive comments on Jenna's cooking with Fross' expression showing how much he did not appreciate the remarks.

Lucy got back to the drifts late and Fross told her she could warm up some leftovers. She thanked him and explained that she had helped Jenna make spew stew and had already eaten. Maxx's ears perked up and asked, "Is that what we're having tomorrow?"

"That and crasberry cake."

"Is the cake as good as her tarts?"

"I think it's better."

Alice smirked at Maxx and stated, "You and your appetite."

# Chapter 5 Pilot Ray Oseeka

In the morning as the mulching and the cutting crew prepared for work, Ann took Lucy aside to explain, "Zeff and Maxx want you to stay close to Jenna."

"Sure, but why?"

"Pregnant women make Maxx nervous."

"I didn't think anything made him nervous."

"After he was born, his mother miscarried twice. Her regrets have always stayed with Maxx."

For the first seven weeks after Llelu's group had arrived, things went relatively well. Both crews had picked up speed and began to be more productive. Then on the first day of week eight, there was a noticeable change in the intensity of the suns. Both crews stopped what they were doing and stared skyward. The cutting crew quizzed Ben about the phenomenon.

With some reluctance, he looked at their faces before explaining, "Somewhere the planet's been attacked, and the globes have repositioned to neutralize the threat. Another vessel has been turned into what you classify as a ghost ship."

Zeff asked, "What ship?"

"There's a council meeting scheduled in four days. In two days, I'll leave for the city and will get any answers they have."

"Four days? Ben, they should be meeting right now."

"What's been done now is done. When the globes return to their positions, it'll mean the attack has been neutralized."

When Lucy and Jenna were delivering the mid-day meals to the chipper crew, the suns' intensity changed. Ann asked what was happening. Jenna explained about the attack and told them that Ben was the local member of the council and he would ask about the attack at the next meeting.

With that, Jenna gave Ann a pained expression and fell to her knees. Immediately, Ann ordered Alice to give her a hand

and sent Lucy to the house for blankets and to tell Connie to go to *Defender* and put the med deck online.

As Ann left on her tree tug, she called Zeff on her comm and explained about Jenna. Ben was beside him and heard. Immediately they got on their tree tugs and headed to the chipper. When they got there, Ann was kneeling by Jenna's right side as she lay on a skidder holding her newborn son on her chest.

Ben got on his knees and quietly asked Jenna, "Are you good?"

"And our son as well."

As they talked, Alice told Zeff that the umbilical cord had been wrapped around the baby's neck and it was a simple thing for Ann to remedy. Then she explained that they would be taking Jenna and the baby to the med deck for a checkup. Zeff glanced at the group that had gathered as both crews stood waiting for the news. He called Llelu and Alice over to him and explained, "Ben, you'll ride in the skidder with the family. Llelu will drive the tug."

"I'm glad Ann was here. Jenna and I, appreciate her help," Ben smiled.

Jenna looked up at Zeff. "A little rest and I'll be fine."

"Lucy will stay with you until Ann says otherwise."

When they got to *Defender*, Connie and Wicks had a hanger door open and Llelu drove the tree tug in. Ben helped Jenna into the lift and up to the med deck. Alice washed the baby as Ann took care of Jenna while Lucy stood ready with clean clothes for Jenna and diapers and blankets for the baby.

When Alice handed the baby back to Jenna, she asked, "Have you decided on a name?"

Jenna glanced at Ben, "Allen Russell Simon."

"Allen after Zeff, Russell after Maxx and Simon's our last name," Ben explained.

Alice smiled, "It's a beautiful name. Zeff and Maxx will be honored."

"Won't your relatives be disappointed?" Ann politely queried.

"Ben will explain to my father, and he'll understand."

Ben smiled, "Our daughter will be named Ann Alice Simon."

"Are you two sure?" Ann questioned.

"We're quite sure."

Maxx called on the comm link, "Ann, we're all waiting to see Jenna and the baby."

"Tell them to be patient." Ann looked at Ben and Jenna. "I have a question. When we took a blood sample from Jenna, there was something different. I'm not sure if it's normal or not."

Ben looked at Jenna to explain.

"It's hereditary in a few of our kind."

"Meaning?"

"When our ancestors agreed to leave Mars, they were given an injection against space sickness and streamers disease. It's referred to as the M Marker and is passed down from generation to generation in the blood. For us, it's normal and our son will carry it with him."

Alice commented politely. "M for Matagam. A cure for space sickness, I wish we had that."

Ann looked at Jenna. "Are you two ready to show off your son?"

"We're ready."

They took the lift down to the hanger and Ann had Jenna with Ben sit in the skidder. Then Llelu moved it out slowly so everyone could gather around. As the group gazed at the family, they each gave congratulatory comments.

Ann looked for Zeff, wanting to tell him the name Ben and Jenna had chosen. She called him on her comm link. "Zeff you're missing this. Where are you?"

"Engineering. Get down here."

When Ann got to engineering, Zeff, Connie and Wick's expressions showed their concern. Ann asked, "What's the problem?"

"Remember I fixed the short-range comm. Well, it recorded a transmission," Connie explained.

"From whom?"

"*Venture* was the ship that attacked the planet."

"And the crew?"

Wicks solemnly deduced, "Odds are *Venture's* a coffin ghost ship with the crew sleeping their way into eternity."

Zeff detailed, "*Venture* wasn't traveling alone, and they got a long-range distress call off to *Rapture*. It said the heat of the suns was interfering with their on-board systems. Then the transmission stopped mid sentence."

Ann thought for a moment. "*Rapture* will be on its way to investigate."

In a guarded tone, Zeff surmised, "If they come across *Venture* and see it's been turned into a ghost ship. With the warning, if I was the captain, I'd plan a night attack."

"Does the planet have night defenses?"

"I've got no idea, Ann. We'd better ask Ben."

Ann thought of Ben, Jenna, and their newborn son, "Not today, Zeff. They're so happy, I don't want to spoil it."

"If I was the captain, I'd be searching for *Venture* and looking for answers before planning any attack."

"Wicks, let's hope you're right," Ann said.

Ann looked at Zeff with a disenchanted expression, "I think you'd better get out there and congratulate Jenna and Ben. They named their son Allen Russell after you and Maxx."

Connie suggested they congratulate the happy couple. When they got outside Ben asked everyone to celebrate with him and Jenna by taking the rest of the day and the next day off as rest days.

That night, Zeff, Ann, Connie, and Wicks took Maxx and Alice, along with Llelu, back to *Defender* to explain about *Venture* and its distress call to *Rapture*. They all discussed the possible negative outcomes. Then the group went silent while reflecting on the friends they had made and the possible coming attack that could ruin their relationships.

Alice suggested Connie try using the ship's transmitter to send a message to the four missing fighters. Connie said she had tried with no success and explained sending a signal straight up offered little difficulty. The problem was that the trees and the escarpment blocked directional signals. Llelu suggested he could go back to the escape pods on a tug and bring back the others and the pods. Then they could use the pods to direct *Defender's* signal. Connie pointed out pods were designed as single flight crafts.

Maxx commented with a grin. "The escarpment isn't the problem, it's the solution. Put a remote relay on it and we can turn it in every direction until we get a reply. Those pilots have to be somewhere."

Ann asked, "Zeff, what would you have them do?"

"Connie and Wicks will stay with the ship and listen for *Rapture's* transmissions. Then they can send a message that we're here and safe and there's no need for any aggressive action. At the same time, the fighters fly up so the pilots can explain in person."

Maxx's skepticism showed. "That's hoping the fighters are flight ready and the pilots aren't in that alien holding area in the south."

Zeff replied, "I'll ask Ben to find out when he goes to the council meeting."

* * *

In the morning, the crews gathered in front of the portal and Maxx asked, "What's on your minds?"

Llelu spoke for them, "Jenna and Ben deserve time with the baby. We might as well work and show them we appreciate them as friends."

Maxx called Zeff on the comm and asked him to join them and hear the crews' requests. When Zeff and Ann came out, Maxx had Llelu repeat himself. As he explained, Zeff's thoughts were on the threat to *Rapture*. He smiled as he told his crew, "It will mean a lot to them." Then he quietly commented to Maxx, "Carrots."

"Jenna's food," Maxx replied.

After the crews left, Connie and Wicks went to *Defender* to put together a repeater to position on the escarpment. Ann went to Ben and Jenna's to see how the family was doing. She explained why the crews decided to work. Ben thought he should give them a hand and Jenna wanted to make the midday meal. Ann said no to both. She told Jenna that she and Lucy would make the meal. When it was time to deliver it, Ben and Jenna with the baby went with Ann and Lucy to thank the crews. In response, Llelu thanked them. He explained that he had been brought up being passed between foster homes. He admired their relationship and the joy that being parents gave them.

When the meal was finished, Ben asked, "I appreciate what you're doing but I think we all should go to the lake for the rest of the day. Jenna would enjoy it."

"Fresh air will do Jenna and the baby some good. Any objections, Zeff?" Ann responded.

"As usual, the doctor's orders override a captain's."

At the lake Zeff took Ben aside. "The sun and those two globes are very effective daytime defenses. Does the planet have night defenses as well?"

"How often have you and Ann sat out at night and looked at the stars and moons?" Ben asked.

"Moons, they're reflectors as well?"

"Matagam Pagwa wanted Yovex and her sister planet Xevoy protected."

"Sister planet?"

"It's uninhabited and a hundred and eighty degrees opposite the middle sun of Yovex and on the same orbit."

"Why didn't Matagam and his people settle there?"

"The same answer I gave you for them not settling here. Some evil people were looking for him and his people. If they found him, it could put our people in harm's way. He wanted an uninhabited H-type planet. A planet that had certain elements for his research and where they wouldn't put anyone else at risk."

"If that last ship got a message off, your planet could be in harm's way."

"I'll bring it up at the meeting. Zeff, if you'll please excuse me, I want to be with Jenna and Allen Russell."

"One other quick point. Could you ask if any aliens have been detained since we arrived?"

"I had already planned on asking."

Zeff felt guilty about not being totally honest with Ben. That evening when he got back to the drafts, he and Maxx met with Frohm and Wick. They reported that the relay was in place on the escarpment, and they had sent a test message to all three hundred sixty-degrees with no replies.

In the morning, Ben waited for Zeff to arrive before leaving for the city. "Please don't push the crews too hard. There's still three months before the first snows of winter are expected." Then he kissed Jenna and the baby goodbye and left on his power-glider for the city and his council meeting.

Quietly Jenna informed Zeff, "Ben respects you more than he says. He's not big on expressing his feelings."

"He's a good man and you're a very fortunate woman."

Jenna smiled and nodded as Zeff left to see how the cutting crew was doing.

* * *

After each workday, Zeff and Maxx checked with Connie and Wicks to see if they had received any replies. On the afternoon of the third day of the second week, Connie called, "Zeff, go to the private channel."

He changed settings. "What is it?"

"A response from Ray Oseeka. I gave him our co-ordinates. All going well, he'll be here at about fifteen-hundred."

"As soon as he gets here, have him put his fighter in the hanger and get it refueled. Anything from above?"

"Nothing as of yet."

"Maxx and I'll see you at fourteen-hundred, out."

At 1330 hours, Zeff told everyone to call it a day. With so much daylight left, the crews were happy to comply. When Ann and Alice questioned the early quitting time, Zeff told them to meet him and Maxx at *Defender*. Once they got there, Connie played back the conversation with Oseeka. After listening to it, Alice asked Connie to play back a certain part.

"Mary and Sam's fighters burned up on entry. Must have been problems with their heat deflectors. Beth crashed about a mile from me. I gave her a proper burial and decided to sit tight."

There was a moment of silence after which Zeff asked, "Ann, how about you and Alice going up to the mess to make tea. See if you can find something to snack on?"

"It will give us something to do."

"Maxx and I will be outside watching."

When they got outside, Maxx spoke with a tone of remorse, "Half our crew's dead, a third's missing. Not the letters to write home either of us want to write."

Zeff took his time before replying, "The official report will be easier. I can live with being demoted or washed out. Visiting the families and explaining what happened, that will be the killer. I shouldn't have put it that way."

"As you go, I go. We'll see the families together."

The two men sat down on the ground and remained quiet as they thought of how many families they would have to visit. Half an hour passed before Ann and Alice came out carrying tea and military survival muffins.

Alice explained, "Connie and Wicks are on their way. I guess we've all gotten used to eating outside."

As they sipped the tea, Maxx bit into a survival muffin and turned his head to spit it out. "There was a time when I could stomach fleet food."

"Not up to Jenna's standards?" Alice questioned.

"She's spoiled us."

"After some hard work, food always tastes better."

"Not these or Fross'."

Ann stated, "None of us have ever been in better shape. Whether it's Jenna's food or Ben's work ethic, the crew is in good shape physically and mentally."

"The way the war was going, our life expectancy here is better than it would've been with fleet," Wicks interjected.

Ann's comm link sounded, "Ann its Llelu. After the lake, I went to check on Jenna. She thinks something's wrong with little Allen Russell."

"Tell her I'm on my way."

Alice stated, "I'm coming with you, Ann."

Maxx added, "Alice, keep us informed."

Frohm stood up and looked at Wicks, "I'll check the systems from engineering. You get up to the med deck and make sure there aren't any problems."

* * *

Twenty minutes after Ann and Alice left, a fighter buzzed the top of the trees above *Defender*, then put down vertically close to it.

The pilot started to get out of the fighter, when Maxx spoke in an angry tone "Oseeka, you were told to land and put it in the hanger. Why do you think the damn door is open?"

Oseeka did what he was told and walked outside and stated, "The ship's a wreck. I thought you'd be happy to see me."

"We are. We might have a medical emergency."

"Who's hurt?"

"Jenna's baby and we're waiting for Alice to let us know."

"I don't recall any Jenna on the crew?"

"One of the locals," Maxx clarified,

Oseeka nodded and asked, "How many of the crew made it?"

Maxx detailed how many were with them and the number missing. Oseeka asked respectfully.

"Have you tried looking for the missing?"

Zeff interjected with orders, "Maxx, you and Oseeka get that fighter fueled up."

While they went to the hanger, Zeff finished his tea as he waited for Ann or Alice to contact him. Ann's comment that none of them has ever been in better shape physically or mentally played on his mind. Then Wicks' statement that life expectancy here was better than with fleet, seemed to echo Ann's sentiments.

Maxx and Oseeka came out of the hanger and walked over to Zeff with Maxx suggesting, "Let's go to Jenna's. It beats sitting around here."

"We'll be at Jenna's," Zeff informed Connie.

Wish her well from me and Wicks."

"Copy, Zeff out."

Oseeka asked, "Does that include me?"

Maxx's tone softened as he replied, "It's time you meet one of the locals and her son, Allen Russell. The kid's named after Zeff and me. You'll ride in my skidder."

When they got to Jenna's, Lucy and Llelu met them outside.

Zeff stated with abruptness, "Lucy, you were told to stay with Jenna and the baby."

Llelu interjected, "When you told everyone to knock off early, Jenna told Lucy and me to join the others at the lake."

Zeff paused, "Okay, so how's the baby?"

"Ann thinks it's a reaction to some sort of bug bite. He must have been bitten the other day when we were at the lake."

When Ann came out of the house cradling Allen Russell in her arms, Zeff pondered the sight of her holding a baby.

"There's a rash and some swelling on his inner thighs. To be safe, Ann wants to take him back to the med deck," Alice explained.

Maxx asked politely with conviction, "Jenna, please keep Lucy and Llelu with you. If you think they need some time off, we'll have someone else stay with you."

"Sorry for over reacting."

"Jenna, you didn't over react. Just please have someone with you at all times while Ben's away," Zeff interjected.

"You sound like a father."

Zeff glanced at Ann, "Not yet."

Ann steered clear of Zeff's implication by introducing Oseeka to Jenna.

After saying hello, Jenna said "He's far too skinny. Lucy, please put some stew and some desserts together for him."

"Make it to go. Oseeka can eat when we get back to the ship," Maxx stated.

# Chapter 6 The *Rapture*

When they got back to *Defender*, Ann, Alice, and Lucy took Jenna and the baby up to the med deck. Wicks listened as Ann outlined the tests she would be doing. Then he went down to engineering and explained things to Connie. She had him check the backup systems while she kept the primaries online. Zeff, Maxx, Llelu with Oseeka, waited outside.

As Oseeka was eating the meal Lucy had put together, he asked, "EXO could you have Fross take cooking lessons from Jenna?"

Sarcastically, Maxx asked, "Zeff, what sort of carrot should I use?"

"Some people you motivate with carrots. With Fross, use a big stick."

Oseeka stated, "Tell him it would help with his social standing with the crew."

"I doubt he cares. I'll have the big stick ready."

It took Ann and Alice thirty minutes to run and verify the tests. Their final analysis confirmed Ann's original suspicion of an infection caused by an insect bite. She used an open comm frequency to tell the others.

Zeff replied on a private channel, "Have Lucy and Llelu take the baby home and tell them to stay there. The rest of us are going back to work."

"Alice and I will clean up here. See you later, Zeff."

After Alice and Ann cleaned up the exam room, they had tea in the mess. As they sat, Ann asked, "What's with the grin?

Alice grinned, "The idea of a family on this planet has crossed our minds. Far away from war and death, settling down here has its definite merits."

After visiting, Alice left to check on the mulching crew while Ann went to see Jenna and Allen Russell.

When Zeff, Maxx, and Oseeka got back to the cutting crew,

Oseeka spent the time with Maxx getting lessons on how to safely use the tree tugs.

An hour before quitting time, Jenna used Lucy's comm link to ask both of the crews to come to the house. Llelu and Lucy had set up sawhorses with long planks as tables. Jenna spent the time making dinner with their help. When everyone got to the house, they saw the tables were full of cooking and baking. The crews helped themselves to the food and sat on stumps, the ground, wherever.

As Oseeka was eating and socializing, he appreciated the relaxed comradely that the crew had developed. He glanced over to Ann holding Allen Russell and the expression on Zeff's face.

Maxx and Alice walked over to Oseeka and she asked, "How's the food?"

"It couldn't get any better. If Jenna had a sister that could cook like her, I think I'd be in love."

Alice glanced at Sandra Buffet, one of Fross' galley staff, "How well do you know Sandra? She's glanced over at you twice."

Oseeka turned his head to look, "Buffet? We haven't really talked."

"It might be time you did."

"What's she like?"

"She's got a pleasant personality and a good sense of humor."

Maxx winked, "She seems interested. What are you waiting for? Pilots are supposed to be fearless."

After Alice gave Maxx a stern look, he added, "Well, I feel sorry for anyone who puts up with Fross all day. Grab some food, use a tug and treat her to a picnic at the lake."

"Can I tell Buffet it's an order?"

"If your charming personality doesn't work, then definitely."

When Oseeka turned and looked at Sandra, Maxx challenged him, "Good pilots don't lose their nerve."

Oseeka walked over to Sandra and they began talking. Alice looked at Maxx, "How about we do the same thing? I'll get the food and meet you at our tug."

Jenna sat down beside Zeff and Ann. "Do you want me to hold the baby?"

Ann smiled knowingly, "Zeff needs the practice. We should start cleaning up." She handed the baby to Zeff, "You take good care of little Allen Russell."

Zeff asked, "Where's Lucy and Llelu?"

"They've started in the kitchen."

After Ann and Jenna left, Zeff walked around with Allen Russell in his arms and talked with members of the crew. After a while, his nose noticed a disagreeable poignant stench. He took the baby into the house and mentioned it to Jenna.

"Lesson two of being a father is diaper changing," Ann interjected. "Come with me."

When the baby had been washed, dried and fitted with the second clean diaper, Ann grinned, "A little crooked, but not bad for the first time."

"Do I have what it takes?"

"With proper training, the possibilities are there."

* * *

During the following three days, work progressed. Allen Russell's rash cleared up. On the fourth day, Zeff and Maxx were discussing how to deal with a damaged tree that was hung up on another one.

Connie called on the comm. "Zeff, you'd better get back to the ship. I've picked up parts of conversations between *Rapture* and *Raven*."

"Can you make contact?"

"Too far away for what Wicks and I patched together. I figure twelve hours before I can make continuous contact."

"Be right there, Zeff out." In a puzzled tone, he said "First *Venture*, now *Rapture* and *Raven*, three full-size battleships."

Maxx commented, "Definitely not what I send for a rescue."

"Maybe twelve hours? Get Oseeka on the comm and have him meet us at the ship."

When the three of them got to *Defender*, Zeff asked Oseeka, "Is your fighter fueled and flight ready?"

"Yes, sir. What's the objective?"

"Connie picked up part of a conversation between *Rapture* and *Raven*."

"Two very big nests full of angry birds."

Maxx stared at him. "Listen to your captain's orders."

"You'll fly up to meet *Rapture*. When you're close, make contact. Make it plain to who's in charge that this planet is inhabited and the people are friendly. And, under no circumstances, are they to take any offensive actions." Zeff paused briefly. "Get permission to go wheels down, then when you're on board, ask to talk to the captain face to face. Make it very plain that he understands he's not to take any offensive actions. Make it damn plain."

"May I quote you, sir?"

"If he doesn't listen, you have my permission to use stronger language and say you're quoting me."

Maxx interjected, "You remind whoever's in charge, *Defender* is down here. She might not be able to get off the ground, but her weapons array is totally functional."

"Meaning?"

"If he asks you that, you ask him if he's an idiot."

Zeff cut in. "Oseeka get that bird out of the hanger and wheels up. Deliver my message and make it very blunt and damn plain."

Oseeka left and hovered the fighter around and out of the hanger. Then he lifted it vertically above the trees and pushed the controls all the way forward.

* * *

Zeff questioned Maxx, "Are our weapons array totally functional?"

"Connie and Wicks have been working on them. I might've stretched the truth."

Zeff tapped his comm link. "Connie, what's the status of our weapons array?"

"We can fire them just not sure what we'd hit. Targeting systems need work."

"Thanks, Zeff out."

"Zeff."

"Yeah, Connie."

"Message from Oseeka. He wants spew stew and root tarts

when he gets back. He asked if the EXO would personally see to placing the order with Sandra Buffet."

"Tell him I'll get Maxx right on it."

Maxx responded, "That cheeky young twit."

"If he makes it back, he'll deserve it."

"What say we call the crews and tell them to knock off early?"

"After you place Oseeka's order with Buffet."

"You realize it'll be between zero four and zero five-hundred before we can expect to hear from *Rapture*? It'll only be just beginning to get light."

Zeff thought of a night attack, "Better talk to Connie and Wicks."

When they got to engineering, Zeff explained, "I need a couple of favors from you."

You want us to take turns staying by the radio all night and when *Rapture* calls, stall them until daylight," Connie said.

"You got it."

"Any suggestions on what we're to say?"

"Tell them I died and Maxx is acting captain and he's got a hangover."

Maxx laughed, "That's not going to work. Is Oseeka supposed to be quoting a dead man? Connie, you and Wicks think of something and make it believable."

When Zeff and Maxx got back to the drifts, Ann was outside and told Maxx, "Alice is on the escarpment waiting to finish your family discussion." After Maxx nodded and walked away, Ann asked, "What's wrong?"

"Pardon?"

"Zeff, we've known each other for five years. I can tell by instinct."

He explained about battleships *Rapture* and *Raven* and sending Oseeka as an envoy. Ann took him by the hand. "It's going to make for a short night."

At 0440 hours, Zeff's comm alert sounded. "Connie?"

"Zeff, a certain rear admiral wants to talk to you. I delayed him by saying you've just had your gall bladder removed and you're resting."

"Pardon?"

"Gall bladder removed. He gave me an hour to get you on the comm."

"Gall bladder? Which rear admiral?"

"Three-in-One."

"Oilskin?"

"The one and I hope the only."

"I'll be right there."

Ann opened her eyes and asked, "Whose gall bladder?"

Zeff explained and then called Maxx and told him it was time.

Maxx asked, "Who's the captain?"

"Don't know but Oilskin's in command."

"What's that butt sitting, button-pushing moron doing out from behind his desk?"

"I'll be sure to ask him. Now get ready."

"Alice says she coming."

"Fine, then bring her."

Ann responded with humor, "As the attending physician, I'd better be close at hand to answer any medical questions."

When the four of them got to *Defender*, Wick was waiting outside, "He called again, and Connie told him the doctor was helping you to get dressed."

As they walked into engineering, Oilskin was on the comm link to Connie. "Understood, sir. As soon as the doctor gets the captain down here, I'll notify you and have him on the comm. Out, sir."

Alice turned to Ann. "He's a real piece of work in need of a total frontal lobotomy?"

"What did he say?"

"It's his attitude and his words like 'listen, dearie, when a man says…' He's totally demeaning. I wouldn't talk to a child like that."

Zeff asked Connie, "Contact *Rapture* and I'll talk to him."

"Zoyia, it's Connie Frohm, please inform Three-In-One that Zeff is holding."

The next voice was Oilskin's, "Zeff, your pilot wants me to have *Rapture* stand down."

"With due respect, both *Rapture* and *Raven*. As long as you don't take any aggressive actions, you'll all be safe."

"Are you aware of the circumstances? The last transmission from *Venture* came from above that planet. We found it floating in space as a ghost ship."

"Sir, I feel that I need to make a couple things clear." Zeff said. "Please do not attack the planet! The inhabitants are friendly and peaceful."

Oilskin raised his voice. "Zeff, I'll make things clear. I've been on *Venture* and all systems including life supports were fried and offline. The crew was frozen stiff. Captain Arbutus and I went through the academy together."

In the background, Maxx stated a fleet-wide known fact, "Political connections are what got those two through the academy, not intelligence."

Wicks started laughing and Zeff gave him a cold hard look. Oilskin asked, "What was that last bit?"

"Interference, sir, may I ask?"

"What?"

"First *Venture*, now *Rapture* and *Raven*, on a rescue mission, sir?"

"What's left of our Zolleck fleet is searching for planets to inhabit. Your illusion of a rescue is secondary."

When Maxx heard the statement, he motioned to Connie to put conversation on the open channel.

Oilskin continued talking off handily, "You knew the war was going badly. Update Zeff, we lost. Now we need a planet to re-settle on."

"How many civilian craft are with you, sir?"

"We lost the damn war, Zeff. We did not have time to put together a civilian convoy. It was all I could do to get away alive."

"Sir —"

"I'll get back to you, out."

With an expression of disgust, Maxx stated, "He ran to save his own cracked butt. Rear admiral, now I understand the term."

"Your illusion of rescue is secondary. It makes me feel so appreciated," Alice stated with sarcasm.

Llelu walked in as Connie asked Maxx, "Should I keep the comm open?"

Zeff thought Connie meant the link to *Rapture* and answered with attitude, "Yeah, I'm sure Three-In-One will have more to say."

Llelu asked Zeff, "How did the Rear Admiral get known as Three-In-One?"

"Oilskin was the Minister of Defense for a short period."

Maxx stated, "Three years."

Zeff nodded and continued, "In those three years, he put the military under one umbrella. Naval personnel were transferred to Space Fleet while ground forces traded places with everyone. His motto was a Three-In-One military would save money and be more effective."

Maxx piped in, "He couldn't get it through his thick, fat skull that each arm of the military is a career choice and not a job. The concept that you had to have confidence in the ones you served with to stay alive and get the job done was a foreign notion to him. The guy did more damage to our military than any enemy."

Connie detailed to Llelu, "At one point, they assigned a naval gunner to me as my apprentice engineer. Nice guy but he didn't know a sonic coupler from a sound meter. Totally off the books, Zeff got the trade reversed."

"How'd he do that?"

"The guy's still on our roster. Fleet still pays him as an apprentice engineer." Connie paused and added, "I guess none of us are getting paid now."

As Llelu considered, Zeff stated, "We've run four short since then. I want a crew who works well together and is dependable. There isn't a man or woman that I'd trade off this crew."

Maxx questioned, "Does that include Fross?"

Zeff was about to comment when Connie Frohm answered the comm and stated, "Yes, sir, he's standing right here." Connie pointed to Zeff to take the comm.

"What can I do for you, Rear Admiral?"

"Your pilot, what's your name, son? Your pilot, Oseeka, is standing beside me, and he says he's quoting you."

"Was he respectful and polite, sir?"

"He certainly was not."

"Then he's probably quoting me."

"He says if I attack the planet, I'd better kiss my six goodbye."

"I'm sure I said, 'kiss your cracked ass goodbye.'"

"That's insubordination."

"Very true, sir."

"Damn right, it is. Your pilot says *Defender's* weapons array is functional. What's that supposed to mean?"

"That our weapons can be fired, sir."

"Do I detect hints of a threat?"

Zeff choose his words purposely, "I wouldn't hint, sir."

"We're close enough for our long-range scanners to scan that planet. Other than *Defender*, I don't see other ships or weapons."

"Think of *Venture*, sir. I doubt you want *Rapture* to be a ghost ship."

"If that planet's responsible, I'll start by smashing its biggest cities to rubble."

"Rear Admiral, please allow Oseeka to make his choice of staying on a potential ghost ship or returning to the planet."

"Why would I do that?"

"You've already lost the war. Now you're about to lose your ass. Oseeka should have the right to choose where he's going to die."

"If he's stupid enough to want to die under the bombardment, I'm going to unleash. It's his choice."

Oilskin looked to Oseeka for his answer. "By your leave, sir, I'll be going."

Oilskin snapped at him. "Get off my ship. I'll blow a creator big enough to bury your fighter and you in it." Then Oilskin questioned Zeff, "Are you giving the rest of your crew the same choice?"

"Sir, *Rapture's* scanners should be able to pick up *Defender's* position. When you're in range, please send down three shuttles to our position. A hundred miles south of our position is a mud volcano. Fifty miles west of it is where eight of our escape pods landed. If you'd have three shuttles search that area, they might be able find the rest of my crew."

"Am I to understand that you haven't even looked for your crew?"

"We've been preoccupied cultivating a rapport with the locals. Their good will and assistance have been crucial to our survival."

Oilskin could not comprehend Zeff's attitude, "Your priority is to your crew."

"It was, sir. Doctor O'Casey says they're in better shape now than ever. Sixteen of the crew from the pods found their way to *Defender*. I can't answer why the rest decided to sit tight."

Oilskin hesitated before commenting, "When we're in range, I'll dispatch the shuttles. Once they're back on board, that planet's getting blasted. Oilskin out."

"The man's an idiot. Odds he doesn't know what a mud volcano is." Maxx stated firmly.

In a very quiet tone, Connie confessed, "Maxx, I don't know what a mud volcano is."

"Connie, mud volcanoes exist on most H-Type planets. They form when a combination of mud, fluids, and gases erupt at the surface and form massive mud flats over the ground."

Llelu questioned, "Is Oilskin typical of the rear echelon?"

"He wouldn't be if Zeff had taken the promotion he was offered," Maxx retorted.

Llelu's eyes focused on Zeff as he detailed his reasons of refusal, "Politics, Llelu. Oilskin had political backing and I would've been there as the fall guy."

"You don't know that for sure."

"Reality check, Maxx. When Bert White was the Minister of Defense before Oilskin, he offered me the promotion. If I had taken the move, you would've gone with me and White warned me that we would be sheep for the slaughter."

"And Alice and Ann?"

"Just us."

Maxx thought of Alice, "In that case, I'm glad you turned it down."

Alice commented, "Both Ann and I appreciate it."

"In fifteen minutes, all of you are to meet us outside."

Lucy called on her comm, "Zeff, you do realize you're on an open channel?"

Zeff glanced at Maxx as Lucy continued, "We all heard every word of your conversation with Three-In-One."

"I know now. Thanks, Lucy." Zeff stared at Maxx. "The things Oilskin said will have a negative effect on morale. Next time think before you issue orders behind my back."

"I did. The crew needs to know the truth. How else can they make a decision?"

"I would've explained it to them."

"No offense, Zeff, but it's better they hear it straight from Oilskin's mouth."

Wicks added, "Maxx is right. None of us would want to believe we lost the war and command ran away leaving the civilians as fodder. Would you have believed it?"

Zeff considered Wicks' point. "Let's head outside."

Outside, the crew was standing around talking and waiting. As Maxx glanced at them, a flight technician who had arrived in Llelu's group asked, "Zeff, those three shuttles you requested. You're not really going to order us to leave on them? Are you, Capitan?"

"What I'm ordering you to do, is make your own decisions. You all heard what the Rear Admiral said." Zeff paused to find his words. "I'm honored to be your captain, but this goes beyond my military or moral authority."

"Oseeka made his decision and he's on his way back. When those shuttles arrive, each of you'll have to make yours," Maxx said.

"If the Rear Admiral does what he said and attacks the city, none of us will be welcomed on this planet," Zeff added. "We'll be seen as the enemy. We'll have no way off and might be forced to live in hiding."

Connie reminded them, "We'll be putting Jenna, the baby, and Ben in a very difficult position."

There were conversations amongst the crew until Jones raised his voice. "Shut it. All of you." He waited until he got their attention before continuing, "Life on the run is life. Frozen dead on a ghost ship is dead. Now ponder that scenario."

The group went silent as they thought. Zeff knew that it would take three hours for the shuttles to arrive and three more for them to get back to *Rapture*. "You have a few hours to make your decision. Think it out carefully."

"When you talk to Three-In-One again, will we be allowed to listen?" Sandra asked.

"You're damn right. Now you heard the captain, think it over," Maxx retorted.

"Everyone up to the mess. Fross, you get your people making something edible to eat," Ann intervened.

With the idea of Fross cooking, there were some negative moans and comments. Maxx stated, "Try to do better than those survival muffins."

# Chapter 7 The *Raven*

A half-hour after Zeff had talked to Oilskin, he and Maxx stood outside *Defender* waiting for Oseeka. Lucy and Jenna and the baby pulled up in a tree tug. Lucy explained, "Zeff, after listening to your conversation with the Rear Admiral, Jenna wanted us to be with the crew."

"They're in the mess trying to decide what they're going to do. Fross has made something, hopefully edible. You might as well head up."

"Zeff, I know you have nothing to do with what's going on. My prayers are with you and your crew." Jenna spoke compassionately.

"Thank you, Jenna."

* * *

An hour later, Oseeka landed his fighter vertically near *Defender*. When he saw Maxx's expression from the cockpit, he then maneuvered the fighter into the hanger and set it down. Oseeka climbed out and walked outside, "Am I ever glad to get off that ship. Three-In-One's not flying with his stabilizers fully engaged."

"What happened up there?"

"EXO, it's strange. The pilots and the flight deck guys aren't happy. I haven't ever seen a crew more on edge."

"Oseeka, I asked you what happened. What did Oilskin say?"

"I said I was quoting Captain Allen Zeff and called Oilskin an idiot. He threatened to create a crater big enough to bury me and my fighter."

"We heard that, what else?"

Oseeka hesitated before answering. "Anyone who doesn't get on those shuttles will be officially charged with treason, as if ..."

"What do you mean by as if?" Maxx asked.

"The deckies told me there are only five full-size carriers and three cruisers left. The rest of the fleet was destroyed defending Avanac while the rear echelon ran."

"Who was left defending our home world?" Zeff questioned.

"According to those guys, only ground forces and they were getting pummeled by four Catherian Fleets. By now any resistance would have been crushed."

Maxx told Oseeka, "Most of the crew is in the mess. Join them and get some food."

"Did you give Buffet my message?"

"Zeff ordered me to."

After Oseeka walked away, Maxx asked, "Are you going to call Oilskin?"

"After the shuttles arrive. Right now, I'm not in the mood."

"There are two crews up there. Richard Dobbs is captain of *Raven* and he's not a bad guy. I'd say he's level headed."

"Dobbs left Avanac in the middle of a fight. What's that say about him?"

"He was following orders?"

Zeff thought of the crew of *Raven* before responding. "You know Dobbs. Call him and see if he's free to talk."

They went to engineering. Maxx called *Raven* to request to speak with Capt. Dobbs. "Dick, can you talk freely?"

"I'm in my quarters with my EXO. We've been listening to Zeff's tête-à-tête with Oilskin. You might suggest he use a private channel in the future."

"It was open by my orders. I wanted the crew to hear Oilskin's raving stupidity."

"Say what's on your mind, Maxx."

"Did you see *Venture*?"

"Three-In-One made the senior officers put on space suits and do a float through. What kind of a weapon does that?"

"The kind you don't want to be on the receiving end of. Just don't fire on the planet and put some distance between you and *Rapture*. If Three-In-One opens fire, you don't want to be near him."

"How do I do that without him targeting *Raven*?"

"Tell Oilskin you want to reposition fifty miles west of the mud volcano to look for the rest of *Defender's* crew."

"I guess he can't shoot us down for asking. I suppose it's worth a try."

"Tell him you'd be in a better position to cover his shuttles."

"His ego might buy that."

"Dobbs, it's Zeff. If he fires on this planet, it'll be the second last thing he'll ever do."

"Second last, what's the last thing?"

"Dying."

"Dick, it's Maxx. Do you have any rear echelon brass with you?"

"They're on *Rapture* along with their political correctness security chaperones."

"Get your ship moved and do it quickly. Maxx out." He looked at Zeff. "We've got about forty minutes before the shuttles arrive. Let's go up to the mess and see if Jenna's made something edible. Those darn survival muffins should be wrapped with warning labels saying 'Caution Hazardous to Taste Buds.'"

When they got up to the mess, Ann was standing by the galley door holding Allen Russell. She nodded to Maxx and motioned to the kitchen. Ann walked over to Zeff and they found a table off to one side.

Zeff's expression was full of awe. Ann asked, "What's with the look?"

"You holding the baby is the only bright spot in my day."

Ann glanced down at Allen Russell then passed him over to Zeff. He looked at the baby as Ann spoke with a fondness. "Odds are we're not getting off this planet and raising a family here does have some genuine appeal."

The baby's tiny fingers gripped Zeff's thumb. "He's got quite the grip."

"So was that a yes?" Ann asked.

"I was counting how many times I've asked you and now you're asking me," Zeff smiled.

She looked at the attentive way Zeff was holding Allen

Russell, "I think you'd make a good father and husband. And yes, Captain Allen Zeff, I'm asking."

"You're serious?"

"Very serious."

Maxx, Alice, and Jenna joined the table and Zeff's expression prompted Alice to ask, "And the good news is?"

"Ann's asked me to marry her."

"Say again?"

"You heard me."

"And you had the good sense to say yes?"

"Of course."

The three of them congratulated the couple. Then Jenna asked, "In your society, does the woman always ask the man?"

Alice explained, "Zeff's proposed five times to Ann. I guess it was her turn."

"May I ask why you procrastinated so often?" Jenna asked Ann.

"I was raised with the belief that marriage had no escape pods. I needed to be sure Zeff was as committed as I was."

"After four rejections and he's still asking, I think he'd proven that."

When Maxx looked around the room with the idea of making a formal announcement, Zeff asked him to hold off until the shuttles had arrived and the crew had made their final decisions.

Ann noticed Sandra and Oseeka talking by the galley door. "Those two seemed to have hit it off. Zeff, when it's time, you as captain, could join those two together."

Alice suggested, "And when you two do it, we'll have to make Maxx an acting captain. The way Zeff's holding little Allen Russell, I can see he'll be busy being a father."

Llelu and Lucy came over to the table and Llelu put down a pot of tea and cups. Lucy placed a small platter of buns and explained, "The buns are called winter tree tops because of the thick white icing covering the dark, rich carrot cake. EXO, they're safe to eat. It is Jenna's recipe with her supervising us."

EXO Maxx made a questioning expression before picking one up. As he started to sample it, Oseeka walked past their table and went out into the corridor. Five minutes later he came back in and informed them, "A shuttle's inbound."

Zeff started to handed a smiling Allen Russell to Ann, "Don't get ahead of us, I think Jenna would like to hold her son."

He smiled. "Listen up. Oseeka says—" Zeff stopped mid sentence and asked, "A shuttle?"

"One's all I heard, sir."

Zeff continued to speak to the crew, "From now to when it and the other two land, you'd better have your minds made up. There'll be no opportunity for second chances. Now I want you all on the ground. Those leaving form a single line beside the shuttles. Your mild-mannered EXO Maxx and I salute you and thank you for being part of our crew."

Maxx stood up. "You heard the captain, move it people!"

* * *

When *Defender's* crew got outside, they watched as the shuttle landed. After the door opened, a commander and lieutenant commander got out and sized up the group. When the commander spotted Zeff, she went over to him, saluted, and made the introductions, "Captain Allen Zeff, I'm *Rapture's* EXO Commander Stephanie Bozzar. This is Squadron Leader Flight Lieutenant Bart Cassel."

"An EXO and a squadron leader?" Zeff questioned.

"Only one shuttle?" Maxx asked.

Zeff made the introductions, "Stephanie, Cassel, this is my EXO Russell Maxx."

"If I'd be allowed to explain, sir?"

"Go ahead, Stephanie."

"You requested six shuttles and six left the ship. Five were shot down before they entered the planet's atmosphere."

Zeff knew *Defender* had not fired and glanced up at the three suns that were still in their normal positions. He asked, "By whom?"

"*Rapture* on the Rear Admiral's orders."

Maxx barked, "Why the hell would he do that?"

"Some of the flight technicians and deckies saw the shuttles as a chance to escape."

"Escape?" Zeff questioned.

"There are four teams of political correctness security people on board. After we found *Venture,* eight of the pilots mutinied. They were charged and found guilty. Their penalty was execution by airlock extraction."

Maxx spoke in disbelief. "They were sucked out into space alive?"

Stephanie continued, "The Rear Admiral went on ship-wide comm to announce it as a warning to the rest of the crew. No one doubted his intent."

Oseeka's words that the Rear Admiral was not flying with his stabilizers fully engaged resonated through Zeff's mind.

"Why wasn't your shuttle shot down?" Maxx asked.

"We, the Lieutenant Commander and I, didn't have any passengers on board."

"When does Three-In-One expect you back?"

Cassel looked directly into Maxx's eyes. "ASAP! That's unless you intend on holding us as hostages."

Maxx grinned as he spoke. "Either one of you take one step toward that shuttle, you'll both be shot."

Stephanie and Cassel handed their sidearms to Maxx. She asked, "What now?"

Zeff replied, "Good question." Then he called Ann over and asked her to take them up to the mess.

"What are you planning, Zeff?" Ann asked with suspicion.

"I'll cover their sixes and tell Oilskin that I've taken them hostage. Do me a favor, take the rest of the crew back to the mess. Maxx and I'll figure something out."

When Ann got to the mess, she introduced Stephanie and Cassel to Lucy, Connie, Jenna, and Allen Russell. Alice and Llelu went into the galley to make fresh coffee and ice more winter-capped buns. Then they brought them out for Stephanie and Cassel to sample.

When the others had gone up to the mess, Zeff and Maxx sat outside with their backs against *Defender's* fuselage discussing tactics. Zeff stated, "I didn't ask any of the crew if they'd made up their minds."

"After what Cassel and Stephanie said, was there a need to?"

"Still, I should've asked."

"What are you going to tell Three-In-One?"

Zeff pondered his response. "We-I took Stephanie and Cassel hostage."

Maxx corrected him. "We took them hostage. The question is why?"

"As a bargaining strategy."

Maxx shook his head. "He's shot down five of his shuttles. That strategy won't fly."

"Did you have to say won't fly?"

Maxx ignored the comment. "Try this, we took them hostage to keep them alive."

Zeff smirked as he suggested, "I think I'll wing the conversation."

"And you had to say 'wing the conservation.'"

When they got to *Defender*'s bridge, Zeff called up to *Rapture*.

"Captain Allen Zeff of the *Defender* requesting to speak to the Rear Admiral."

"Please hold, Captain."

After five minutes, Zeff finally got a response from Oilskin. "How soon will that shuttled be off the ground?"

"Not in the foreseeable future, sir."

"What do you mean?"

"I've taken it and your officers hostage."

Maxx grabbed the comm. "We've taken Bozzar and Cassel hostage."

Zeff took the comm back from Maxx as Oilskin yelled, "Who the hell is that?"

"A member of my crew trying to cover for my actions, sir."

"Loyalty to the point of stupidity. The only reason you called was to tell me you're holding my shuttle hostage?"

"No, sir. I just thought I'd take a shot at talking some sense into you. Now I realize it would be a waste of ammunition."

"When we take that planet, if by some miracle you're still alive, I'll have you shot. And it won't be a waste of ammunition."

Zeff responded with attitude. "Captain Allen Zeff of the battle cruiser *Defender,* out, sir." He looked at Maxx, "Now what?"

"There's still Dobbs on *Raven*." Maxx changed the frequency. "EXO Commander Russell Maxx of the *Defender* for Captain Richard Dobbs."

"Please hold, sir."

Dobbs replied immediately. "What do you want now, Maxx?"

"I'm sure you're aware *Rapture* shot down five of its shuttles."

"Yeah, we witnessed it."

"Did you distance *Raven* from *Rapture*?"

"Three-In-One went for it. We're in position south and west of the volcano mud flats."

"What do you see?"

"Your escape pods but no heat signatures. I've sent down two shuttles to take a closer look."

"Let us know what you find."

For reassurance, Dobbs asked, "Are you sure we're far enough away from Oilskin?"

"As long as you don't fire on the planet, you'll be alright. Maxx out."

"If Oilskin wants to do as much damage as he claims, *Rapture* will need to get closer to the planet," Zeff concluded.

"A psycho like Oilskin will want to watch it amplified on his forward screen."

"I figure we've got two hours before he fires. We'd better ask Jenna how to get word to Ben." Zeff called Ann on a closed comm link. "Ann, I need to talk with Jenna, would you bring her down to engineering?"

"We'll be right down."

Ann brought Jenna, Alice, Connie, Stephanie, and Cassel with her. As humor, Zeff asked, "Ann, should we wait for any others?"

Jenna responded, "I asked Connie and Bart to come. They've explained a great deal of the situation. Now what may I do?"

"The Rear Admiral in charge is—"

Maxx interrupted, "His stabilizers aren't fully engaged."

Alice explained, "What Maxx means is the man's mentally unstable."

Zeff continued, "We need to warn Ben he intends to bombard the city. The council needs to act first and fire on that ship."

"That's not possible. The council doesn't control the defenses."

"Then we need to speak to who does."

"The defenses are automated. They're designed to activate only after an attack has been initiated."

"Then someone needs to reprogram them."

"Zeff, you don't understand. We have no control over them. They've been protecting our planets from the days when Matagam Pagwa's people were here. The ancient books tell us that his people put the defenses in to protect the planets. We don't know how they work."

Maxx questioned, "Matagam who? People have to die before the defenses kick in. What good is that?"

Zeff focused on Connie, "The weapons array."

"We can fire but other than putting them up, I'll have little control in the direction they go."

"What about heat seekers?"

"Odds are they'd head toward the suns and disintegrate."

Zeff began to get really frustrated, "Jenna, how do we contact Ben?"

"My tree tug has a communicator to the council."

When they got outside, Jenna reset the emergency comm setting to the planet's standard frequency. Then she called Ben and waited for a response.

"Jenna, how are you and little Allen Russell?"

"We're fine, dear. Zeff asked me to call. He wants to know if the council has noticed there are two ships above the planet."

"The defenses have alerted us."

Jenna handed Zeff the comm. "Ben, it's Zeff. The bad news is one of the ship's commanders plans on attacking the city."

After Zeff explained the situation, Ben replied, "I'll have the council activate a city-wide alert. I appreciate you warning us."

"Ben, I suggest you go pro-active with your defenses before the attack."

"Not possible, Zeff, we don't control them. Jenna can explain that."

"Ben, thousands will be killed."

"Sadly, some lives will be lost but there's little we can do. Zeff, I have to get back to the council and give them your warning. Please put Jenna back on the comm."

He handed Jenna the comm.

"I love you, dear, and our son. I'll get home when I can, take care."

"I love you, see you then."

Maxx stared at Zeff and stated, "A planet of peace-nicks? They should have a least one war-nick to advise them. Now what? We wait?"

# Chapter 8 The Outcome

After Jenna talked to Ben, she and the others went back up to the mess. Zeff and Maxx sat down by the tug to wait and surmise about possible outcomes. All of their theories ended with multiple deaths on the planet and the loss of the crew on *Rapture*. The loss of Oilskin, the other rear echelon cowards, and the four political correctness teams were considered acceptable collateral damage.

One of Maxx's ideas was to have Dobbs use *Raven* to bluff Oilskin. Tell him he was sending his shuttles chaperoned by his fighters to free the crew of *Rapture*. If Oilskin refused, *Raven* would attack. In Zeff's opinion, the result would be too many deaths with Rear Admiral Oilskin firing on the planet in a fit of madness. Zeff's idea was to co-ordinate a mutiny at the same time with Maxx's plan. The question was would Dobbs agree to co-ordinate with the mutiny? Zeff smiled a shrewd grin and stated, "Stephanie and Cassel?"

"The *Rapture's* EXO and squad leader, what about them?"

"We send them back in Oseeka's fighter. They tell Oilskin they escaped and when they're on board, they organize a mutiny. Stephanie would have to get the weapons officer onside while Cassel organizes the flight technicians and deckies. The political correctness teams will offer the most resistance. Maxx, there could be too many casualties."

Maxx responded with a big grin. "While Oilskin is preoccupied with Dobbs, it'll give Stephanie and Cassel time to organize the mutiny. Then they capture Oilskin and the rest of the rear echelon. Death by airlock extraction for being cowards in deserting their posts in a time of war."

"It almost sounds feasible and legal. Oilskin doesn't fire on the planet and *Rapture* isn't turned in to a ghost ship. A lot less casualties than letting Oilskin fire on the planet."

"Now if we can talk Dobbs, Stephanie, and Cassel into it." Maxx pondered.

Zeff got on his comm and asked Ann to send Stephanie and Cassel out to see him. Then he had Maxx go to engineering and contact Dobbs and run the idea by him.

When Ann came out with Stephanie and Cassel, Zeff detailed the idea in full.

Stephanie nodded with confidence, "The majority of the crew will go along with it. There may be some causalities but that's better than losing the whole crew."

Cassel interjected, "We can count the pilots and the deckies being in on it, so let's do it."

"We'll wait for Maxx and see if Dobbs agrees."

Stephanie stated, "It doesn't matter. I like the idea. Cassel can get things organized below decks while I'm on the bridge bantering with Oilskin. We can do this with or without Dobbs."

Ann questioned, "And if it doesn't work, you and Cassel will be killed."

Stephanie replied, "I shouldn't have left in the first place. I owe it to the crew to go back. Zeff, do we have permission to steal Oseeka's fighter?"

He smiled. "Who asks for permission before stealing anything? Five minutes after you are wheels up, I'll complain to Oilskin so he'll know you're on the way."

They hovered the fighter out of the hanger and took off vertically. Maxx came up from engineering questioning, "Was that Stephanie and Cassel?"

Zeff explained Stephanie's and Cassel's motivations.

"What did Dobbs say?" Ann asked.

Maxx shrugged, "Noncommittal, he'll think it over."

Zeff asked, "Did his shuttles find our crew?"

"Not as yet. Odds are they're in the alien zone in the south."

Zeff checked his watch. "Time to report to Oilskin."

They went down to engineering and Zeff called up to *Rapture*. "Zoyia, it's Allen Zeff for the Rear Admiral."

"Zeff, it could be a while."

"Pardon?"

"He's in his quarters and not in the mood to talk. Zeff, may I contact you when he's less agitated?"

"If you would, thanks, Zoyia."

Ann stated bluntly, "That bastard –"

Zeff asked Maxx, "Do us a favor, go talk to Alice and cool off. Then bring down some coffee."

"The way I feel, it might be a while before I cool off."

When Maxx left, Ann stated, "Zeff, I'm glad you're a reasonable man."

Zeff questioned, "If Oilskin's taken alive, how would a reasonable man handle things? I'd like to act on Maxx's suggestion, but for some reason I can't."

* * *

Connie and Wicks came down to engineering with coffee and root tarts. Connie placed the tray down. "Maxx told us to bring you something edible. Jenna's keeping herself busy baking and the crew's been doing a lot of talking."

Connie hesitated so Wicks started, "Zeff, what Connie is getting at is this. We'd all like a meeting."

"After I've talked with Oilskin, I'll come up and explain."

"You were on an open channel with Zoyia and the crew heard what she said," Connie added.

"The guy's a pig and the crew should know what Zeff's up against," Wicks stated.

"You two go back and tell the crew we'll be up after I talk with Oilskin."

"Zeff, you know we're all with you."

"If Oilskin targets *Defender* first, that could be a mistake."

Another twenty minutes passed before Zoyia called. "Zeff he's on his way up to the bridge, I'll tell him you're holding."

"Thanks, Zoyia."

Five minutes later, Oilskin snapped, "You've got some nerve. What do you want now, Zeff?"

"Just to inform you that about forty minutes ago your EXO and that squad leader escaped in Oseeka's fighter. I can only guess they're headed your way."

"Why are you telling me?"

"They've clearly made a choice to die unless you've reconsidered."

"Don't be stupid and don't call me again—"

Zeff switched channels on the comm. "*Raven*, this is Captain Zeff of the *Defender* for Captain Dobbs."

"Would you hold, Captain?"

"I'll hold."

Two minutes went by before *Raven's* comm officer's voice was heard. "Captain Dobbs is ready, sir."

"Sorry, Zeff, I was watching my screen."

"Have you made a decision, Dobbs?"

"When your fighter took off, six of my shuttles shielded and went wheels up loaded with armed personnel. In about five minutes, I should be contacting Oilskin. This better work, Zeff."

"Did you listen to my conversation with Zoyia?"

"Regrettably, yes."

"When it's over, we'll have to do something with him. Think about what."

"I've got a few ideas but I'm not saying them over the comm," Dobbs replied.

"Thanks, Dobbs. Zeff out."

Zeff left Ann by the comm while he went up to detail the plan to the crew. When he finished, Fross asked, "If it fails, what then?"

"First, people on this planet will die. Second, *Rapture* will be a ghost ship, and third, we'll probably be on the run as enemies."

"What about escaping on *Raven*?"

"That's one slim possibility. Captain Dobbs told me they're short on fuel."

Maxx stated in a clear voice, "We'd better hope that Stephanie and Cassel are successful."

The mood of the crew was pensive. They feared failure as much as they feared to be optimistic.

Jenna was concerned for her friends and had a quiet word with Zeff. "Those mining drifts your people live in were made by Matagam's people to extract cesium and yatterblum. As you know, they're the base elements of solid fuel. If your plan succeeds, then those ships would have the fuel they need."

"I'll hold off mentioning it to the crew until the outcome is known."

Next Zeff asked Maxx to stay with the crew while he went back to engineering. He got two coffees and root tarts, then went back down to wait with Ann. It was ninety minutes of nervous anticipation before they got word.

"Captain Zeff of the *Defender*. This is Comm. Officer Lieutenant Zoyia of the *Rapture*. Are you there, sir?"

"What's the status, Zoyia?"

"Stephanie Bozzar is being treated in the med center. She asked me to inform you that we've taken our ship back, sir."

"And Cassel?"

"Sir, he's busy processing prisoners."

Ann cut in. "Zoyia, it's Dr. O'Casey, how's Stephanie?"

"She took a round in her thigh and less mobile than she'd liked to be. The medic says she's fine. He wants to keep her off her feet for a couple of days."

"Zoyia, patch me through to her?"

"When you're ready, Zeff."

"Stephanie, how are you?"

"Pissed that I got shot, but it was well worth the outcome. Sorry about the language, sir."

"Good job and congratulations to your crew."

"Thanks, sir. I'll pass that along."

"Stephanie Bozzar, you're acting captain and I'd recommend Bart Cassel as your EXO."

"Sir, Fleet doesn't promote females to captains."

"I just did, but if you don't want the position then name an alternative."

"That's not what I'm saying, sir."

"Good. Now about Cassel as EXO?"

"I'll let him know, sir."

"Get three day's rest and stay off that leg. On the morning of the fourth day, I want you and Cassel on *Defender*. Each of you have two copies of your after-action reports written for me to review. Zeff out." He turned to Ann. "We need Jenna to contact Ben."

"You should go up to the mess. Let the crew know the news."

"Have Maxx do it. You get Jenna and meet me at her tug."

Ann hugged Zeff. "Promoting Stephanie and Cassel, that was a nice touch."

She went up to the mess to give Maxx the news to pass along to the crew. Then she and Jenna went down to the tug to meet Zeff. Jenna contacted Ben and had Zeff explain what had happened, "Ben, the commander of that ship I warned you about, the threat has been neutralized. I believe your planet's out of harm's way."

"Good! I'll let the council know it's thanks to you and your people."

Zeff handed the comm back to Jenna so she and Ben could talk privately. Then he and Ann went over to *Defender* and sat down beside it to relax and let their anxieties unwind. Shortly after, the crew came down to congratulate Zeff.

"Nice job, sir. One question remains." Oseeka said.

"And what would that be?"

"How's my fighter?"

Zeff shook his head at the young pilot's question, "Why don't you fuel up that shuttle and take Buffet for a ride to find out?"

"Seriously?"

"Yes, now get out here."

After Jenna finished talking to Ben, she spoke to Ann while Zeff was talking to Oseeka. When he finished, Ann had Jenna address the crew.

"Ben and I are very grateful for the way things have turned out. We'd like you to take the next few days off in recognition of our gratitude. When Ben returns from the city, I'm sure he'll have good news you'll appreciate."

"Three days, then back to work," Maxx responded.

The crew thanked Jenna and then dispersed while discussing how to spend their time off. Zeff went back to engineering and called *Raven* to thank Dobbs and asked him to attend the meeting on *Defender* with Stephanie and Cassel.

For three days, everyone relaxed on the escarpment or at the lake as their tensions dissipated. Their biggest question was where they would be heading after leaving Yovex.

On the morning of the fourth day, the cutting and mulching crews went back to work. At 0900 hours, Zeff, Ann, Maxx, and Alice met with Stephanie, Cassel and Dobbs in the mess of *Defender*. As instructed by Zeff, Stephanie gave a copy of her detailed report to Alice while Cassel gave his report to Ann. Then Stephanie read from her original report of the events of the mutiny on *Rapture*. Zeff asked Cassel if her version was correct. He corroborated the facts and that the report was true and accurate.

Next, Zeff had Cassel read his report. When he finished, Dobbs confirmed it lined up with his boarding party's account. Zeff sat back and thought about the events. Then he asked Alice and Ann, "You've been following along with the written reports. Are there any differences or omissions?"

They agreed that Stephanie and Cassel's reports were accurate. Zeff considered his options, then stated, "I want some changes made. Alice and Ann take notes, then rewrite the reports."

Zeff paused to think out the changes. "The part where EXO Stephanie Bozzar shot the Rear Admiral, it will state that Oilskin took his own life instead of facing numerous misconduct charges. Where Cassel and the other pilots jettisoned the political correction teams out the airlocks, it will read they were all killed in the retaking of the ship. Then their bodies were jettisoned into space as proper protocol states. As for the other members of the rear echelon, two died during the retaking of the ship and one followed Oilskin's lead and committed suicide. At the bottom of the report, put the statement: 'All actions were authorized by Capt. Allen Zeff of *Defender*.' I think that's about it. When you have them written up, have Stephanie and Cassel sign them along with me as the Commanding Officer in charge."

Stephanie countered, "Zeff, that's not what happened. My report is factual."

"A little too factual. The record needs to show you and

Cassel being officers acting within your moral and legal rights following my orders retaking *Rapture*."

Ann asked, "What happened to the original captain of the *Rapture*?"

Stephanie answered, "Captain Rollins was on the surface getting his family when Oilskin ordered us to run."

There was a pause as they considered Rollins' fate. After a moment or two, Dobbs finally broke the silence. "If we still had a rear echelon, we'd all be court-martialed. I'll gladly sign the revised statements."

Cassel spoke quietly. "The pilots, crew, and I thank you, Captain Zeff."

"Do I detect an unspoken but?"

"With all due respect, and I mean, all respect. What now, sir?"

"Jenna and Lucy are in the galley making lunch. After we've eaten, Jenna's husband, Ben, should be arriving. Your questions will be answered by him."

Ann and Alice left for the set room to rewrite the statements. Until lunch was ready, Zeff and Maxx took Stephanie, Cassel, and Dobbs outside to teach them how to handle tree tugs.

Dobbs asked Maxx, "Why are we doing this?"

He pointed to Dobb's belt line, "Because it's healthier than sitting around waiting for lunch. You've put on weight, Dick."

An hour and fifteen minutes later, Lucy called Zeff on an open comm to tell him and Maxx that lunch was ready. Maxx had Stephanie and Cassel park their tree tugs.

With a broad smile, he informed them, "You're in for a real treat."

When they got up to the mess, one of the tables was set in a buffet style. Ann was holding Allen Russell in her arms and Zeff paused to smile at her. All of them lined up with their plates. When they were seated, Jenna bowed her head thanking the Creator for her new friends, the protection of the two planets and the food. Then she raised her head and said, "I hope you'll enjoy the food."

Maxx stated with enthusiasm, "Spew stew with winter tree top buns, who wouldn't?"

Lucy added, "There's also root tarts."

After they finished eating, Dobbs stated, "Zeff, you certainly know where to crash. Jenna, thank you for a wonderful meal."

Maxx and Alice gave a hand clearing away the dishes as Zeff, Stephanie, Cassel and Dobbs went over the rewritten reports. When it was agreed they were written the way Zeff had asked, each of them signed them. Alice came out of the galley with fresh tea followed by Maxx with a tray of soft butter raisin cookies.

Fifteen minutes later, Ben walked in and apologized. "Please forgive me. I'm much later than I had hoped. There were some things the council needed to ratify before I could leave."

Jenna introduced Ben to Stephanie, Cassel, and Dobbs. When they were seated, Ben explained, "Jenna called me after you neutralized the threat to our planets and told me your ships are short of fuel. Plus, Jenna says you're in search of a home. There's a second planet in our system called Xevoy. It orbits the same path as our planet Yovex, but on the opposite side of our middle sun. The planet is uninhabited and would have much the same climate as this one. The council has authorized me to offer it to your people as their new home."

Dobbs questioned, "One of our kind threatened to blow your biggest cities away. Why offer us a home?"

"First of all, the council's grateful for Zeff's warnings. If there had been an attack, his warning could have saved thousands of lives. Second, the council is very thankful for the way things turned out. Understandably, you will want to visit Xevoy before making a decision."

Ben saw the bewildered looks on Stephanie, Cassel and Dobbs faces. "Jenna called the night of the event and told me how Stephanie and Cassel risked their lives in coordinating the re-taking of *Rapture*. Commander Bozzar, it is my and Jenna's sincere hope that your wound heals rapidly. Jenna told me the part Capt. Dobbs' people played. The council took note of the serious considerations you must have given before authorizing your people's actions."

Bozzar queried, "How were you able to talk your council into all of this?"

Ben smiled as he looked at Jenna, "Added to what I've already explained, my wife is a good judge of character. Her father is head of the council and he trusts his daughter's instincts."

They turned their heads to look at Jenna. She answered with a timid smile, "You, your species, is only the second one to treat us as equals and to help. From helping with the logging to neutralizing the threat, you've acted as true and valued friends."

Ben picked up the conversation. "Zeff, twenty-nine of those believed to be of your crew are in the detention area. In four days, they'll be brought to the house for you to identify. I've been assured they are being treated well."

"Ben, Jenna what can I say. Thank you isn't enough?" Bozzar spoke with humility.

Dobbs added his gratitude. "The crews of both ships will be relieved to know we have a destination. Thank you."

"We thank you for what you've done."

Jenna nodded to Ben to continue. "Zeff, Jenna, and I hope you and the others of your original group will stay. We've become very fond of you all."

"You understand it'll be up to each individual to make their own choice."

Cassel asked, "Ben, if we live on the other planet Xevoy, would we be allowed to visit?"

"We hope you will. Your people are considered citizens."

Jenna looked at Ann holding Allen Russell. "There are twenty-three of you who have become like family to Ben and me. If you decide to stay, the lumber from the trees will be more than enough to build small homes for each couple."

Alice smiled at Jenna, "Hopefully with more than one bedroom?"

"Two to start, you can always build on as needed as your family increases."

Dobbs took a shuttle back up to *Raven* so he could inform his crew that they had a planet called Xevoy to land on and start making new lives for themselves.

Stephanie and Cassel left in a shuttle for *Rapture* to give their crew the good news about Xevoy and the new beginnings it offered.

After they left, Maxx stated, "Zeff, I can't wait to hear our crew's reaction when you tell them."

"Correction, Maxx. You'll tell them."

* * *

Dobbs and his crew in *Raven* surveyed the planet Xevoy for three days before deciding to choose a point at the forty-ninth parallel on the east coast on the major continent to start their settlement.

During the same three days, newly-promoted Capt. Stephanie Bozzar with her newly appointed EXO Bart Cassel and their crew on *Rapture* choose a point on the west coast at the fifty-fifth parallel.

Both captains reported back to Zeff and Dr. O'Casey about the locations. For three weeks, the crews of *Raven* and *Rapture* were trained on the tree tugs and how to harvest trees safely.

When Cassel questioned Jenna on all the new tugs, skidders, and saws, she explained, "The council has paid for them and one new mill for each of your locations on Xevoy. What they ask in return is *Rapture* be brought back to Yovex when the initial building is finished on Xevoy. That way there will be a ship on each planet to run shuttle services between the two planets."

# Epilogue

Three years after the confrontation over Yovex with *Raven* and *Rapture* was resolved, Ann and Zeff sat together on the escarpment under the night sky holding hands.

Ann asked him, "Remember when we soared among the stars and traveled between galaxies?"

"All too well. I remember it was a time of war and the scary ride down in *Defender* before crash landing and skidding to that sudden stop. *Defender* was a good ship with a good crew. The crews of *Raven* and *Rapture* have adapted well to life on Xevoy."

"We were younger then and life here has been good," Ann reconciled her thoughts.

Zeff smiled, "Second thoughts?"

"There are so many beautiful things we haven't seen. I've wondered about the stories Ben and Jenna told us of Matagam Pagwa's people … haven't you wondered?"

"Old stories have a way of turning into legends and growing into fantasies or exaggerated myths."

"We've seen the drawings in the cave and read the Book of Chronicles written by the ancestors. Three suns and how many moons – there has to be a trail to follow."

"What are you suggesting, Ann?"

"*Raven* is on Xevoy, and we have *Rapture* here. I miss them so much …"

"*Raven* and *Rapture*?"

"Maxx and Alice are the people I miss most. It's nine months now since Alice and the baby passed."

"I think about them often myself."

"I remember the day we got the message that Alice's hand had lost its grip on the ladder to the escarpment while holding her infant son and that they had fallen to their deaths."

"And three months later, Maxx followed them when he took

his own life." Zeff spoke softly to console Ann. "We could take *Rapture* for some short tours."

"In a month, it'll be our second anniversary. We could spend the time getting *Rapture* ready."

Zeff gave Ann a compassionate smile. "Just the two of us?"

"I was thinking of Oseeka and Buffet in *Raven* and us in *Rapture*. They're a little younger than we are ..."

Zeff squeezed Ann's hand, "Tomorrow you talk to them, and I'll explain things to Ben and Jenna."

# Bleak Realities

# Planet and Character List

## Planets
Izbax
Vulzar
Yenna

## Yenna
Rear Admiral Jonathan Flynn Military Headquarters

### Transport Ship *Resolute Bay*

#### The Black Sentry – Elite Ground Force
Major Jason Donavan (Able Unit)
Major Drake Esposito (Bravo Unit)
Capt. Brook Emerson (Delta Unit)
Capt. Victoria Wilson (Charlie Unit)

#### Med. Techs.
Lt. Fred Wood
Lt. Peter Defoy

#### Radio Men
Trooper Troy Gross
Trooper Tory Nesium

#### Sniper Unit
Capt. Gwen Hoi
Master Sgt. Grant Taunt "Taunt-Toe"

#### Sniper Teams
First Lts. Pam Longbow and Amie Longbow
First Lts. Tracy Canz and Brie Canz
First Lts. Lin Tian and Jing Zhang
First Lts. Jill and Joan Larson

#### Lieutenants
Lt. Paul Sparling, Unit A
Lt. Tamzil Knox Unit B
Lt. Kevin Zack, Unit C
Lt. Bob Bonnel, Unit D

#### Sergeants
Sgt. Hnayu Peng
Sgt. Vince Luangwa

### Lance Troopers
Lance Trooper Wayne Phoss
Lance Trooper Al Frizz

### Troopers
| | |
|---|---|
| Kim Choi | Mary Gibson |
| Roy Glen | Terry Horton |
| Peggy Marques | Sara Taku |
| Carl Tobias | Ross Visotzky |
| Phin Hwan Yang | Pam Young |

## Vulzar, Tweeb Outpost

### Command Ship *Tide Hornet*
Fleet Admiral Wavell
Rear Admiral Jonathan Flynn

### Troop Carrier *Granby*

### Tweebs
Comm. General Zaunk
Doctor Zerb
Karl Moors, Scientist
Laura Farmane, Research Tech.
Zaivour Valgoski, Research Tech.
Marion, Research Assistant

### Elros
Ganter, Leader
Mosey, Ganter's mate
Pippa, offspring of Ganter and Mosey
Clare, Yaugur, Enza, Kinya, Hugo, Lilly

### Trirobs
Slayer, male Trirobs Leader
Bitcher, female Trirobs Leader
Trasher, son of Slayer and Bitcher

### Orebs
George, flock patriarch
Sherry, flock matriarch

### Bec
Harlan, leader
Julie, Harlan's wife
Tyler, Harlan and Julie's son
Ryan and Shue, village leaders

**Borven Baboons**
Moore, leader
Tabla, Moore's mate

**Beavpines**
Stump

**Ruse Owls**
Gus

**Oncilla cats**

**Mongrels**

# Prologue

The Black Sentry was an elite ground force from the planet Yenna. Vulzar is a Treeb outpost planet used for scientific research and hunting big game animals. The original 144 members had suffered catastrophic losses against the Tweebs on the planet Vulzar. Unknown to the surviving four members, the original incursion force had been betrayed by a high-level command officer in their own military. For Majors Jason Donavan, Drake Esposito and Captains Brook Emerson and Victoria Wilson, the horrendous experience was etched into their psyches. They had never been the same. After two years of numerous physical and psychological examinations, followed by repeated evaluations, the four had been cleared for active duty.

Major Donavan was called into Rear Admiral Jonathan Flynn's office. Donavan was offered a chance to rebuild the company and finish their original objective. As an incentive, Flynn authorized Donavan to pick the people he felt had the experience and fortitude to see the mission through. Donavan asked Flynn for time to talk to the people he wanted and to do some planning before accepting the offer. Flynn gave him a month to pick his people and another two months to prepare for deployment.

Donavan started by picking Esposito, Wilson, and Emerson as they were the other three surviving members from the Black Sentry's betrayal on Vulzar. Next, Donavan sought out Med. Tech. Lt. Fred Wood, Master Sgt. Grant Taunt, and Capt. Gwen Hoi. The three of them were highly decorated veterans. Wood, together with Taunt and Hoi, gave Donavan the names of other veterans.

Over an eight-week period, Donavan and Esposito with Wilson and Emerson taught their handpicked units the basics of the Tweeb language and the natural dangers of the Vulzar jungle. The Black Sentry's original objective had been to extract six genetic scientists off the Tweeb planet of Vulzar. After two years, the prospect of the scientists still being alive was at best remote. The scientists had gone to Vulzar to learn the Tweeb's advanced techniques in gene splicing, DNA amalgamation, and physical enhancements.

Seven days before the company's departure date, on Wood's advice, Donavan organized an evening social for the women and men of the Black Sentry. The prime objective was to create a cohesive bond within the force. With that objective in mind, the party went into the early hours of the morning. Out of the 144 members, few of them were fit for duty that day.

Taunt promised Donavan, "Everyone will be in uniform and be ready for inspection at 0700. Even if they have to be held upright with bayonets, they'll be there."

* * *

In the morning at 0700, the company was standing in front of their barracks at attention ready for inspection. Donavan, Esposito with Taunt, followed Rear Admiral Flynn as he reviewed the troops. The Rear Admiral asked, "There seems to be a high number of females. Are you sure they're what you want?"

Donavan replied, "Master Sergeant Taunt, the Admiral has asked a question. Would you care to answer him?"

"With due respect, Admiral, you pick a man from another company and one of our ladies. My money will be on the lady."

"I take that as a challenge, Master Sergeant. Have your four best female snipers on the firing range tomorrow morning at 0800. Let's hope they don't prove to be an embarrassment to you."

"With respect, sir, we'll see."

After the admiral finished reviewing the troops and left, Donavan told the company to stand easy. "In an hour, I want you in the assembly hall. Dismissed." Then he spoke with Taunt as Esposito listened, "0800, I wonder who he'll pick as his shooters."

Taunt replied, "Son, you let Wood and me pick the snipers

and those girls are the best. With one eye blindfolded, they can out shoot any man on this base. If we use Flynn's face as the targets, I'd guarantee one hundred percent accuracy."

Esposito commented, "Taunt-Toe, you explain things to them and have them ready mentally."

"After I tell them about Flynn's attitude, they'll be ready, sir."

* * *

At 1900 hours, the company was in the assembly hall where Donavan had Taunt address them. "This morning during the Rear Admiral's review, a challenge was given. He made it emphatically clear he has no confidence in a woman's ability as a sniper. At 0800 hours, there'll be a competition between the men the Admiral picks and our ladies. Our company will be there as witnesses. That is an order, not a request."

After some good-natured remarks supporting the women, Wood raised his voice. "Settle down, you're here to be briefed."

Esposito stood by the wall and pointed to the projected images as he talked. "In five days, we deploy to the planet Vulzar using glide suits down to a clearing in the jungle. As soon as your feet are on the ground, peel off the suits to your jungle fatigues. The *Resolute Bay* will drop seventy-two clam shells before we jump. They're your priority. Our first objective is a small Tweeb fort. We'll take it to protect our six. We don't need to be fighting a rear action on our way to our second objective. We'll be crossing the Wishbone River where Elros are known to bathe in the mid-afternoon heat. As you will see, Elros are genetically-engineered crossbreeds between elephants and rhinoceroses. The females are very protective of their young and are to be feared more than the males."

Taunt interjected humorously, "As in any species."

When the remarks and laughter died down, Esposito continued. "Half of our company is female. You'll have their backs because you'll depend on them to have yours. I hope I've made myself clear on that point. Our final objective is a Tweeb research facility. We don't have any Intel on it. If any of our scientists are still alive, we get them out. Command wants documentation on the Tweeb's techniques in gene splicing and physical enhancements."

"As you're aware, only four of us made it off Vulzar. Four out of one hundred and forty-four. We can assure you the Tweebs are ruthless and are not to be under estimated," Donavan pointed out.

With Donavan's reminder, a hush of reality filled the room.

Then Esposito continued, "The *Resolute Bay* is a new ship with four jump bays. Two on the port and two on the starboard. Your sergeants will make their final inspections during the flight. All but our four female snipers are dismissed."

Taunt motioned for the snipers to move forward. Then he gave them his words of inspiration. "Each of you is better than any man in the whole damn army. In the morning, you'll prove it."

Esposito gave them his advice. "You party hard and you shoot even better so don't underestimate yourselves."

"Taunt and I picked you because you're the best. Need I say more?" Wood stated.

Hoi stated, "You were trained by Taunt-Toe, so kick butt."

Donavan smiled. "You're dismissed. Get some rest."

After the snipers left, Esposito asked, "Taunt-Toe who'd you put your money on?"

"Lin and Jing have the best accuracy for distance and the Longbow sisters have the patience snipers need."

"What about the Lawson sisters?"

"Third, tied with Tracy and Brie Canz."

Donavan asked, "What are their shortcomings?"

"As a group or individually?"

"Start with the Lawson sisters."

"Jill's short of patience and Joan's always going for the perfect head shot."

"And Brie and Tracy?"

"Tracy's too worried how Brie's doing."

"Flynn knew about the party and he's banking our girls being hung over and at a disadvantage. What he hasn't taken into account is his guys' cockiness," Wood said.

Taunt emphasized, "Our snipers are very fit and attractive

which will work to our advantage. The Admiral's snipers will be thinking of the ladies more than their targets."

As Wood, Taunt, and Hoi were leaving, the snipers were waiting in the corridor. Brie Canz spoke for them, "We weren't at ease dropping but we heard what was said. Thank you, sir."

"First Lieutenant, you don't address a master sergeant as sir. Now what are all of you doing here?"

"We'd like to be on the range at zero-six-thirty to sight in our weapons. If that's okay with the master sergeant, ma'am?"

Taunt replied, "Knockoff the sir. I'll be there."

Lin Tian spoke politely. "Master Sergeant, sir is said with respect to you personally."

Wood grinned, "Ladies, please keep the sirs to officers when Flynn is here. He'd take personal offense to hearing the master sergeant called sir."

* * *

Morning came early for the members of the Black Sentry. The whole complement turned out to witness how their snipers would fair against Rear Admiral Flynn's chosen men.

When he arrived with his men, Donavan went through the rules. Each of the shooters would get one shot from three different positions: standing, kneeling, and prone. A coin was tossed to determine who would go first. The men won the toss and elected to have a woman shoot first in an altering progression of woman and man.

At the end of the standing shooting, the women had a slight eight to seven lead with a technicality to be discussed at the end of the contest. After the kneeling shots had been fired, the score was women sixteen and men fourteen with a second technicality to be inquired into. At the end of the prone shooting, the women had hit all twenty-four targets, the men twenty-one.

Flynn ordered the competitors to stand in front of him with Donavan and Taunt beside him. Then he asked Taunt, "Who's the senior of your group?"

"First Lieutenant Pam Longbow, sir."

Flynn pointed as he asked, "First Lieutenant, I want an

explanation why you and those two each shot one of the men's targets and I want it now."

"As you order, sir." Pam turned and told Lin Tian and Jing Zhang to account for their actions.

Lin spoke first, "That's the way Master Sergeant Taunt trained us, sir. Snipers work in teams and cover for each other's misses."

Flynn's expression questioned as he looked at Jing. "What do you have to say?"

"Here the enemy is only a target. In the field, he's real and represents a threat to both snipers. The threat needs to be neutralized."

Flynn turned his face to Pam and asked, "I suppose I'd get the same answer from you."

"We were shooting to honor Master Sergeant Taunt's training and the genuine respect he shows for us, as females and as soldiers

Flynn turned to look at Taunt. "Congratulations," he said grudgingly.

Taunt replied respectfully, "Sir, all the targets were hit, I'd call that a tie."

Donavan interjected, "Admiral, Master Sergeant Taunt stresses excellence in his training with a coordinated team effort. Snipers depend on a bond of unity."

Flynn replied with a gruff attitude. "They're trained to do a job and each of them should be able to do it without excuses."

When Flynn walked away, Taunt gave his snipers the nod to relax and shake hands with the male shooters. Some of the men were good sports and asked about the Master Sergeant's training while a couple of them asked certain ladies out socially. The ladies respectfully gave the excuse they were restricted to base. Taunt waited until the men left, then informed his team. "Tomorrow you and your spotters be at the River Front Hotel at twelve-hundred and be in your civvies. Now get some breakfast."

Donavan and Esposito spent that afternoon going over the details of their deployment with the company for the tenth time. Both men wanted the mission etched deep into the minds of the Black Sentry's members.

At 1200 hours the next day, the snipers walked into the River Front Hotel restaurant. The Maître showed them to the side room where Donavan was waiting with Wood, Taunt, and Hoi. Taunt was the first to speak, "Ladies, we congratulate you."

"What Taunt-Toe's saying is you made him look good, and with his looks, that's some difficult accomplishment." Wood said.

Joan Lawson respectfully asked, "If I may ask, Taunt-Toe?"

"The Toe of Taunt's boot. It's a nickname given to him by the male snipers he's trained. In no way is it meant as a derogatory remark to his heritage." Donavan replied with a grin.

At the end of the luncheon, Emerson reminded them, "We deploy the day after tomorrow. You are to be back on base at twenty-one-hundred."

# Chapter 1 Hit the Ground

On the seventh day of the fifth month, the members of the Black Sentry were dressed in their jungle green and brown camouflage as they boarded the transport ship the *Resolute Bay*. During the four-day flight, each of the sergeants inspected their platoons while speaking in the Tweeb language of the planet Vulzar. Then nine hours before entering Vulzar's atmosphere, the troopers tried to sleep or at least rest their eyes. Able and Charlie units were in hangers A and C on the starboard side of the ship. Bravo and Delta Units were in hangers B and D on the port side. Taunt went to each of the hangers with his message of confidence to the sniper teams.

Just before *Resolute Bay* entered Vulzar's atmosphere, the troopers put their blue and white glide suites on over the jungle camouflage. High above the landing site, the clamshells containing weapons, ordnance, and supplies were kicked out.

The members of Black Sentry jumped from their hangers to feel the air rushing against their bodies and helmets as they dropped toward the surface. Their objective was to scrutinize the dense vegetation as they aimed for their designated drop zones.

Suddenly, pieces of red-hot jagged debris rained down from above. Severed and torn body parts to plummeted to the ground. A missile had struck the *Resolute Bay* and it had exploded above them. Out of the 144 who had jumped, only 122 landed alive. They had been detected by the Tweeb forces. There would be no element of surprise going forward.

They peeled off their glide suits to their jungle fatigues. Each of them checked the 9mm sidearm strapped on their thighs and the Bores knife on their belts. Unofficially, but in accordance to Taunt's orders, each of the snipers had a small sharp throwing knife on each ankle.

Donavan assigned Delta to set a perimeter around the drop zone. Able and Bravo had the grim task of searching for the wounded and bringing them in. Med. Techs. Lts. Wood and Defoy and five troopers set up a triage area to attend the twenty-five injured as they were brought in. Donavan had his radioman Troy Gross send long-range subspace distress calls back to their base on Yenna. Both of them knew it would be days to weeks before receiving any response or help.

Many of the clamshell's parachutes were destroyed by the debris of the explosion of the Resolute Bay. Capt. Victoria Wilson's Charlie Unit was ordered to search for as many clamshells as could be found. After long hours of searching, Capt. Wilson reported Charlie Unit had found twenty-nine of the clamshells intact, six others busted open, and the rest were unaccounted for. Out of those found, eleven contained weapons and ammunition. One had medical supplies, four had blankets and rain slickers, and another five contained military rations.

After a head count of troopers was taken, Donavan divided them evenly between the four units with twenty-eight in each unit. Then he gave the order to set up camp for the night. Esposito's Bravo Unit and Wilson's Charlie Unit would keep searching the area for clamshells while Defoy and five troopers would stay to attend the injured.

In the morning at 0700, Donavan's Able Unit and Emerson's Delta Unit set out for first objective of the small Tweeb fort. The humid temperatures along with the thick ground cover under the jungle's triple canopy made progress painfully slow. The natural dangers of the jungle ran from twenty-six-foot-long bone-crushing snakes to giant poisonous spiders. The vegetation held its own lethal variety of killing-on-contact plants. The worst dangers were the ones that paralyzed instantly while four-inch-long flesh-eating ants cleaned a body to the bone as the victims lie helpless and motionless. On the previous deployment to Vulzar, twelve of the force had been lost to the jungle's natural defenses.

It took Able and Delta twelve hours to reach the outward perimeter of their first objective. From the cover of the jungle, they looked across the two-hundred yards of the semi-cleared opening to the ten-foot-high, eight-sided log wall which encircled the inner compound. Donavan had Emerson spit her unit in half with fourteen troopers to the port side and fourteen to the back side of the fort. Donavan divided his Able Unit in the same manner with them on the front and starboard side.

After thirty minutes of watching without any signs of movement, Emerson contacted Donavan. They agreed she would enter the fort with half of her unit through the back gate with Donavan entering with half of his unit through the front gate.

Once inside, Donavan sent his sniper teams, the Canz sisters with their spotters, and eight troopers up to the catwalks. Donavan and Emerson slowly moved with their backs to the wall to come together and second guess the emptiness of the fort. They talked while their eyes moved across the courtyard. Then they used their comm links to call the second half of their units to enter the fort.

Lt. Paul Sparling called Donavan on his comm from the catwalks to report that no movement outside the wall had been detected. Emerson's Lt. Bob Bonnel and his people were inside the fourth building when Bonnel called on his comm to ask Emerson and Donavan to come up to the Officer's mess. When they got there, Bonnel pointed to a notice on the bulletin board:

Death comes from above
in the night skies on the silent wings.
Woe to those who stand the night watch.

Emerson questioned, "Do you think Tweebs have nightmares as bad as mine?"

"I hope so. Lieutenant Bonnel, have you checked every floor?" Donavan asked.

"Every floor, Major."

Donavan stated, "This place has been deserted for at least a year. Before we spend the night here, recheck for hidden passages and booby traps." He contacted Lt. Sparling and told him to leave the spotters with the snipers and take the rest to check the ground inside of the walls for tunnels. He called Taunt, "Taunt-Toe, have the barracks double-checked. We'll be spending the night and it would ruin my morning if I woke up dead."

Taunt walked into the barracks and read the posted notice:

They come from underground quietly
at night while you sleep, not making a sound.
Woe to those who sleep with both eyes closed.

Taunt contacted Donavan and Emerson to come and see the posting. After they got there, Emerson questioned, "Two postings, two different deaths. The first one from above and this one from below. Jason, being back on this planet brings its own set of nightmares. I don't need any help from cryptic notes. When we're finished here, I want to check the officer's quarters."

After Donavan and Emerson walked out into the hallway, Trooper Ross Visotzky commented to Taunt, "I'm glad I'm not under her command, she's a real whack job."

"Visotzky, I suggest you keep comments like that to yourself."

"Sergeant Major, she's going to get people killed."

"Or get herself killed."

"By the Tweebs or one of us."

"That's enough, Visotzky."

In the hallway, Emerson asked Donavan, "I'd rest easier with us in the same room."

"If you're that fragile, have Trooper Peggy Marques bunk with you."

"That would make me look weak."

After thoroughly checking the building, Donavan sat down with Emerson in the ground floor common room to draw up the night guard roster. As they finished, Bonnel informed them that dinner was ready. Emerson's unit was first to eat.

Donavan had Able come in for dinner second. He detailed his orders to have one person staying awake in rotation through the night. After dinner, he did a slow walk along the catwalks to check with the sniper teams. The first two pairs were sisters Joan and Jill Lawson with their partners. They reported that nothing had been seen nor heard.

When Donavan reached Brie and Tracy Canz with their partners, the five of them used their night-vision goggles to scan the clearing and the perimeter of the treeline.

After they discussed the situation, Brie looked at Donavan with disappointment. "Not a very auspicious start."

"Hopefully a bad start can only get better. Do any of you want coffee?"

With a hint of sarcasm, Tracy asked, "How's Lady Emerson doing?"

"I believe Capt. Emerson is resting comfortably in quarters."

Brie smiled at Donavan. "I'd appreciate a coffee. If you brought one for yourself, we could talk for a while."

When he returned with the coffees, they walked slightly away from Tracy and the others. Brie stated, "Please excuse my sister. We've always had to look out for each other."

"Brie, I admire the bond you two have. Tell me you realize there's nothing between Brook and me."

"Only four of you got off this planet the first time. Brook thinks there should be some sort of bond between the two of you."

"It's called survivor's guilt. The four of us share it."

* * *

In the morning, Donavan walked into the mess and over to those who had pulled the last of night duty. They informed him everything had been quiet. He went over to join Lts. Sparling and Bonnel.

Sparling asked, "Do we move out to our second objective or wait for the Esposito and Wilson?"

"Let everyone eat and have them ready to leave at zero-ten-hundred. I'll have Gross radio Esposito."

At 0830 hours, Donavan and Gross stood on the catwalk and radioed Esposito. Donavan explained the fort had been deserted for some time and at 1000 hours they would be heading for their second objective. Esposito said Bravo and Charlie would head out at 0900 hours to meet them on the other side of Wishbone River. After a short discussion, Esposito and Donavan decided they would leave Med. Tech. Defoy with five troopers to care for the injured.

With a feeling of relief at 1000, Able and Delta left the abandoned Tweeb fort. The messages on the walls and the unknown reason for the fort being deserted had caused an uneasy sleep for most of the troopers.

Death comes from above<br>
in the night skies on the silent wings.<br>
Woe to those who stand the night watch.<br>
They come from underground quietly at night<br>
while you sleep not making a sound.<br>
Woe to those who sleep with both eyes closed.

# Chapter 2 Wishbone River

After leaving the Tweeb fort, it took Able and Delta four hours of cutting through the jungle undergrowth in eighty-five-degree temperature to reach Wishbone River. The water of the three-hundred-foot-wide meandering river did little to refresh the troopers. Knowing that the Elros were documented to bathe in the river during the mid-afternoon heat made the thought of crossing it even more challenging.

Donavan had Sgt. Taunt remind both units of the Elros. Even though Taunt spoke quietly, his tone conveyed the firmness of his words. "Listen up. Elros are a genetically-enhanced mixed-breed of elephants and rhinos. The adults have two curved tusks beside the top of their trunk and one long horn protruding out from below it. They have big flat feet so don't get stepped on. The bone spikes on their ankles are for fending off predators that try to immobilize them by gnawing on their tendons. In short, they're damn dangerous, so keep your distance."

Donavan gave the units a half-hour's rest while he and Lts. Sparling and Bonnel surveyed the river and glassed the far banks. With no sign of the ill-tempered Elros, Donavan gave the orders for Able to split into two columns. They formed lines ten feet apart with eight feet between them. Delta crossed between the two lines.

Donavan stood in the middle of the river and watched as the troopers slogged through the waist-high water to the far bank. Donavan observed a female Elros with a yearling wade into the water off the bank that the units had just left. Knowing the defensive nature of a female with calf, Donavan stood holding his rifle at the ready and, without turning his head fully, he used his peripheral vision to scan the banks looking for the dominate male. He knew that the herd leader would be nearby. He glanced behind to see if all his people had made it to the shore. Lts. Sparling and Bonnel had waded out and were on either side of him.

Sparling quietly stated, "The sniper teams have their sights set and Lieutenant Canz requests you join her on shore, sir."

Slowly the three men made their way to the bank and stepped onto shore. Donavan nodded with respect to both sniper teams for covering them. He took one last look across Wishbone River and saw what he figured was the dominate male Elros watching the troopers. Sparling looked at the big Elros and commented to Donavan, "That one's huge and there's something uncanny about the way he's watching us."

"Like he's evaluating our behavior?"

It was another three hours of heat and humidity before they reached their second objective, a village of thatched huts. Both units divided in twos to observe the village from all four sides. After fifteen minutes with no sign of any movement, Donavan led his Able Unit to the far side of the village while Emerson kept her Unit in position. Able carefully checked the village hut by hut for inhabitants and booby traps.

When Donavan and Sparling met in the village square, Sparling asked, "First the fort, now here. Where the hell is everyone?"

Donavan questioned as his eyes scanned the area. "The way this place is overgrown, I'd say it's been abandoned for a number of years."

"Our next objective's eight hours away. Do we wait or move on?"

"We'll wait for Esposito and Wilson, then move out in the morning. Put spotters in the trees and do continuous sweeps of the perimeter."

Donavan called Emerson to bring her unit in and gave the orders for them to rest but to stay diligent. He and Emerson found some shade to sit under as they continued to scan the village while they talked. Emerson restated her uneasy feelings. "One deployment on this planet was enough. Why did I sign up for a second? Jason, it's getting to me."

"You're the one who asked to be included, so don't lose your nerve now."

Two hours went by before Esposito contacted Donavan to tell him they were three miles northwest of the village and surrounded by a curious herd of Elros. Donavan told Esposito to have the troopers to be as still as possible. Then he explained to Emerson, "You keep both Units here. I'll take the Canz sisters to meet Wilson and Esposito's Units."

"Are you crazy? Why do that?"

"The fewer people coming up behind a herd of Elros will lessen the chance of it stampeding into a frenzied mass."

"If you leave, people will expect me to be in charge."

"Listen to Bonnel, then give the orders."

* * *

As Donavan, Brie, and Tracy Canz got closer to the outer ring of the Elros, the ones closest turned their heads to look down at them. A female raised her trunk and gave a low trumpeting sound. The Canz sisters kept their eyes focused on the ankle spurs of the Elros as Donavan glanced at Wilson and Esposito. He slowly motioned for them to have their people gradually lower themselves to the ground into a duck squat. He turned his head and used his peripheral vision to size up the patriarch of the herd. It was the same one that had been behind the female with calf at Wishbone River.

Donavan squatted and looked up cautiously at the patriarch Elros' white diamond mark on his forehead. At the same time, Brie looked up at the female as the Elros cautiously used her trunk to sniff the air.

The big male bent his front legs while lowering his head and used the end of his long trunk to rub the middle of his back. Donavan quietly stated he had the feeling the big male was looking directly into his eyes. Brie quietly replied she had the same feeling from the female. When the calf ambled up to Brie to sniff her, she cautiously and gently laid her rifle on the ground and patted the calf's trunk. The mother Elros lowered herself to the ground and stroked her back with the tip of her trunk.

The male Elros made a low sound with his trunk and two females with a male came forward. The male looked at Esposito while the females looked at Wilson and Tracy Canz. Then the three Elros bent their front legs and lowered themselves to the ground and stroked their backs.

Wilson guessed, "Donavan, either they all have the same nagging itch or they're offering us a ride."

"Giving us a ride or taking us for a ride. Where and why?"

Esposito responded with humor by asking the patriarch Elros kneeling in front Donavan, "Hey, big guy, where do you want to take us and what do you charge for the ride?"

"Southeast in the direction you've going. My name is Ganter and I'll discuss the fee with your leader."

"Donavan, is it heat stroke or did he just answer me?"

Esposito stared at big Elros as it remarked, "Humanoids! Such a fragile species and so war-minded. Yet they think they're the only intelligent species in the universe."

Brie asked the female, "Do all Elros speak?"

"We're a social species that live in a herd with a leadership structure. Different forms of communications such as sign, sounds and words are used depending on the circumstances. How many languages do you speak?"

"Three—may I ask your name?"

"Mosey. And you're Brie Canz."

Donavan inquired, "Ganter, why are you offering us a ride?"

"At the river, you could have defended yourselves without cause, instead you chose to back away slowly. The safety of the herd is my responsibility and I appreciated your choice of passive non-action. Your people's noisy movements have drawn the attention of the Mongrels and that has given them reason to pack up for a hunt."

"Mongrels? We have no Intel on them."

"A fierce breed of dog which were genetically crossbred from Doberman pinschers and pit bulls. Not the type of breed you'd keep at home as a pet."

Brie looked at the unprotected ankles of the young Elros calf with its immature tusks and tiny horn. "Your young would be at risk."

Mosey, the calf's mother stated, "Unfortunately, we lose many of our calves to those beasts. If you rode on our backs with your weapons ready, we'd all travel much safer."

Tracy Canz commented to Donavan, "Those Elros must be fifteen feet at the shoulders. From up there, we'd have good visuals with a tactical advantage."

Ganter said, "We protect our young by forming two circles, sadly, always at a cost."

With her trunk, Mosey pointed to the scars on Ganter's legs. "He doesn't back down and has our females form the inner ring behind the males. I like the way your kind allows females stand with their males."

Brie replied sympathetically, "If we had our young with us, I'd respect Ganter's formation. If we don't want to get eaten alive, we'd better do what the Elros say."

"How do you propose we're going to get up onto your backs?" Donavan questioned as he sized up the Elros.

"With trust." Ganter gently curled his trunk around Donavan's waist, picking him up and settling him behind his shoulders.

"That was unexpected."

Mosey asked Brie, "If you're ready?"

Brie nodded and the next thing she knew she was on Mosey's back. "Soft hands. I mean trunk. It's a whole different perspective from up here."

Donavan asked, "What about the rest of our people?"

Using his trunk, Ganter pointed to Tracy Canz, Wilson, and Esposito. The male Elros picked up Esposito as the females picked up Tracy and Wilson. "As long as your people trust and remain calm, enough of my herd will approach with due care and pick them up."

"Due care?"

"In other words, they'll try not to step on anyone."

Donavan used an open comm link to tell the troopers to gather up their ordinances and get ready for a low-level air lift.

Ganter clarified, "We'll go to the village to get the rest of your species, then head southeast."

Donavan contacted Lts. Sparling and Bonnel to explain and advised them to have the troopers ready.

As the herd of Elros came through the jungle toward the village, the spotters in the trees reported their movement. Both

Units of the Black Sentry came out to see the spectacle. When Ganter and Mosey talked, the troopers were dubious. Trooper Carl Tobias asked loudly, "Who's the comedian trying to be a ventriloquist?"

Donavan responded in a cold tone, "Get on or get stepped on, your choice."

"Men on the males and ladies on the females. If you don't know the difference, my Elros will educate you." Ganter stated in a firm voice.

After the Elros knelt and the troopers were seated, Ganter led out. An hour later, they came to a large grassy clearing where they stopped to survey the area. Four of the largest males walked the perimeter and signaled with their trunks. Ganter nodded to Mosey and she led the females and young Elros to the center of the field. As the young fed on the tall grass, the females formed a circle around them. With their backs to the females, the males formed an outer ring encircling the inner.

Donavan had been counting as he watched as one hundred and sixty-four Elros moved into position. "Ganter, how long will we be here?"

"Tactics, Donavan. The Mongrels will be on us shortly and it'll be easier to fend them off in the open."

Donavan used an open comm link to inform his people to be ready. Within ten minutes, four groups of five Mongrels were skirting the herd from the treeline. Donavan asked, "Is that all there is?"

"Don't you scout out your enemy before an attack? Elros' feet and ears are very sensitive, so watch the herd."

The Elros stood with their big flat feet on the ground while their trunks were up sniffing the air with their large floppy ears straight out, listening. When four of the male Elros pointed with their trunks, Ganter explained, "They're feeling the vibrations with their feet and it seems there are four packs. One is downwind getting your people's scent. The yelping is the Mongrels conveying the presence of humans to the packs' leaders. That will caution them briefly but they will attack."

"How many in a pack?"

"Fifty to seventy-five."

"You're sure they'll attack?

"It's been a while since they're bellies were full. Two months ago, I lost two males, one female, and a calf to them. They're hungry enough to be bold."

One hundred and eighty degrees from his position, Donavan heard the echoes of rifles being fired. Then Taunt reported, "Donavan, some of those things were starting to get brave and move in. We got three of them."

"Everyone listen up. We're expecting four packs of fifty to seventy-five Mongrels in each. Ready your under-barrel grenade launchers and try to thin out those dogs before any of them get closer than a hundred yards."

Taunt stated, "If those Mongrels are looking for a meal, we'll give them one. They can feast on the bodies of their dead."

In between the trees, Mongrels could be heard barking and howling as they conveyed the deaths of the three dogs. Then all at once they went silent.

Ganter explained, "They'll be on the move. The question is which tactic will they use."

Donavan used his comm to issue his orders to Esposito, Emerson and Wilson. "When the dogs were yapping, you should have been able to get a general fix on their positions. Use your grenade launchers to blow the trees above, below, and around them."

The specialists of each Unit fired three grenades into the trees causing them to splinter and the branches to plummet to the ground. The maneuver killed and wounded an unknown number of Mongrels while scattering the packs. A few moments later, the leaders could be heard barking orders.

Ganter stated, "Donavan, you've made them very angry."

"If it forces them into the open, it'll give my people clear shots. Can you tell what they're saying?"

"Only certain words, Donavan. I'd expect three of the packs to do a full-frontal attack to draw our attention while the fourth pack crouches down in the tall grass to sneak up."

"If it was me, I'd have them come from downwind so you wouldn't be able to catch their scent."

"What's your point?"

"When the main attack begins, I'll have my people use incendiaries to light up the grass downwind. It will force them to back off or come at us full-on. Either way, it will expose them."

Ganter's ears perked up, "Only three Mongrel packs barking. I believe the fourth is on the move."

Donavan called Taunt. "The wind is at your back. How's barbecue sound to you?"

"Understood, son."

Taunt passed the order to fire three incendiaries and when they hit the ground, the fire formed a wall of flames and smoke blowing back on the pack. The sound of burning Mongrels' barking and whimpering was heard as the flames rushed over them. For insurance, Taunt had his troopers fire three more incendiaries into smoke behind the Mongrels. He was hoping to have the flames encircle the dogs.

When the other packs launched their assault, Ganter trumpeted to his herd to lower their heads, keep their trunks raised and have their horns ready. At the same time, Donavan gave the order to fire at will. Even with the grenades blowing large holes in the packs, the Mongrels raced fearlessly at the outer circle of Elros. When the dogs got to within a hundred yards of the herd, the grenades stopped and the Units fired automatic weapons.

Amongst the carnage of their own, the Mongrels were relentless in their assault. A number of Mongrels rushed past the male and female Elros to get at the young calves. The female members of the Black Sentry used their sidearms to kill as many dogs as possible.

When one of the Mongrels dug its teeth into Mosey's hind leg above her ankle spikes, Brie Canz had Mosey lower her trunk so she could slide to the ground. Not wanting to risk injuring Mosey's leg, Brie used her Bores knife to slit the Mongrel's throat. As it dropped lifelessly, Brie turned to see Mosey use her front ankle spurs to wound a second Mongrel as it tried rushing past her heading toward Brie. She threw one of her ankle knives into the forehead of the Mongrel and her second knife into the chest of the snarling Mongrel running beside it.

A well-aimed shot pierced the forehead of a Mongrel Brie had not spotted. Brie looked up to see her sister Tracy point at a Mongrel that had a young Elros by the end of its trunk. Before they could react, Tian was on the ground with her Bores knife drawn and was piercing the dog's jugular. Zhang slid down her Elros' trunk and joined Tian and Brie on the ground in defending the calves. The rest of the snipers got to the ground to defend the calves and their sisters in arms. The eight snipers stood valiantly with their 9mm in one hand and their Bores knives in the other as they shot and sliced the snarling onslaught.

The snipers' spotters immediately joined them to stand shoulder to shoulder with their female counterparts. Most of the rest of the troopers stayed seated on their Elros while running up the attrition count. The male Elros used their horns and tusks to spear Mongrels while kicking others with their ankle spurs.

When the howling of the pack leaders called a retreat, the troopers continued to fire on the Mongrels as they tried to quickly distance themselves from the herd. Donavan was on the ground firing at the dogs as they retreated. Ganter put his wounded trunk around him and raised him up on his back.

"Ganter, you're bleeding."

"Your people fight well."

"It was a team effort."

In his own brand of humor, Ganter stated, "Elros are used to being fired at, not fired from. I like the difference, Donavan."

Donavan heard Brie use her comm to call Wood, the Med. Tech. He responded with a quickened voice, "How bad are you, Brie?"

"Not me. One of the calves got the tip of its trunk chewed. Zhang's tending to it. I want Wood to look at Mosey's leg."

Ganter turned and walked back to Mosey. He rubbed his trunk with hers and stated, "You're hurt."

"Brie killed the beast before any real harm was done."

Wood arrived to tend to Mosey's leg and spoke to Donavan

with war-time humor, "The Army's malpractice insurance won't cover this."

"I doubt Mosey will sue the Army or you. When you're finished, check with Zhang. She's tending to a calf's trunk."

When Donavan and Wood finished talking, Brie reported Tian and Zhang's actions to them. From all around, troopers were reporting on their comm links to their senior officers. Ganter turned so Donavan could survey the Mongrel bodies and body parts that littered the blood-soaked grass.

Then Ganter stated, "They're not above eating their own but I doubt they'll be back. My friends from above take pleasure feasting on Mongrel flesh."

"Friend from above?"

Mosey spoke before Ganter could explain, "We should be leaving now."

"Your leg?"

"Wood said he'd check it when we stop for the night."

Brie inquired, "Which direction?"

Ganter stated, "There's a mud bath five miles to the south. The water comes from a warm mineral pool and the mud bath will help Mosey's leg. Donavan, the pool is for your people to bathe in. Their body odor is rather strong."

Brie smiled. "Jason, it would be nice to wash the blood off."

# Chapter 3 Mosey's Influence

The morning after the battle with the Mongrels, Ganter along with five of his herd brought Wood, Tian, and Zhang back to Donavan's camp. When Donavan asked Ganter about the village and the fort being abandoned, the big Elros shook his head and explained, "That village has been empty for more than a year because of attacks. As for the fort, it was abandoned due to fear of ongoing attacks from the Orebs and Trirobs."

"Orebs?"

"Our friends from above. Orebs are large orange-eyed birds that were engineered by genetically crossing two species of eagles and bats. They have exacting eyesight for hunting in the day and finely-honed sonar for hunting at night. Along with their iron-strong pointed beaks, they have blade-sharp teeth and retractable talons. The Tweebs developed them for two selfish reasons. First, to cull the Mongrel population and, second, as an aggressive game bird for off-world hunters to shoot."

When Esposito asked Ganter what the Elros were breed for, he replied, "To be hunted. The rich off-worlders pay for the experience of killing us and hanging our heads on their walls. It's said they hang their hats and coats on our tusks and horns. I see it as a sign of their arrogant, primitive dominance."

"Ganter, were the Mongrels breed to track the Elros?" Zhang spoke with some hesitancy.

"Very correct, Miss Zhang. You now understand the purpose of three of this planet's specialized species."

"You mentioned Trirobs."

"If you're fortunate and very quiet, you may meet one. Pray you don't meet them en masse. Miss Zhang, isn't there a happier topic or question you'd like to ask?"

"Okay, Ganter, when did the Elros learn to talk?"

"A fundamental probability that the Tweeb geniuses probably

overlooked. They spliced humanoid brain cells and stem cells into the original Elros. The Tweebs wanted to offer their off-world clients the very best hunting challenge they could. It was in their own arrogance that our path to freedom was found. When you can understand and listen to what is being said and you don't talk, it gives you an advantage. Elros have stern rules preventing divulging their competence of language, both understanding and speaking."

"But you talk to us."

"At the river, Donavan backed away from Mosey with her calf without one shot being fired. With that, I saw the value of compassion in your leader." Ganter paused before he asked, "Excuse me, Miss Zhang, but I have to ask Donavan, what are your intensions?"

"The Tweebs are holding some of our troopers and we're here to extract them."

"One hundred and twelve of you against 395 Tweebs. Good luck with that."

Capt. Victoria Wilson stated. "Ganter, I'm sure you'd do the same if Mosey or a calf was being held captive."

"I wouldn't risk the whole herd. How many have you lost already?"

"Too many."

"And those black arm bands, Miss Wilson, what do they signify?"

"The last time we were here, there were 144 of us. Only Donavan, Esposito, Emerson and I were evacuated out."

"There aren't as many this time. What happened?"

"Our ship exploded above us while we were in glide formation. Our dead and wounded are at our designated landing zone."

"Two incursions onto Vulzar, and both with negative outcomes. Donavan, has it ever occurred to you that someone doesn't want you to succeed?"

Donavan retorted, "We were allowed to pick every member and they're all seasoned vets."

"Who allowed you to do that?"

When Donavan did not answer, Ganter considered his words

and changed the subject. "The females of my herd spoke with me this morning about your females. Mine are most honored to carry yours on their shoulders."

Donavan asked, "Wood, how's Mosey's leg?"

"The mineralized mud helps. With a couple of days rest, she'll be able to keep up."

"Ganter, what if the Mongrels attack in the meantime?" Donavan asked.

"Little likelihood of that. They don't maneuver well in the deep, soft, thick mud."

Donavan thought about how vicious the Mongrels were. "Ganter, if you hadn't picked us up and those Mongrels would have caught us unprepared . . . I'd like to leave Zhang and Tian with you until Mosey's leg is healed. Then you could bring them to us."

"Where are you planning to be?"

"The fort where our people are being held."

"Again, good luck with that."

When Ganter and his Elros left to rejoin the rest of his herd in the mud flats, Esposito was eager to get on to the next objective. He tried to convince Donavan he should take Bravo Unit on a reconnaissance. He estimated it would take twelve hours of hard trekking to reach the Tweeb fort. As Donavan thought about his people being on foot and the Mongrel menace, Wood interjected, "Son, your people have earned a day or two rest. Then you might try talking Ganter into giving us a lift."

"Sounds good, Wood." Esposito contact Defoy and see how things are at the landing zone with the wounded."

"I'll give him the heads up about the Mongrels."

When Esposito walked away, Wilson asked, "Donavan, why did you lie and tell Ganter we're here for troopers and not the truth about us being here to get our genetics scientists and the blueprints of the Tweebs work?"

"He doesn't need to know."

"The Elros, Mongrels, and Orebs are products of generic manipulations. Ganter knows what other species the Tweebs have redesigned. It'd be a big help if we knew."

"How do you think Ganter would react if he knew our genetic scientists came here to learn the techniques of the Tweebs? He'd see us as the same as them."

Wilson retorted, "You should have told him."

"I'm going to talk with Lieutenant Sparling. You and Emerson, tell your lieutenants we're staying here for a day or two."

Most of the troopers spent the mornings soaking their sore muscles in the mineral rich waters of the pool. Then they stretched out and relaxed under the shade of the giant teak trees.

At 1400 hours of the second day, the sentries reported that Ganter with some of his herd were approaching. Donavan with Sparling walked out to meet them with Sparling asking, "Back again?"

Ganter answered resolutely, "Females can be quite persistent."

"Pardon?"

"Mosey feels you'd stand a better chance with our help."

"What about the rest of the herd?"

"There are eighty-two Elros in the mud baths with the young. As long as they stay in the deepest parts, they should be safe."

"Ganter, you should stay and protect them."

"The Mongrels have a bigger problem. The Orebs have put the run on them so they could feed on the dead and wounded. The dogs that were barbecued have given the Orebs a new taste preference."

Donavan remarked, "It sounds like you and Mosey have a good relationship."

"I lead the herd with Mosey tactfully pointing me in the direction she would have me go. At a good pace, it'll take us seven hours. Night would be the best time to do reconnaissance."

"I'm not sure why you're helping, but I'm glad you are."

Ganter motioned with his trunk toward Brie, "Donavan, some women are worth listening to. Where a lady such as Miss Brie is concerned, it's something an intelligent male of your species might consider trying."

Donavan raised his eye brows as he said, "When are you planning on leaving?"

"We'll all leave at noon today. I suggest you have Esposito's people flanked on both sides and have his rear protected."

At 1130 hours, Donavan gave the order to load up. Wilson shot him a sharp look and told Donavan to walk with her. When they were a discrete distance away, she stated, "Before we leave you, tell Ganter the real reason we're here."

"We need his help and I don't want to jeopardize it."

Wilson's disappointment showed in her expression, "If you won't, I will."

When she walked back to the massive Elros, he peered down at her, then bent his front legs and turned his head to see eye to eye with her. "You're upset. What has Donavan said?"

"There's something you should know."

"The real reason you're here."

"Originally some of our geniuses came to Vulzar to learn the Tweebs techniques of cross breeding and species enhancement. When they didn't return, we were sent to extract them and our troops were massacred. That was our first incursion on this planet. Ganter, this time we're here to find any survivors and the scientists."

Ganter glanced at Donavan, then he focused back on Wilson. "The Tweebs don't restrict their research to animals. There's a distinct possibility they've experimented on your troopers and your scientists."

Donavan interjected, "What gives you that idea?"

Ganter answered while staying focused on Wilson. "The Tweeb genes' atrocities are without limits. They've experimented with a number of different off-world species. Miss Wilson, where does Donavan think our brain stem cell splices came from?"

"Thus your ability to speak and understand."

"Like I told Donavan earlier, a product of brain stem cell splicing."

"That's why you can relate to us."

"Some of us more than others. Mosey has the ability to sense a female's feelings with intuition. Miss Brie is the main reason she has encouraged me to offer you our help."

"Brie?"

"Empathy and compassion are only two of Mosey's strong points. She is honored to carry Brie as her rider."

Donavan spoke with kindness, "Ganter, after you get us close to the fort, I want you and Mosey to go back to the mud baths to keep the calves safe."

"Mosey can be most persistent."

Donavan used his comm to tell Brie Canz to report to him immediately. When she got there, Mosey bent her front legs and turned her head to look at Brie with one eye as she watched Donavan with the other. "The herd saw how you and the other women defended our calves. I'd be most honored if you were to ride on my back."

Mosey curled her trunk around Brie's waist, picked her up and set Brie carefully down behind her broad shoulders. Ganter wrapped his trunk around Donavan's waist and abruptly picked him up and firmly placed him on his back.

Donavan commented, "I think I'm in for a bumpy ride."

"If you'd rather walk, I wouldn't mind.

Mosey stated gruffly, "Ganter?"

As the rest of the Elros hoisted their riders up, Wilson commented, "Ganter, make it a very bumpy ride. Major Donavan deserves it."

* * *

It was a long, bumpy ride for Donavan before Ganter stopped thirteen miles short of the Tweeb's fort. Once the troopers were on the ground, Donavan called Esposito, Wilson, and Emerson to join him in listening to Ganter's explanation.

"This is not just a fort, it's the Tweeb's primary scientific experimental facility. It's where they do stem cell transplants and blend DNAs along with more despicable things. The place is called the Citadel. Its walls are twenty feet high, six feet thick at the base and tapered to two feet at the top. They're built from sandstone cut from the quarry forty miles away."

Donavan stated, "We were told it was a fort, not a complex."

"Surprisingly, Donavan, someone has misinformed you."

Wilson questioned, "With walls that thick and high, what are they expecting?"

"If all the Elros herds stampeded log walls like the first fort, it would be trampled underfoot. Between the treeline and the walls, there are camouflaged pits the Tweebs dug as traps for us Elros."

Esposito asked, "How big is the place?"

"Two miles wide and five miles long. The Tweeb population fluctuates."

"So, what's your idea, Ganter?"

He curled the end of his trunk around a stick and drew in the dirt as he talked. "Tonight, you send troopers to the front and side walls to count the lights and note the placement of the communications ovals. There's at least one oval half way along each side wall. Don't go past the halfway point of the side walls."

"Is that a threat or an order."

"Esposito, take it any way you like. Just don't do it."

"After we do the recon, then what?"

"Donavan, I told you the walls are made from stones cut from a quarry forty miles from the Citadel. There the Tweebs have machines called crawlers. In the morning, you send Emerson's people to bring the crawlers along the road close to the Citadel but not close enough to be heard or seen. While she's doing that, we and our daughter, Pippa, will talk with the Trirobs."

"Again, with the Trirobs?"

"Donavan, Trirobs are a cross between weasels and mongooses. Their pelts are bright red on their right side and bright orange on their left side. Their backs and stomachs are a glossy black. The females have silver triangles inlaid on their black backs. Female venom is deadly and acts quicker than the males'. Both females and males have razor-sharp retractable claws on all four paws. They slice flesh like lightening in the black of the night sky. For the size of them, they're fiercer than the Mongrels. From nose to the end of their tail, they're only ten inches in length."

"Why are they called Trirobs?"

"The tri colors of their pelts: red, orange and black. The Tweebs call them throat chewers because it is the first place a Trirob lunges for. Their fangs are as sharp as their claws and the throat is the quickest kill with the least damage to their prey's flesh."

"And for some reason, you think they would help us?"

"The back half of the Citadel is built over their birthing dens."

"What insanity would make the Tweebs build over the birthing dens?"

"Trirobs migrate and after mating has been done, then they return to the birthing dens. The Tweebs built over the dens when the Trirobs were at their furthest point of migration."

"Great warning but how's that help?"

"Do you listen, Donavan? The Citadel covers a part of the Trirobs' birthing dens."

"And?"

"Birthing season is almost finished. The females will be hungry. The males will be looking for food for them and their pups. Pippa may be able to have the Trirobs agree to create a diversion inside the Citadel."

Donavan gave Ganter a sarcastic look. "So we'll just go out back and explain things to the Trirobs and they'll be more than happy to help. Of course, we all speak a common language."

"Jason Donavan, your attitude needs a serious adjustment."

"You're the one who warned us how deadly those throat-chewing Trirobs are."

Ganter shook his head. "In between the trees behind the back wall of the Citadel is an area where the Trirobs post guards. Approached properly, they can be talked to. I'll need you standing beside me as a sign of trust and good will."

Unconsciously Donavan slowly stroked his throat before replying, "On the ground beside you—with those throat chewers at my feet?"

"Wilson and Pippa will be there."

"Why them?"

"Pippa spent seven days and six nights with Bitcher, the Trirob's matriarch. Three years ago on their way back to the birthing dens, a group of Trirobs were attacked by a troop of badgers. Their canines are longer and sharper than lions. Bitcher was wounded and crawled away to birth her pup. The day after the attack, Pippa was foraging and heard Bitcher snarl a warning at her. Trirob's don't give warnings. Pippa saw she was pregnant and gathered some Dryrotum flowers and placed them within reach of her. Pippa stayed with Bitcher for three days before she gave birth to her young and then four days after."

Donavan questioned Ganter's logic. "With those Mongrels around, you let Pippa wander alone and stay with her?"

"Pippa was young and had a habit of wandering off, it took me two days to find her. Even then she wouldn't leave."

"So, you think some of the Trirobs will remember her?"

"Bitcher will and her young might. I stayed with Pippa and gathered crapples for them. They're highly nutritious and Trirobs are partial to the juice of them."

"I've got the picture. Wilson, I stand on the ground handing out crapples to Trirobs while you and Pippa talk over old times. So why am I uneasy with the idea?"

Ganter tilted his head. "The crapples are a good idea. We'll need a couple of gunny sacks to carry them."

"Better idea, have Emerson hand out the crapples. She wouldn't be much of a loss," Esposito smirked.

Donavan replied, "Esposito, your unit and the snipers have recon tonight. I'll tell Emerson to get her people ready to leave for the quarry at first light."

After the others had left, Ganter asked, "Donavan, you understand why I suggested Emerson go get the crawlers?"

"It'll be an easy assignment for her?"

"So, you have the same doubts about her as Mosey and I have. In the morning you and I shall take a walk. I expect we'll have company."

"Like who?"

"The Orebs. George and Sherry watched us since we met."

"George and Sherry?"

"George is the patriarch and Sherry is the matriarch of all the Oreb flocks."

"I haven't seen any birds watching us."

"They've noticed you and your people and that's what counts."

# Chapter 4 The Trirobs

An hour before first light, Ganter used his trunk to wake Donavan. "I trust you slept well and I'm not disturbing you."

Mosey nudged Brie and spoke quietly, "When Donavan and Ganter leave, we need to talk in private."

"I can take a hint. Come on, Ganter, let's check on Emerson's Unit and see if they're ready to leave."

After they saw Emerson's Unit off, they walked over a large clearing where Ganter told Donavan to sit and look and listen.

"What am I looking for?"

"Donavan, are you beginning to catch on that someone doesn't want you to succeed?"

"What makes you so sure of that?"

Before Ganter could answer, two Orebs glided almost silently into the clearing and landed. Ganter introduced Donavan to Sherry and George, the leaders of the Oreb flocks.

Sherry began the conversation with a compliment. "Barbecued Mongrel was a new treat that our flock much enjoyed. Are you planning on serving more anytime soon?"

With wide-open eyes, Donavan stared at the massive size of the two birds. "I'm really glad we made you happy."

"We understand you plan on attacking the Tweebs," George interjected.

"That's the idea."

"If you can get the Trirobs to help and shoot out the floodlights and their communications dishes, our flocks may be persuaded to assist you."

"Why would they?"

"Strength in numbers. Alone none of us have the numbers."

"How many species talk?" Donavan asked Ganter.

"All of them but only an enhanced few of them in languages you would understand." Ganter looked at George and Sherry.

"This morning Donavan and I will have Pippa speak to the Trirobs. After that, we'll let you know if they're willing."

"The floodlights have to be out before we'll risk our flock." George reminded Donavan.

"We'll do our best to make sure they're out."

As George and Sherry lifted off, Ganter told Donavan, "Pippa and Miss Wilson are waiting."

They met up with Wilson and Pippa three miles east of the Citadel. Then they all made a wide circle around back to pick crapples. When the Elros caught scent of the Trirobs, Pippa asked Donavan and Wilson throw some crapples in their direction.

The Trirob guards who were observing them moved cautiously in the direction of the fruit that had been thrown toward them. The two Trirobs who had been watching the humans were soon joined by a dozen more. Pippa explained she was a friend of Bitcher, their matriarch. Then she told Donavan and Wilson to toss more crapples toward them. The Trirobs watched them fall to the ground, then eight encircled the humans' feet. Donavan and Wilson had watched as they moved closer, snarling to show their teeth.

Wilson asked Pippa. "Have you chosen the right words? Do they understand we come as friends?"

"They'd be on your throats if I hadn't. Empty the gunnysacks at your feet and slowly lower them to the ground. Then stand with your hands open at your side with your palms facing forward."

After Wilson and Donavan did as Pippa said, two of the Trirobs slinked up to them and sniffed the sack, the crapples, and then the ankles of Wilson and Donavan.

Donavan tried humor to keep his tension at bay. "Ganter, if my throat gets ripped out, I won't ever talk to you again."

"You're doing fine and be quiet."

It was ten minutes of stress before a pair of large adult Trirobs came to assess the situation. The male stood beside the female as she stared at the humans and then spoke to Pippa. After what seemed to be a lengthy conversation, the pair boldly scampered up to Wilson and Donavan. They sniffed them and then each snapped up a crapple with their extended claws and sliced it in half. They shared half and threw the other half toward the closest of the other Trirobs.

Pippa explained, "They've accepted your offering and by throwing half to the others, they've shown that you can be trusted."

"Is there much more to talk about or can we get going now?"

"Where are your manners, Donavan? It would be socially impolite to leave while our hosts are still eating." Ganter said sarcastically.

Bitcher asked Pippa why they had come. She explained they needed a diversion in the Citadel so the humans could attack the Tweebs. Bitcher and her mate, Slayer, talked it over and pointed out that many of their kind would be killed. As the two adult Trirobs attentively watched the humans' expressions, Bitcher asked Ganter why the humans wanted to attack the Tweebs.

Ganter explained how many humans had been killed by the Tweebs and that revenge was their motive. The word revenge was a thing the Trirobs understood.

Slayer looked at the crapples by Donavan's feet, then let out a gurgling noise that sounded like fluid in his lungs. It was his invitation for the Trirobs watching to come and get the crapples.

As they scurried to get the treats, Donavan asked Ganter. "What's going on?"

"With the questions you ask, maybe Miss Wilson should be in charge. Both of you stand absolutely still and don't make any sudden movements. All they want are the crapples."

Four of the Trirobs stood erect on their hind legs and stared up at Donavan's and Wilson's faces while munching on the juice-filled fruits.

Donavan asked, "Do we look at them and smile or what?"

"Smiling would show your teeth and that would be taken as a sign of aggression."

"Fine. I'll keep my mouth closed."

"It's about time."

Pippa, Bitcher, and Slayer continued their conversation and

when it was finished, Slayer gurgled a sound for the others to back off. Ganter and Pippa bent their front legs and carefully knelt to the ground. Pippa explained, "Slowly walk five feet in front of us and then stand perfectly still."

"What are you planning?"

"Donavan, we're leaving. Do you want a walk or ride?"

Wilson and Donavan did as they were told and the Elros used their trunks to pick them up. As Donavan rode on Ganter's back, he asked, "So did they agree?"

"Pippa promised you'd show them good faith."

"Didn't Wilson and I do that when we stood on the ground."

"Bitcher and Slayer want you to kill the floodlights on the back wall. After you do that, they'll talk with Pippa."

"Nice names for their leaders: Bitcher and Slayer."

"Would you rather they have friendlier names like Joe and Flow?"

* * *

While Donavan and the others were being questioned by the Trirobs, Emerson's unit had made it to the quarry looking for the machines Ganter had called crawlers. Sgt. Hanyu Peng, with Troopers Mary Gibson and Carl Tobias, had found the three crawlers parked in the bottom of the quarry on the far side of the pit. Gibson's father had been a mechanic and she figured out how to start and operate the crawlers. After showing Peng and Tobias, the three of them impressed the rest of Delta Unit by driving the crawlers up the ramp to Capt. Emerson and dropping the blades as a salute near her feet.

Emerson felt that her authority had been threatened and belittled by the action. She ordered them to shut the crawlers down. Then she verbally dressed down the three of them in front of the rest of the unit.

When she finished, Bonnel politely asked to speak to her in private, "Capt., dropping the blades in front of you was done as a salute. I seriously think you should apologize to them."

Emerson's hands were shaking as Bonnel spoke. She started to rub them together as she responded, "Lieutenant, I have nothing to apologize for. The three of them needlessly put my life at risk. You can tell them their actions will be reported to Donavan with my recommendation that they be charged with insubordination."

"Capt., I'd like to say this with all due respect, this is not going to happen."

Lt. Bonnel walked away leaving Emerson vibrating. He went over to Gibson and asked, "I'd like you to try to settle Emerson down. Please try and talk to her. Maybe woman to woman would be less threatening."

"Donavan's the only one that can do that, but I'll try, sir."

Twenty minutes later, Gibson reported back to Bonnel who asked, "What happened?"

"I did as you suggested and tried to talk rationally. She kept repeating how Donavan should be here to support her and how much trouble Peng, Marques, and Tobias are in. I made the mistake of saying the Major would understand the blades were dropped as a salute. Emerson used a derogatory expression comparing me to a dog."

"I'll put in an official report to Donavan. Please have those crawlers fired up. I'll try talking to Emerson and then we're heading back."

"Sir, she's the one who should be reported. It's you that runs the unit."

"Gibson, I'm out of sleeping tablets, would you have any to spare?"

She smiled slyly at him as she handed him all she had and asked, "For Capt. Emerson, sir?"

"Precisely."

* * *

It was 1600 hours when Bonnel reported back to Donavan. First, he explained the three crawlers were parked off the road two miles from the Citadel. Second, he reported Emerson's conduct and the language she had used to Trooper Gibson.

Donavan asked, "Where's Emerson now?"

"Resting in her tent, sir. I left Sergeant Peng with Troopers Gibson and Tobias with the crawlers. The rest of Delta is settling in."

"Good work, Bob, get some rest."

When Bonnel left, Donavan decided talking to Emerson could wait until morning. His priority was to convince the Trirobs of his commitment. He used his comm to have the snipers and Taunt join him and Esposito for a briefing. When they arrived, he told them that they would be under Taunt's direction to take out the floodlights. Next, he reminded them to keep their Elros well out of range of the Tweeb's weapons.

"With the Elros well back in the jungle, it means being on foot. So tread softly and try not to step on any of the Trirobs. Donavan and I have been up close to them and I'm telling you their teeth and claws are razor sharp," Wilson added.

Next Donavan called Sparling and Esposito's Lt. Tamzil Knox and had them deploy with five men each. Sparling was instructed to take out the communication ovals on the west wall while Knox would take out ones on the east wall in conjunction with the snipers' harassment.

At 1900 hours, the Elros lowered Taunt and his snipers and their partners to the ground between the trees at a safe distance behind the rear wall of the Citadel. Once on the ground, Taunt quietly gave them his orders. "Ladies, be safe and remember to keep your butts down. Men, all eight in and all eight out. Promise me?"

Tian commented, "We love you, too, Master Sergeant."

"If I were twenty years younger, my ego would've taken your comment seriously."

Tian used good-hearted humor in replying. "Experience comes with age, sir, and I'm sure at your age, you've got the experience."

Taunt responded in kind, "First Lieutenant, take my advice and save your future personal experiences for a man your own age, who truly loves you."

As the sniper pairs moved closer to the Citadel, they used their night vision glasses to scan the ground and trees for the Trirobs. They first noticed the slender tri-colored furry creatures standing on their hind legs peering down at them from the branches. After a short pause, snipers proceeded to the treeline and fanned out along the two-mile length of the wall and chose their positions.

As Amie Longbow and spotter, Wayne Phoss, were in the prone position sighting in their rifles, she felt something on the back of her right leg. It moved over the length of her backside up to her right shoulder. Then sniffed her hair and jumped onto the ground in front of her to stand on its hind legs to stare curiously at her. With the thought of them being called throat chewers, Amie felt a lump in her throat. The Trirob turned to look toward the back wall and then turned and looked back at her. In Amie's mind, it seemed to be smiling. Then it moved to a position six feet parallel off her right shoulder and settled down as if to observer her.

At the designated time, the snipers began to take out the floodlights and the soldiers on the wall. The Tweeb soldiers randomly returned fire into the treeline. The Trirob beside Amie moved in tight to her side flat against her thigh. She could feel its body twitch as the bullets hit the ground and trees close by. Slowly, Amie stretched her right arm back and put her hand on her little companion to calm it. Then she went back to shooting out floodlights.

After fifteen minutes, the Tweeb's return fire stopped. The small Trirob moved up beside Amie's face and stood on its hind legs looking at her. Slowly Amie reached out her hand and gently stroked it.

In the morning after the sniper teams rendezvoused back at camp, Taunt brought Amie Longbow to meet with Donavan and Esposito to brief them. They stared at the sight of a Trirob perched on Amie's right shoulder.

"That's not a pet and you're not keeping him," Donavan said.

The young Trirob started chirping and Amie's Elros Clare translated that his name was Trasher.

Donavan saw the bandage on Amie's arm. "Why hasn't Wood tended to that?"

"It is only a splitter from where a bullet grazed a tree. Pam patched me up. Sorry for not reporting it, sir."

The young Trirob began chirping again with Clare

translating. "Trasher says his parents are Bitcher and Slayer. They say tomorrow night will be the dark of the moon and a good time to attack."

"I'll have Mosley let George and Sherry know," Ganter interjected.

Donavan outlined his plan to Clare so that she could tell Trasher and he could explain it to his parents. Donavan directed that the scientists and the Citadel's commanding officer be taken alive which prompted Ganter to challenge him.

"The basement level of the Zavtar Building is where the experiments are done and where the cages that hold the results are. Once you see what Tweebs do, I'm hoping you'll change your attitude."

"Sir, I should be taking Trasher home," Amie suggested.

"Taunt and Pam will go with you. Ask Trasher to thank his parents."

After they left, Esposito questioned, "Ganter, after last night, do you think the Tweebs will call for re-enforcements?"

"I doubt it and if they did, it would take two days for them to get here."

"Two days?"

"The nearest base is on the coast and the commander here is quite arrogant. He prides himself in being self-sufficient. All you've done is to shoot out the floodlights and a couple of comm dishes. It's not like you've made a full-out assault on the place."

Donavan used his comm to have Bonnel join them.

When he arrived Bonnel explained. "Sir, the metal boxes on the crawlers are full of explosives used for blasting rock at the quarry. We could load one of the crawlers with the explosives and drive it backwards into the front gate. Then use the other two to push the debris out of the way."

"Good idea but who is going to operate the crawler?"

"Sir, it was Trooper Gibson's idea. She's quite gutsy and intelligent."

"Have her rig the thing up and have it ready for tomorrow night. Then find Capt. Wilson and get back here for a briefing."

"And Capt. Emerson, sir?"

"I'll brief her later, alone."

"You said you were allowed to pick the best, yet you still brought Emerson? Seems odd your command board would agree to that," Ganter questioned.

"Rear Admiral Flynn and the base psychologist thought revenge would help Emerson's emotional sense of balance."

"How do you, Wilson, and Esposito balance things?"

"The three of us talk."

"And Emerson?"

"She's a bit of a loner, always has been."

"And that's why you try to compensate."

"I know what it's like to be a loner."

"What do you intend to do now?"

Donavan took his time before replying. "The officer in command of the Citadel should have some answers." He looked at Bonnel. "Lieutenant, what's been said here is to be kept totally confidential. Major Esposito and I know you and Sergeant Peng are holding Delta together. Please continue to do so."

"I'll have Gibson get the crawlers ready and find Capt. Wilson. We'll report back to you, sir."

When Bonnel reported back with Wilson, Donovan detailed the plan for the night attack on the Citadel. They were instructed to detail their units.

# Chapter 5 Inside the Citadel

Six hours before the attack on the Tweeb Citadel, Ganter asked Donavan, "You have secured a way for Miss Gibson to get off the crawler and safely make her way back to the treeline?"

"I'm sure Bonnel and Mary Gibson have thought of that."

"If one of my females was putting herself in a precarious situation, I'd want to be darn positive."

Donavan used his comm to check. "Bonnel, Ganter needs to know how Gibson's escaping from the crawler and getting to the treeline?"

"Sergeant Peng has identified one of those pits the Tweebs dug as traps for the Elros. He has Troopers Kim Choi and Peggy Marques ready to hit it with grenades to open it up. With your Able Unit concentrating their firing across the length of the front wall, Gibson will dart from the crawler and jump in the pit for cover. Anything else, sir?"

"I think Ganter is satisfied. That's all, Bonnel."

Ganter looked skeptically at Donavan. "Miss Gibson's putting her life on the line in the hope she'll make it to a pit for safety without being shot in the back and you're satisfied with her chances?"

"The floodlights will be shot out and the Tweebs will be firing blindly."

"And if it were Miss Brie?"

"What do you suggest we do?" Donavan asked sarcastically.

"Have Taunt with two troopers support Marques and Choi with grenade launchers. After the pit is exposed, have the four of them concentrate on the top of the wall. With your unit's rifle fire, it will force the Tweebs to keep their heads down. Then Miss Gibson will have a running chance of living."

Donavan called Taunt on his comm and explained the plan. After they spoke, Taunt thought about the safety of his snipers.

He contacted each of them and told them to be sure to have their spotters close to them. He confirmed that the Orebs and Trirobs were informed and ready.

* * *

With the dark of the moon, the crawlers were in place and the four units of the Black Sentry moved into position to start their attack on the Citadel. Able Unit concentrated their firing across the length of the front wall while Charlie Unit's objective was the left wall. At the same time, Bravo Unit's goal was the right wall. At the signal, Gibson lifted the blade of the crawler loaded with explosives and moved to the front gate. She locked one track and spun the crawler around and backed it tight against the gate. Then with the detonator in hand and as chunks of the top wall were falling, she jumped off the crawler and scrambled to the exposed pit. After catching her breath, she pushed the button and lifted her head high enough to watch with approval at the explosion and as the parts of the gate flew upwards and backwards into the Citadel.

With the explosion and the floodlights out, it was the signal for the Orebs and the Trirobs to attack. The Orebs glided silently and unseen down towards the Tweebs. They reached the catwalks, picking up Tweebs in their talons while pecking holes in the tops of their heads with strong pointed beaks. Then the Orebs dropped the bodies from great heights to the ground.

The Trirobs entered the Citadel from tunnels below ground connected to their birthing dens. Their primary objective was the Tweebs inside the buildings. Bitcher and Slayer deployed one hundred of their adult males to complete the task.

At the same time, Sgt. Peng and Trooper Tobias moved their crawlers forward to clear the debris from the front entrance.

George, the patriarch of the Orebs, dropped a Tweeb body in front of Donavan as a signal for Delta and Able to enter. Once inside, Emerson's Unit went right to clear the right catwalks and the secondary buildings. Wilson's Charlie Unit went to the left catwalks. Esposito's Bravo Unit had the task of clearing the streets and ground floors of the buildings.

Donavan's Able Unit went directly for the Zavtar Building

where the experimental laboratories were. Able entered the building, checking it room by room. After the ground and top floors were cleared, they headed down to the lower level.

Taunt was the first down the stairs with his rifle at the ready. A tall smug man in a white lab coat stared at him and emphatically stated, "We're non-combatants and I demand you guarantee our safety."

Taunt motioned with his rifle as he gruffly spoke. "Park your ass and speak when spoken to. If you don't, I'll escort you to the catwalk for the Orebs to peck holes in your head."

The man was sitting down as Donavan got to the bottom of the stairs. He looked at the three men and two women in lab coats. "Is that all of them, Taunt?"

"So far, sir. The tall twit seems to think he is their spokesman."

"Get him on his feet and we'll have him show us around."

Taunt motioned with his rifle. "The Major wants a walk through and you'll answer his questions or end up as bird food."

"First, I want a guarantee of my personal safety before I'll go anywhere or answer any questions."

Bitcher and Slayer jumped down from the top of a coat rack at the bottom of the stairs and sat upright on their hind legs.

"Keep those blood-thirsty rodents away from me," the tall scientist yelled

The other four in lab coats recoiled in their chairs and stared at the Trirobs. Taunt bent down and put out his arm. Bitcher climbed up and laid across his shoulder and peered at the scientist.

Taunt stood up and commented. "It's birthing season and the females are looking for food for their pups. So it's your choice, bird food or baby food."

"You wouldn't dare."

"I take dare as an invitation to do something."

Taunt looked at Troopers Visotzky and Taku and told them, "Tie his hands to the chair and gag him. I don't want Bitcher or Slayer hurt while they're feeding."

One of the women spoke. "I'll give you the tour and answer your questions on one stipulation."

"What's that?"

"You promise that you won't assault us before killing us?"

"Your name?" Donavan interjected with raised eyebrows.

"Laura Farmane and my co-worker is Zaivour Valgoski."

"You have my word."

Farmane led Donavan and Taunt with Bitcher and Slayer following from the foyer through the canteen and into the laboratory. Donavan and Taunt stopped immediately and stared at four species tethered on the tables. The first had its stomach spread open revealing his intestines. The second was face down with its back bone and shoulder muscles exposed. The third was a man with the top of his skull surgically sliced open with probes stuck into his brain. The fourth was a massive owl-like bird. Its chest was clamped open with its beating heart exposed.

Once Donavan regained his composure, he demanded an explanation. "Tell me what insanity is going in here?"

Farmane pointed as she spoke. "She's a Maraden monkey. They carry only one fetus at a time. The scientists are trying to increase her capacity."

"The damn thing's alive and awake," Taunt retorted.

Farmane was slow to respond. "The scientists measure pain thresholds. They want live accurate readings." Hesitantly, she pointed to the second table. "This is a male Borven baboon. They have five times the strength of a man the same size. The scientists want to know the density of their muscles and bones."

Farmane stopped and timidly looked at Taunt and Donavan before stating, "The third is Hector, a Flordite miner. I'd rather not face him."

"Why not, you are part of the team that did this to him," Taunt retorted.

Farmane closed her eyes as she replied. "It wasn't by choice. Our first night here, six Tweebs soldiers came into our room and assaulted us. In the morning, we were told if we didn't comply with their desires as well as do our jobs, we'd be given to the soldiers."

"I'll take care of all three of the bastards." Taunt stated with vigorous anger.

Donavan stated, "Right now I could easily consider looking the other way."

Taunt settled down. "Two of you and three of them?"

Farmane explained, "The morning after, Marion, the third lab assistant, took a scalpel and tried to cut Doctor Zerb's jugular. She was given to the soldiers and we never saw her again."

"Is Zerb that tall talkative twit?"

Farmane nodded in the affirmative.

Taunt looked at Donavan. "I want an hour with the three of them."

When Donavan motioned to the fourth table, Farmane was slow to respond. "He's a Camowl. Originally, they were Great Horned Owls. Their DNA was altered with that of the Orebs. Then some stem cell splicing with chameleons. They have the ability to change the color of their feathers to match the surrounding environment."

In a tentative tone, Donavan asked, "What's behind that door?"

"The cages, sir."

In a disgusted tone and with serious reservation, Donavan asked, "What's in the cages?"

"Living specimens."

"Show us."

As Farmane walked by Hector, the Flordite, she turned her head so as not to look at him. When they went into the large room, Donavan and Taunt gawked at the cages. There were humanoids wearing hospital gowns, four to a cage. They had been altered mentally and stared outwardly as though there was no life left in their souls.

Farmane looked at the floor while she explained, "The two males are failed experiments in grafting Borven baboon DNA. Stem cell splicing was tried without success. The females had their reproductive organs removed. They were transplanted into the female Maraden monkey. The first attempt was rejected. It's not known if the second attempt has been accepted yet."

As they walked the two hundred yards of the room, Farmane broke down and cried. Taunt put his arm around her to support and steady her.

Donavan stared at a pair of perched owls staring back at him.

They had the look of wanting to kill him given the chance. "I've seen enough. We'll go back to the foyer. I want a few words with those so-called scientists."

When they got back into the laboratory, they found Hector the miner, the Maraden monkey, the Borven baboon, and the horned owl had their throats chewed. Donavan and Taunt glanced around for Bitcher and Slayer and then walked Farmane through the canteen and out to main foyer.

Bitcher and Slayer were sitting on their hind legs as Bitcher spoke with compassion, "Call it euthanasia or mercy killings. Our venom acts quickly. You wouldn't have done it so we had to."

Slayer explained the rest of their plan. "Once your people have witnessed these atrocities, the rest of the living dead will be given their peace."

Donavan stared at them without response. Then he looked at Farmane and the other female lab assistant. "Taunt, have Troopers Visotzky and Taku escort the male non-combatants to a catwalk and tie them securely until we join them."

"Understood, sir."

When they took the scientists out, Donavan looked at the women and asked, "Suggestions, Master Sergeant?"

"Sir, I'd have the Lawson sisters take charge of the women."

"You stay with the ladies while I go outside and get them on the comm. When the Lawson sisters get here, you explain things. Then meet me on the catwalk."

After Donavan left, Taunt tried to reassure the women by explaining that the Lawson sisters were respected officers that did not suffer misbehaver from any man.

When Donavan got outside, he called Joan and Jill Lawson on his comm and told them to report to Taunt in the basement of the Zavtar Building. While Donavan stood scanning the street scene, the fire fight inside the walls continued.

Lt. Sparling walked up to him, "Sir, Med. Tech. Lieutenant Fred Wood wants to see you by the main gate."

"Right after the Lawson sisters get here and I give them their orders."

Sparling commandeered a Tweeb vehicle to take Donavan to see Wood. As they got out of the vehicle, Wood walked over to them to report there had been three casualties so far. The last name Wood gave was that of Emerson. "Jason, she was hit though the forehead with one of our own rounds. I'm going to report it as a friendly fire incident."

Donavan nodded, "My fault, I should've left her out of this."

"Son, she had repeated psychological evaluations and was clear for duty."

"I'll sign off on your report as a friendly fire incident."

Donavan and Sparling walked slowly to the vehicle to drive back to the Zavtar Building. They walked up to the catwalk to question the scientists. Trooper Visotzky had his fifteen-inch Bores knife drawn.

"I want answers first," Donavan stated.

Sparling, Taku, and Visotzky used the laser lights of their rifles and flashed then skyward. In two minutes, the Orebs, George and Sherry, landed on the wall.

"Problems, Donavan?"

"Could you convince these men to answer my questions?"

George spread his wings, rose into the air and dug his sharp talons into Doctor Zerb's shoulders pulling him a foot off the catwalk. As Zerb screamed, Sherry ran her pointed beak through the scientist's hair.

Taku repeated Taunt's original threat, "Bird food or baby food. Think about it. If Zerb doesn't talk, one of you is next."

"I'll talk."

Taku looked at Donavan. "With your permission, sir."

"At your pleasure, Trooper."

Visotzky looked up at George and Sherry, "We don't need that one."

George flew off with Doctor Zerb in his talons. Sherry stayed. Donavan began questioning his own moral code.

Visotzky began the interrogation, "What's your name and position?"

With a tremor in his voice, Moors answered, "I'm Karl, Karl Moors. My field is stem cell research."

Taku asked Donavan, "Is there some place you should be? I was thinking Capt. Wilson might have prisoners she might want you to question."

Donavan nodded the affirmative and contacted Wilson on his comm. She told Donavan that she and Luangwa were questioning Commander General Zaunk, the Tweeb commander, in Zaunk's office. When Donavan and Sparling arrived, Wilson detailed everything Zaunk had told them to that point.

As Donavan listened, Sparling pointed to the stuffed pair of Trirobs on Zaunk's desk. Donavan nodded and started his own line of questioning in the form of statement, "This is the second time we've been on this planet and both times we've met with disaster. Someone has been giving you Intel on our deployment and troop strength. I want to know who and why."

Zaunk replied in a frosty, factual tone. "The why is that our scientists wanted a new variety of specimens. As for the who, think about who sent you and allowed you to pick your best for our scientists."

They all knew Zaunk was referring to Rear Admiral Flynn. Sgt. Luangwa stated, "Sir, he's one cold son of a bitch and keeps reminding us of the rules regarding the treatment of prisoners."

Donavan vocalized his contempt. "George has your Doctor Zerb. Sherry is waiting patiently for Karl Moors."

"Who are George and Sherry?"

"The patriarch and matriarch of the Orebs and they have a fondness for the tender gray matter in Tweeb heads."

"Need I point out that I'm an officer and a gentleman in the Tweeb army?"

"An officer is accountable for his men's actions and a gentleman would not have allowed any violations. Now shove any idea of prisoners' rights up your ass."

With that remark, Wilson, Sparling, and Luangwa stared at Donavan. They had not expected him to be so blunt.

Donavan stayed focused on Zaunk, "General, in no definition are you a gentleman. You are the worst excuse for an officer. So I'll list your options. Bird food, meaning being given to the Orebs, or baby food, meaning you'll be given to the Trirobs. The third is an officer's cowardly way out."

Donavan pulled out a 9mm from his left leg holster, ejected

the clip and laid the gun on the table. "There's one in the chamber and I strongly suggest you make use of it."

While the garrison commander tried to stare Donavan down, Wilson stated, "Eat the bullet willingly or be force fed."

Donavan pulled out his other sidearm from the holster on his right leg. "If you don't do it, I will. Now the rest of you wait outside and that's an order."

There was the sound of a shot and the garrison commander's head jerked sideways with splinters of skull, blood, and brains splattering the wall.

Luangwa stated, "Had to, sir, he didn't have the balls. You'd be up on charges and that would be a waste of a good officer."

Donavan looked at Wilson and Sparling, "My after-action report will read that the Garrison Commander Zaunk took his own life. If either of you disagree, state it now."

When three of them remained silent, Donavan called Trooper Taku and asked if she had finished questioning Karl Moors. She replied in the affirmative. Donavan told her and Visotzky to report back to the basement of the laboratory and wait for Wilson, Sparling, and Luangwa. Then he told them to have Taunt give them a tour and introduce them to Farmane. He holstered both his sidearms and walked outside. In the stark cold darkness of the night, he continued to question his torn and tattered moral code.

Sgt. Peng tapped Donavan on the shoulder. "Sir, sir."

"What is it, Peng?"

"Lieutenant Bonnel needs to see you."

"Lead on, Sergeant."

Peng apologized, "Sorry about the transport, sir, but this is all I could find. The lieutenant is in the warehouse building near the back wall."

Peng pointed to a motorcycle and Donavan sat on the back as Peng weaved past the debris and between the dead bodies of Tweebs. When he stopped, Donavan was led up to the second floor. Bonnel was sitting on the floor leaning against the wall with the body of Trooper Gibson to one side.

"Lieutenant Wood has his hands full and I did my best. Sorry, sir."

In a quiet tone, Peng stated, "A sad night for the unit, sir. Gibson was someone we all liked."

"Sergeant, get on the comm and find proper transport and some help."

"Understood, sir."

"Bob, have all the buildings been cleared?"

"I believe this was the last one, sir."

"Then walk with me."

When they got outside, Donavan stated, "You did what you could, accept it. You can grieve when the night's over. Now you're in command of Delta and I need you to set an example for your people."

"Sir?"

"Emerson's dead. At zero-eight-hundred, I want Delta on the main floor of the Zavtar Building. Taunt will be there to give them a tour of the basement. Pass the word."

"Consider it done, sir."

Donavan took the motorcycle and drove back to the Zavtar Building and went down to the basement. Taunt was with Wilson, Sparling, and Luangwa. He explained, "They've had the tour and I was giving them time to deal with their emotions. Next, I'll take them to meet Farmane."

"At zero-eight-hundred, Bonnel will bring Delta for a tour. Can you handle it?"

"I'll handle it."

"At zero-nine hundred, Sparling will bring Able, and at ten-hundred, Wilson will bring Charlie. Can you do it three more times?"

"They need to see this."

Donavan asked, "Sparling, Wilson, Luangwa?"

They nodded the affirmative. Donavan went outside and used his comm to contact Brie Canz. She told him she was on the catwalk behind the motor pool. When he crested the stairs, he found her butt down on the wall. From across the compound, they could hear the sporadic sound of weapons fire. Brie quietly questioned, "What did you find and was it worth it?"

Donavan looked down at the body at her feet. She did not

wait for him to answer. Instead, she stated, "It's Ben Eason. One of those guys no one notices, always kept to himself. The poor bastard bought it from a Tweeb with a rifle on the roof of the motor pool."

Donavan sat down beside her to answer her original question, "In a morbid way, yeah, it was worth it."

She was uncertain of his meaning. "The sun will be up in a couple of hours, what then?"

"Morning seems too far away to plan for. If you're up to it, I want to show you why it was worth it."

# Chapter 6 Coming to Terms

As the bright sunlight of morning began to shine over the eastern wall of the Citadel, Taunt found Donavan with Lt. Brie Canz sitting on the ground floor of the hallway of the Zavtar Building. The sight of them resting peacefully made Taunt hesitate before he nudged Donavan's foot with the toe of his boot.

With eyes half open, Donavan looked at Brie as Taunt spoke quietly to make his presence known. "Bonnel will be bringing Delta for a tour soon. The Lawson sisters should be with them. Who do you want to stay with the women?"

Donavan nudged Brie with his shoulder and she responded softly. "I've been listening. Taunt-Toe, Donavan told me about them."

"They need to be chaperoned."

"And some breakfast."

"Almost forgot. Zhang and Tian have volunteered to make breakfast. It starts at zero-nine-hundred in the officer's mess. I pity them that ate before seeing the lab."

Brie remarked, "I doubt if anyone will be hungry afterwards."

Donavan got to his feet and offered his hand to Brie. As she stood, she asked Taunt, "Where are they?"

"With the Lawson sisters in the chapel. The two of them used to go to the chapel to be alone and pray. The Tweebs weren't much on faith."

When Donavan and Brie got to the chapel, she talked privately with Jill Lawson while Donavan and Joan Lawson stayed with Farmane and Valgoski. While Brie and Jill talked, Donavan was contacted by Wilson. After Brie and Jill rejoined him and Valgoski, the Lawson sisters left for the Zavtar Building. Donavan explained Wilson's message and left leaving Brie with the two women.

Donavan met with Wilson in the motor pool as she sat behind

the steering wheel of a six-by-six truck explaining, "Ganter and Mosey are standing at the treeline. I think they are waiting to gauge your attitude on last night's activities."

"How does anyone gauge what the Tweebs have done here? How do I gauge what I've condoned last night?"

Wilson started the truck and they drove out of the motor pool toward the main gate until Donavan asked her to stop. He looked out the front and passenger windows, then questioned, "Where's the bodies?"

"Before sunrise, the Orebs glided down and picked them up. Sherry told me they were dumping them ten miles the other side of the river. She said the Orebs have started to find Tweeb flesh distasteful. She hoped the dead Tweebs would fill the Mongrels bellies long enough for the Elros to make it to their calving canyon safely."

Wilson continued out of the Citadel through the hole in the wall that used to be the front gate and stopped at the treeline. When they got out of the six-by-six, Mosey spoke first, "Ganter's worried about you and thinks you might be tentative with the actions of the Orebs and the Trirobs."

"Right now, I'm having some difficulties with my own actions."

"Understandable, Donavan, but the deplorable deeds of the Tweebs should outweigh any moral controversy you and your people are dealing with."

"At 1200, I'll be meeting with my people to gauge their responses. After that I'll be better able to comment."

Wilson did an estimated head count of the Elros as Donavan and Mosey talked, "It looks like the whole herd is here."

"George and Sherry report that you suffered casualties," Ganter interjected.

Wilson answered, "Wood's latest reports are that we lost eight with eleven wounded."

Donavan had not read the med. tech.'s latest report and glanced over his shoulder at the Citadel while questioning himself mentally.

After Ganter and Mosey gave their condolences, Ganter asked, "Bitcher and Slayer have a request. They asked me to ask because they weren't sure how you felt about their actions in the lab."

"I can't judge what they did. What's their request?"

"They'd like you to destroy the Citadel. At least the portion covering their birthing dens."

Donavan's expression tightened. "Tell them if there are enough explosives, I'd level the whole damn place."

Wilson interjected, "The stores' warehouse and the armory have the supplies we'll need, sir."

Mosey stated, "If some of the Elros stay on your tire tracks, they'll be able to enter the Citadel. When you've decided whom you want to take, they'll carry them where you want to go."

"You make it sound like you won't be staying with us."

"Migration season has begun. The Trirobs will head north to their feeding grounds. The Orebs will fly southeast and we will be heading northwest to our birthing valley. Donavan, we'll leave you with some males and older females."

"In a way, I'll miss you."

"You and your people should take your time in deciding on your plans."

Ganter stated, "When you set off your explosives, I want to witness the end of this place."

Donavan and Wilson got back in the truck and led the way and then parked by the officer's building and went inside. When they entered the officer's mess, Wilson took her place with Charlie Unit. Ganter, Mosley and forty of the Elros meandered through the streets to see the place their ancestors had warned them about.

Donavan looked around for Brie Canz, with Taunt standing beside him quietly informing him. "Brie is with Miss Farmane and Miss Valgoski will be here shortly. I've sent Lieutenant Tracy Canz to get them."

Donavan waited until the four ladies arrived, then had Taunt introduce Farmane and Valgoski. After that, Donavan got down to his first point of business, "Writing after-action reports may help you to face and deal with what went on there. I expect a report from each of you. For now, we'll start with verbal commentaries. I'll hear from the unit leaders first, then from anyone who wishes to speak." Donavan paused and looked at the faces in front of him, then asked Sparling of Able Unit to speak.

"We did what needed to be done and, in my opinion we did it well. My written report will reflect that."

Bonnel was next to speak, "Delta lost Troopers Mary Gibson, Kevin Craggs and Capt. Emerson. My official report will emphasize the Troopers fought with integrity against the insanity of this place."

Next Donavan called on Wilson of Charlie Unit. She stood slowly and turned to look at the faces of her unit. "We lost Lieutenant Zack, Troopers Young, and Yang. There's nothing that will compensate for their deaths. One night, Kevin Zack and I talked about a woman he had great affection for. She was Wendy Axer, the first officer on the *Resolute Bay*. In my heart, I hope they're together now. I'm truly grateful to each of you for the job you've done here."

After Wilson sat down, Esposito stood. "Two deployments to this planet are enough for a lifetime. Once we leave here, I don't ever want to come back."

When Esposito finished, Wood motioned to Donavan for permission to speak. "For me to stand before you as a med. tech., I'm ashamed to have witnessed what was done here in the name of research. What the Tweebs were doing wouldn't be stopped by any political sanctions and discipline actions. What we did here were necessary actions that needed to be taken."

When Med. Tech. Lt. Wood sat down, Donavan recessed the meeting for a two-hour break. The Canz sisters stayed behind to talk with him. "Brie and I suggest that Laura and Zaivour work with Wood. He can use the help and keeping them busy will help keep their minds off what they've been through."

Donavan told Tracy to run it by Wood and asked Brie to tell Wilson he wanted to see her. When Wilson came in, Donavan asked her to have a seat, "Wood is writing up Brook Emerson's death as a friendly fire incident. I've asked him to write up the Citadel's commander's death as suicide. Unless you and

Luangwa have something to add, that's how both deaths will be officially reported."

"I've nothing to add. I'll check with the Sergeant. If that's all?"

"I want your opinion on some field promotions."

"Of course."

"Sparling and Bonnel to captains."

"Bonnel for Delta is a good choice but I'm not following your reason for Sparling."

"I've too many things on my plate and Able needs a focused leader."

"So you'd be a general?"

"Just a coordinating commander."

Capt. Wilson left the meeting with a knot in her stomach. She knew Donavan suspected she or Luangwa were involved in Emerson's death.

After Wilson left, Donavan walked out of the room to find Brie Canz was waiting. "We're going for a walk," She stated.

"I suspect you'll pick the direction and the subject."

When the two of them got outside, Donavan scanned the catwalk of the eastern wall where Emerson had been shot. Then turned and looked at the western wall behind the motor pool where he had met with Brie the previous night. The fact that she was a first-class sniper moved slowly across his mind.

"I have the uneasy feeling that there's a problem."

"Only one?"

"I mean between us."

Donavan hesitated before answering, "Emerson's death. Brie, it would take an experienced shooter to make that shot in the dark. The idea that one of my people did it intentionally makes me uneasy. The entry point was dead center in the forehead with no powder marks. It was done from a good distance using a night scope. The shooter would've known who the target was."

"Are you thinking it was me?"

"No. I'm saying I don't know who took the shot. Even if I did know, what would it matter?"

"It matters to me what you think."

They stood silently together for a while. Then Brie looked to see what had just caught Donovan's interest and asked, "Why would George and Sherry be perched on the wall?"

"They're watching to see if I'll do as promised."

"That is?"

Donavan explained the promise he had given to Ganter and Mosey about blowing up as much of the Citadel as possible.

Brie commented, "Let us snipers set the charges in the Zavtar Building. After what those bastards did, I want nothing left of that building. We'll set the explosives so the walls implode."

"You got it. Now what did you want to talk about?"

"How are you handling things?"

"I could ask you the same question and we'd both probably lie and say fine."

Brie peered at Donavan, "When there's time, we're going to talk each other through this. I want your word on it."

"Anything else?"

"It will wait."

"We better get back."

Donavan sat at the front alone as the troopers came in and took their seats. Then he asked, "Is anyone willing to go first?"

Pam Longbow stood up. "It was a shit show. Your plan was good. Some of what happened here doesn't need to be reported."

Amie Longbow stood beside her sister, "We owe a debt to the Trirobs and the Orebs. Without their help, I doubt any of us would be sitting here right now."

Sgt. Vince Luangwa got to his feet as the Longbow sisters sat down. "I did a number of questionable things last night. One that I should be up on charges for. It happened in the commander's office and if it comes to me being charged, I'll accept the consequences. Donavan, what I want to know is, are you going to tell everyone what Zaunk said?"

Donavan looked at Luangwa with a puzzled expression. "I don't recall an incident in Zaunk's office you'd be brought up on charges for. Wilson, Sparling, and I were there. If either of them have any recall of what I'm missing, I'd appreciate one or both of them refreshing my memory."

Both of them stated that they had no memory of any chargeable offence.

Donavan continued, "Today I want people to voice their feelings on last night. Tomorrow at 1000, I want everyone here, then I'll share what Zaunk said. Sergeant Luangwa, Captain Wilson and Lieutenant Sparling may be asked to corroborate what was said."

For the rest of the afternoon, Donavan listened to all who were willing to speak. As he was about to dismiss the group, Zhang and Tian asked for volunteers to help with dinner. When six raised their hands, Tian announced dinner would be at 1800.

After the room cleared, Wood walked up to stand across from Donavan, "It was a good start to give them an open venue to talk. It'll help them realize that they're not alone. When they begin to be honest with what they saw in the lab, we'll need to be ready to listen."

Donavan's mind was reflecting on his own actions. "I'm listening."

"Taunt-Toe's one of the toughest men in the group, he'll be ready to help listen."

"What about Farmane and Valgoski?"

"I'm meeting with them and the Lawson sisters tonight. Keeping them busy will help distract what they've gone through. In time, one or both may talk with me. What about you, son, are you ready to talk?"

"Fred, I'll let you know when."

After Wood left, Donavan sat pondering the emotional state of the people under his command. Finally, he got up and went out to find Ganter. Brie was waiting for him in front of the building. "Fred strongly suggested it would be wise if I stayed close to you."

"I guess he's got his reasons."

"So where are we headed?"

"To find Ganter. I promised to keep him informed."

"Mosey said he's outside the main gate."

They took the motorcycle to meet with Ganter. Donavan told Ganter that he was having a second meeting with the troops in the morning. After that, he would have a better idea of what their plans would be.

Brie asked Ganter, "Where's Mosey and why are you standing here alone?"

"Miss Brie, the stories that the elders told in my youth began to haunt me. I needed to be close to the gate."

"It's done with and there'll be no new stories to haunt you."

"There'll still be the memories."

"A healthy mind looks to the future. Soon your females will be giving birth and you'll have a whole new generation to watch over," Brie reminded him.

Donavan interjected, "Ganter, I need another favor."

"I was wondering when you'd remember the wounded you left behind. In the morning, have your people meet me here. Now leave that noisy machine. The two of you ride on me while I look for Mosey."

When Ganter found Mosey, Donavan and Brie dismounted and politely excused themselves so the two Elros would have some privacy. Donavan looked up at George and Sherry sitting on the east wall and suggested, "We'd better meet with Bitcher and Slayer."

"Amie says Trasher's worried you don't empathize with what his parents Bitcher and Slayer did in the lab."

Donavan called Amie Longbow on his comm to ask her where they could meet with Trasher. Amie told him to meet her at the warehouse stores building. When they got there, Donavan told Trasher he wanted to talk with Bitcher and Slayer. The young Trirob jumped from Amie's shoulder and scurried down a hole behind a filing cabinet.

"How are you holding up?" Donavan asked Amie.

"Sir, there's a lot of shit to deal with. Pam and I are going to talk with Taunt-Toe."

"Talk with me as often as you want and let the others know I'm approachable."

Brie added, "Amie, Taunt-Toe taught us that snipers are more than teams. We're family that have each other's backs in and out of combat."

Amie nodded slowly as she informed them that the Trirobs

had suffered twenty-four casualties. Within half an hour, Trasher, Bitcher and Slayer came out from behind the filing cabinet. They sat up on their hind legs and waited for Donavan to speak.

Instead, Brie sat on the floor so she could be more on their level. "Amie told us that you lost twenty-four of your troop. Please accept our condolences."

Bitcher thanked Brie and Slayer commented. "Our fallen aren't left as Mongrel food. We take them below and bury them."

That made Brie consider where they would bury their own fallen.

Donavan followed Brie's example and sat on the floor to talk. "Without your help, we wouldn't have been able to take the Citadel. Thank you and please thank your troops for everything they've done."

Bitcher questioned Donavan's honesty. "Everything?"

Donavan thought about Luangwa shooting Zaunk, the Citadel commander, "Everything."

Amie extended her left arm with her palm up. Trasher moved and stood on it. She stroked his fur as she spoke. "I guess this is good-bye."

The young Trirob tilted his head back. "Every season we return and by then I'll have a mate. I'll always be missing you."

"Be safe, Trasher."

He scurried over to his parents and they disappeared behind the filing cabinet.

Donavan stood. "You made quite the bond with him."

"The little guy was like the younger brother Pam and I didn't have. My father wanted boys."

"Tracy and I got the same feeling from our father," Brie emphasized.

Donavan asked, "Amie, one question. How long have you known Trasher could understand and speak our language?"

"From the first night. He asked me not to say anything. Bitcher and Slayer forbid it. Donavan, it helped build trust with the Trirobs."

"Brie, it's time I thanked George and Sherry."

"We—remember Wood told me to stay close to you."

"Amie I'm sending Taunt-Toe back to get Defoy and the others. I'd like you and your sister to volunteer to go with him."

"Just the three of us, sir?"

Brie interjected, "I'm sure spotters Phoss and Frizz will be happy to go with you."

Donavan glanced at Brie, then added, "I'll have Taunt-Toe pick who he wants. Be ready to leave in the morning at 0600."

"It'll be a pleasure getting away from here."

After Donavan excused Amie, Brie stated, "Tracy and I could go with them."

"I'd rather have you here. Now we'd better go out and see George and Sherry."

When they got outside, the two Orebs were perched on the wall peering down at Donavan and Brie. After Donavan nodded to the Orebs, they glided down and sat on the road.

George spoke first. "Tomorrow the Trirobs will go north. In a few days, the Elros head north and west. When it's our time, we'll fly south. What about you and your people?"

"As yet undecided," Donavan replied.

Brie asked, "How long before the Orebs fly south?"

"As soon as we witness Donavan's promise of destroying this place."

"We promised Bitcher and Slayer we'd fly over their migration route and let them know it's done." Sherry interjected.

Donavan replied, "Day after tomorrow, I promise. George, Sherry … thank you."

"Not necessary, we should be thanking you. Without you, this place would still be a stain on God's creation."

George stated, "A combined effort. The Trirobs, the Elros, you and us. A force that would put any army on the run."

Brie asked, "Will you say goodbye before you leave?"

"We'll do a synchronized flyby to show our appreciation."

After the Orebs stretched their wings and quietly lifted off, Donavan used his comm to contact Taunt. They met at the warehouse stores building where Donavan explained, "I want you to take the Longbow girls back to the landing zone to get the wounded. They've already picked Phoss and Frizz. You pick six more."

# Chapter 7 The Landing Zone

In the morning, Master Sg. Taunt left the Tweeb Citadel with First Lts. Pam and Amie Longbow, Lin Tian and Jing Zhang, along with Lance Troopers Wayne Phoss, Al Frizz, and two other members of the Black Sentry. Their objective was to go back to the original landing zone and rendezvous with Med. Tech. Lt. Defoy and those injured in their initial free fall from the *Resolute Bay*. When they reached the Wishbone River, they rested before crossing it. Meta, Tian's Elros asked her, "If you don't find your way home, would you and the others consider staying with us?"

"Meta, I can only speak for myself. I'd be honored to."

"Elros and you particular humanoids make a very good combination."

"If we did stay, I'm afraid we'd put you and the other Elros in harm's way. The Tweebs will want revenge and be looking for us."

"Mosey has chosen of a place of safety for your people to live. At the far end of our birthing canyon, there's a passageway under the mountains that leads into a valley. A tribe called the Bec live there and would welcome you."

"Who are the Bec and why would they put themselves in danger welcoming us?"

"They are the indigenous inhabitants and were the original stone cutters. Amie, they have no love for the Tweebs and their area is protected."

Taunt gave the order to mount up so they could cross the Wishbone River to make their way to the deserted Tweeb fort to bivouac for the night. When they arrived, the Elros elected to stay outside the compound.

Yaugur, the senior male Elros, explained it to Taunt, "Walls are like cages, we would be uneasy inside. Your people will sleep easier with us being on guard out here."

"Don't Elros sleep?"

"When we close our eyes, our senses stay alert. The ears listen, the trunk sniffs the air, and our feet still register the motions of the ground."

When Taunt's people went inside, they checked the buildings and started to settle in for the night. Radio operator Trooper Tory Nesium was on the catwalk with Taunt and in contact with Defoy. When Taunt finished talking with Defoy, Frizz stated, "Wayne and Amie made supper. I suggest you get some."

"Tell them Nesium will be right in."

"We'd all like to know the rotation for guard duty for tonight."

"I'll handle it. Just have someone bring me a plate of supper."

"As you say, sir."

Twenty minutes after Frizz and Nesium went in for supper, Phoss came out carrying blankets with Amie Longbow holding a plate with supper and a cup of coffee.

Amie stated, "The food and coffee are hot, so relax and enjoy them, sir."

"And the blankets?"

"Taunt-Toe, the three of us will rotate the watch, sir."

"The Elros have the watch. I just wanted to stay within earshot of them sounding an alarm."

"Then, with your permission, sir, the three of us will rotate listening."

"Amie, you're a sweetheart but I'm sure you and Wayne could find a better spot to spend the night."

Wayne interjected, "Master Sergeant, the snipers refer to you fondly as Taunt-Toe. Amie and Pam wouldn't rest easy with you pulling an all-nighter. Pam and Al wanted to come out, but Amie and I said we had you covered. All the women in the Black Sentry value how you back them."

Taunt responded with war humor. "It's safer than being in front of them."

Amie asked cautiously, "Zoowang, does it haunt you?"

Taunt knew for Amie to ask this meant she was afraid what she experienced in the Citadel would haunt her. Taunt settled his mind and the gloomy memories Zoowang held before answering. "Both of you memorize this and pass it along to the others: A healthy mind only remembers the good. Even of this place."

Wayne questioned, "What good is there to remember of this place?"

"Being alive and people you can count on." It took Taunt a minute before he continued, "Brothers and sisters in arms and being with the one you're closest to."

"Zoowang couldn't have left you with too many good memories."

"Amie, like I said, people. Donavan's parents were killed at Zoowang and had asked Wood, me, and Capt. Gwen Hoi to raise their son. There were others like Lady Mere and Dollfuss (Bull) Bullford."

"A trooper called Lady Mere. Was she one of your snipers?"

"Mere was an Army nurse who earned the handle of Lady. She and Wood were the last two people that Bull stayed to evacuate. The hospital had been overrun and Wood with Lady Mere wouldn't leave until the patient they were treating finally gave up the ghost. Bull wouldn't leave without Lady Mere. People you count on, positive events, and being alive."

"How did they get out if the hospital had been overrun?"

"They were operating in the burnt-out fuselage of a troop carrier that had been shot down five miles behind the hospital. All three of them were crazy. We lost too many good people at Zoowang. The surviving members of the Forty Fifth still get together once a year. Sergeant Silaz Park." Taunt stopped talking with his memory of Sgt. Park.

Phoss gauged Taunt's expression before asking, "Who was he, sir?"

"I haven't seen Silaz since ... but every year he sends enough money to pay for our reunion. He used to tell us tales about ghost ships and Matagam Pagwa. Word is Silaz lives on Wabs running a restaurant. Wood and I should look him up one of these days."

"Master Sergeant, you get some sleep. Wayne and I will keep watch," Amie suggested.

Wayne waited until he was sure Taunt was asleep before he spoke. "Amie, did you catch how he didn't mention anything gruesome about Zoowang? He focused on whatever good he could recall. What are you going to focus on as far as this place is concerned?"

Amie used her night vision goggles to look out on the clearing around the fort, then she answered. "You, the others, the friends and allies we've made, most of all . . . other than you and Trasher. I'm going to miss him. What about you?"

"You, the rest of the Black Sentry, the friends we've made with the Elros. And our allies who helped keep us alive, the Orebs and the Trirobs. I think Taunt-Toe is right about having a healthy mind."

At 2400 hours, Taunt's eyes opened wide and alert. He scrambled to his feet. Phoss reacted spontaneously to Taunt's unexpected movement by having his weapon pointing straight at the man's chest. Then he lowered his rifle and apologized, "Sorry, Master Sergeant, I wasn't expecting movement on this side of the wall."

"Don't apologize, your reactions were spot on."

"A bad dream, sir?"

"Phoss wake Longbow and find an empty room inside. Get some sleep and be ready to move out at zero-six-hundred."

"Sir, Amie won't like it. She told me to wake her at zero-three-hundred so she could relieve me."

"Wake her, Phoss. I'm making it an order."

"With respect, sir. Not unless you explain first."

Taunt and Phoss turned their heads to see Amie sitting up holding her nine-millimeter. "Experience has taught me to sleep with at least one ear listening."

After Amie got to her feet, she questioned, "Who is Mary Martha? At one point you were talking in your sleep,"

Phoss asked, "Was it thinking about her that woke you?"

Taunt stared out over the wall before he answered. "Mary Martha Lawrence, a nurse at Zoowang. I was on my knees holding Jack Pine's intestines inside his body while yelling for a med. tech. Mary Martha Lawrence was the one who responded. As she started to get on her knees to help, a bullet pierced her throat and her body collapsed on top of mine. It doesn't do much to keep a relationship together."

"Sorry for asking."

"Amie, at times, you and Wayne will have something trigger experiences better left dormant. Try to focus on the better memories.

By 0530 hours, the members of Taunt's group had eaten breakfast and by 0600 hours, they were mounted up on their Elros and headed away from the Tweeb fort.

Yaugur, Taunt's Elros, led the group to the Elros' migration path. They followed it for four hours before cutting to the right onto a trail that in two hours brought them close to the landing zone. All at once, the Elros stopped, put their ears out and their trunks up.

"Taunt," whispered to Yaugur, "What is it?"

"Oncilla cats."

"Cats?"

"Leopardus tigrinus with brown and black camouflage. Only twenty-three of your inches in length. Scavengers that feed on the dead and wounded. Not a good sign. The Mongrels like feeding on them."

Taunt had Yaugur move beside trooper Nesium, then had him radio Med. Tech. Defoy. "Defoy, it's Master Sergeant Taunt. What's your situation?"

"For the last hour, we've had cat-like things circling. Twice the damn things ran in and attacked the wounded. After five of them were shot, they backed off but they keep circling to find a way in."

"Get your people ready to move. We're coming in on Elros in twenty minutes."

Taunt used his comm link to warn his people about the Oncilla cats and to have their weapons at the ready. "Shoot to kill on sight and be looking for any Mongrels in the area. Nesium, get on the radio and tell Defoy if he hears any shots, it's us taking care of his cat problem."

As Taunt's people approached Defoy's camp, five shots were taken, eliminating five of the Oncilla cats.

Once Taunt's people got inside the camp's perimeter, Defoy

questioned with bewilderment, "How did you tame those huge things?"

As Yaugur bent his front legs to lower Taunt to the ground, he spoke, "A better question would be do you have your people ready to move out."

"That thing spoke."

Taunt got eye to eye with Defoy and abruptly stated, "They're Elros, not things. Do you have your people ready to go?"

Defoy pointed as he spoke. "There's a problem. Ten minutes ago, Horton was bitten by one of those spiders. She's paralyzed."

Yaugur raised himself up and moved to the woman lying flat on her back.

"Taunt, control that thing before he steps on Horton."

"His name is Yaugur and he knows more about this jungle than you ever will know. Now shut it and listen."

Yaugur knelt beside Terry Horton and tilted her head so he could peer into the woman's eyes. Then he used his trunk to convey instructions to Clare, Amie's Elros, and Enza, Pam's Elros. As the two Elros walked away, Defoy retorted, "Where the frig are they going?"

Taunt asked Yaugur, "You have a plan?"

"Clare and Enza will find some Denwa flowers and have Amie and Pam pick them."

Before Yaugur had time to finish his explanation, Defoy reacted. "That thing's not a med. tech."

"I told you to shut your mouth and listen. Yaugur, what's the plan?"

"When they return, have the leaves of the flowers boiled, then make an incision where the spider bite is and lay the leaves over it. Taunt, it's important to replace the leaves when they turn black."

"What happens if we don't?"

"The fluids of the leaves are addictive. Miss Horton will surfer agonizing and prolonged withdrawal discomfort. Sometimes with severe hallucinations."

"Defoy, do you understand Yaugur's instructions?"

"Taunt, do you really expect me to follow some animal's jungle remedy?"

Phoss had his Elros lower him to the ground. "Master Sergeant, I'll do it with Amie's help."

"Good man, Phoss. Defoy, you get the others ready to leave when we're ready. Yaugur, how long before Horton's mobile?"

"It could take as long as twelve hours. I suggest we make the lady comfortable in the bottom half of one of your cam shells. After the treatment, we'll tie it to a female Elros to drag and we'll spend the night at the fort."

"Yaugur, what are Horton's odds?"

"The good news is the flesh-eating ants haven't found her. In the morning, her joints will be stiff and she will need warm water to soak in to relax and loosen them. The warm springs would be best for her."

When the two female Elros returned with Amie and Pam, Wayne told Amie, "I told Taunt-Toe we'd do what needs to be done."

"Clare and Enza have already told us what the leaves are for and how to use them. So what's Defoy's problem."

"His stupid ego won't let him take advice from an Elros."

Amie asked her sister Pam to boil water and start soaking the Denwa leaves. Then she slit Horton's slacks open at the thigh to better expose the spider bite.

Yaugur knelt to take a close look and commented, "Small, it must have been a juvenile. Miss Amie, that makes things more promising."

"Yaugur, will this work?"

"Miss Amie, would I gamble with the lady's life?"

"You're too much of a gentleman to do that."

When the leaves were ready, Yaugur watched and guided Amie and Wayne as they followed his precise instructions. After the leaves had been changed several times, the excess fluid was wiped clean. Amie bandaging the bite. Yaugur asked Torin, Phoss' Elros, and Karn, Frizz's Elros, to take them to find long strong vines to be used as rope for towing the half-clam shell.

As they headed off, Amie spoke with respect, "Yaugur, we owe you Elros so much already and you keep helping us."

"Miss Amie, has Clare told you of the valley beyond the mountains where our calving canyon is?"

"She told Tian there's a way under the mountain into the valley where the Bec live and they don't share any love for the Tweebs."

"The Bec are a race of people about half your height. Do you remember the Borven baboon that was in the Tweeb lab at the Citadel?"

Amie wiped a tear from her eye before answering. "The sight of his suffering will always haunt me."

"One of the surviving troops of the Borven, live in the same valley and they exist in harmony with the Bec. We will take you to meet the Bec. It would be a safe home for you and your kind."

"We might need it if we don't find a way off this planet."

Taunt had spent his time making sure Defoy and everyone was ready to move out. They had the injured loaded into half-cam shells and made as comfortable as possible. Trooper Roy Glenn asked, "Master Sergeant, what are the chances of Horton recovering?"

"Truthfully, Glenn, I'll be better able to answer that in the morning. Trusting Elros is a smart thing to do. I have confidence in their knowledge of the jungle."

When Phoss and Frizz got back with the vines, the half-clam shells were harnessed to the Elros and the group started back to the deserted Tweeb fort.

# Chapter 8 Planned Destruction

The morning after the attack on the Citadel, Taunt's group headed for the original landing zone and the Trirobs left as well. Donavan held his second meeting with the Black Sentry. He began by asking Sgt. Vince Luangwa to repeat his question of the day before.

"Sir, are you going to tell the others what Tweeb Commander Zaunk said?"

Donavan answered by paraphrasing the pertinent part of his conversation. "When I met with Zaunk, I stated the facts that this was the second time we've been on this planet and both times our troops met with disaster. Then I told him I was suspicious someone had been giving the Tweebs Intel on our deployments and at that point, I asked him who and why. Luangwa, can you recall the Commander's response?"

"I certainly can, sir."

"Please repeat what was said."

"That bastard said we were betrayed by the one who sent us here. Then he gave the reason that his scientists wanted a different variety of specimens for experiments. In short, we were to be lab rats."

Donavan listened to the fuming remarks of disbelief and anger from the people in the room. Then he asked for quiet and had Lt. Paul Sparling and Capt. Victoria Wilson verify Sgt. Vince Luangwa's statement. After each of them had substantiated Luangwa's account, Donavan allowed his people to vent off some more of their rage. Trooper Leo Sparks stood and stated, "When we get back, I'm going to find that son of a bitch Rear Admiral Flynn and kill him."

Sgt. Hanyu Peng asked, "How do you suggest us getting back?"

Donavan interjected, "Right now none of us can answer that. Our first task is to destroy this place. Tomorrow we'll use the explosives in the armory to level as much as the Citadel as possible. Then the question is, where do we go after that?"

Jill Lawson motioned to be heard. "I don't understand why the Tweebs didn't call for reinforcements. Yesterday during the break, we did some snooping in Zaunk's office. There are three other garrisons. All of them are on the coasts. Only the south coast seems undefended and would seem to be our safest direction."

After Laura Farmane spoke quietly to Joan Lawson, Joan suggested, "Sir, I think you should hear what Laura has to say."

"Please have her stand."

With some coxing from Joan, Farmane stood. "There isn't a base there because of the climate and the fault lines. For the next three months, the daily temperature will average minus 110 degrees. The fault lines that run along the coast are active. Earthquakes quite often cause two of the volcanoes in the area to erupt."

"In short, no shipping lanes and a no-fly zone." Joan stated.

"I think we'll scratch south off the list. Any other suggestions?" Donavan said.

"Sir, I'd suggest northwest, midway between the coast and our drop zone."

Donavan explained, "The Elros migrate northwest and we could travel with them to the warm springs and set up a base camp. This morning Taunt with his group left for our drop zone to get Defoy and the injured. They're to meet us at the warm springs. After that, we'll make the final decision."

Peng exclaimed, "Why not go to the original drop zone? Then when one of our ships returns, we board it, take control, and go back to kill that bastard Rear Admiral."

Peng looked at Farmane and Valgoski and apologized, "Please excuse my language, ladies."

"Peng, we do that and we'll all be up on charges," Donavan replied calmly.

"With what has happened here, we'd all be up on charges anyway." One of the crew spoke up.

"So what's the alternative, live out our lives here on Vulzar?" a trooper asked.

"If one of our ships did come, we could contact it. Hopefully, the Capt. would be willing to meet with Donavan and listen to what he has to say. He might let him contact Command and see if anyone there would be willing to listen. At least it could mean a ride home."

As low sounds of optimism began to circulate in the room, Wilson rose to speak. "Going home is a nice thought but right now, we have to live the reality. After we raze this bore's nest to the ground, I want to get clear of here. Sooner rather than later. The Tweebs are bound to investigate."

Initially there was silence when Wilson finished. Donavan looked at her and asked, "Have your unit gather all the ordinances and explosives from the armory. Brie and Tracy Canz want to set the explosives in the Zavtar Building. Sparling, have your people empty the stores building of everything we can use. Bonnel, Delta's job is food, find what will keep and have it ready to be loaded. Wood, please have Miss Farmane and Miss Valgoski help sort the medical supplies. I'll talk to Ganter and ask him to pick the Elros we'll need. We'll head to the warm springs with the Elros. Now let's get with it, people."

"Sir? Why don't we use the vehicles from the motor pool?"

"Simple reason, they'd be too easy to track. I'm sure there's a schedule for reporting and when that schedule is missed, the Tweebs will investigate. Wilson, use the crawlers to crush everything on wheels or tracks. I don't want anything left for them to track us with."

Bonnel reminded him, "There's an explosives cache at the quarry and if our people used the vehicles, it'd save time and make a finish of this place."

Wilson nodded. "Sergeant and three troopers will go back to the quarry and get the explosives."

Donavan looked across the faces of his troopers and repeated himself. "Let's get with it, people."

After the room cleared, Donavan left to find Ganter and found him with Mosey on the road by the main gate. He asked, "Would you be willing to take us as far as the warm springs?"

Mosey turned her head to Ganter and nodded her affirmative. Then she told Donavan, "After that, we must head for the calving canyon. The Mongrels know calving season is starting soon and will be on the hunt."

"If the Mongrels know where you go, why not go somewhere else?"

"The calving place is a stone-walled canyon that the Mongrels won't enter. The biggest danger is crossing the Anguish River."

Ganter asked Donavan when the Citadel would be destroyed.

"We'll start this afternoon and the last of the charges will be set off tomorrow around 1000."

"I'll send some of the male Elros for your people to start loading."

"Appreciate it, Ganter. I'd better go back and check on the progress."

Donavan found Wilson's Charlie Unit had already sorted out the ordinances and were waiting on Luangwa to get back from the quarry. Able had cleared the stores building of everything they needed. Delta had emptied the food lockers of the non-perishables. Wood, with Farmane and Valgoski, had organized the medical supplies. The Canz sisters had set the charges in the Zavtar Building. Donavan and Esposito checked all the charges in the building to be sure they would implode so the walls would fall straight down.

As promised, Ganter sent the Elros to be loaded. Then Donavan and Wilson checked the back wall of the Citadel as Wilson explained. "We'll blow the back corners and rear portions of the walls first. Then I'll have the crawlers push the rubble forward off the top of the Trirobs' birthing dens. After that, we'll start on the buildings."

Donavan concluded, "That'll take what's left of today and tomorrow morning."

"It'll be worth it, Donavan."

He gave the okay and then he and Esposito got clear of the blast area. Luangwa pushed the buttons to set off the charges. The sound echoed through the compound as falling walls created dust plumes and a dark cloud over the area. When the dust settled, Wilson thought of Trooper Mary Gibson before sending in the crawlers to push the debris off of the Trirobs' birthing dens.

Their next objective was the stores warehouse and Donavan wanted it done separately to be sure the teams had set the charges properly before blowing the Zavtar Building. The warehouse fell straight down as the base crumbled from the bottom and the thick clouds of dust rose. Donavan noted the late hour and ordered everyone to get a night's rest.

That night as Brie and her sister talked, Tracy commented, "Bonnel and the rest of Delta will be safer and happier with Brook Emerson out of the picture."

"I know Emerson was disliked but I want to believe it wasn't intentional."

"It doesn't much matter, does it? Who really cares?"

"I do. Everyone knows Emerson and I had issues. The last thing I need is having people speculating that I targeted her."

"If anyone says anything, I'll set them straight. I'll say I took the shot."

"You wouldn't."

"It wasn't me but everyone knew she had it coming."

* * *

In the morning, Donavan had Luangwa and the Canz sisters blow the buildings one at a time. The rest of the Black Sentry moved out to the treeline with the Elros to watch the destruction. When it came time to implode the Zavtar Building, Tracy asked Donavan, "With your permission, could we have Farmane and Valgoski do the honors?"

He nodded the affirmative and the Canz sisters walked over to them and explained the procedure. The women looked at each other and wasted no time in pushing the detonation buttons. There was a thunderous sound and ground shaking as a thick dark brown cloud of dust rose. Spontaneously, Farmane and Valgoski hugged each other.

When it came time to blow the front wall, Donavan purposely left seven feet standing on either side of where the main gate had stood. He asked Ganter and Mosey for their approval.

Ganter spoke, "The gate will remain a reminder to the Tweebs that their actions create reactions. I approve."

The Lawson sisters approached them with Joan asking,

"Donavan, we saved some cans of spray paint with an idea. With your permission?"

With some hesitation, Donavan nodded his affirmative. Joan took the left side of the remaining wall and wrote:

Death comes from above<br>
in the night skies on the silent wings.<br>
Woe to those who stand the night watch.

Jill took the right side and wrote:

They come from underground, quietly at night,<br>
while you sleep not making a sound.<br>
Woe to those who sleep with both eyes closed.

Ganter and Mosey nodded as Donavan grinned his approval.

Brie remembered what George and Sherry had promised and looked skyward. The Orebs glided low and quietly over her head and then regained altitude to joined their flocks. As they flew over in perfect v-formations, Brie watched and counted the birds in their formation. Then she asked Ganter, "Did I miss count?"

"Sadly, the Orebs suffered loses."

"They didn't say anything."

"It's not their way."

Donavan gave the order for everyone to mount up. Their first stop was at Thirteen-mile Camp where eight unmarked graves were dug for the members of the Black Sentry who had fallen. As a tribute to the fallen, Wood recited:

**Bleak Realities**

May the grim nightmares of war not be lost<br>
when eyes of mourning are opened to the cost.<br>
For some, they are dreams of great glory<br>
to ride forth for the telling of the story.<br>
For others, they are dark shadows of dismay<br>
that offer few honorees deeds to relay.

"That was written by Jack Pine, a trooper who was killed at Zoowang. What Jack was saying was, most of us enlist with ideals and romantic thoughts of glory. The bleak realities are so different. The dark shadows that cloud our thoughts, they need to be faced and put to rest as much as possible."

Wood gave the nod to Lt. Gwen Hoi to speak. "As most of you know, I was with the Forty Fifth at Zoowang. What

Lieutenant Wood did not tell you was Master Sgt. Taunt was holding Jack when he died. It's a memory that still haunts Taunt-Toe to this day. In Jack's memory, I'm going to recite the last thing he wrote.

**Lament for the Regiment**
The Forty Fifth have lost,
So many have they lost.
And we stand too,
In remembrance of those lost.
And we stand too,
Zoowang on Dulque they fought.
And we stand too,
In remembrance of the cost.
And we stand too,
Women and men both we lost.
Stand too we do,
No matter the cost.

"Again, Jack was reminding us that we'll always remember those who are no longer with us and we should remember them with honor and the comradeship we shared with them."

After spending the night at Thirteen-mile Camp, the Black Sentry members headed to the warm springs to rest and wait for Wood and the wounded. Once camp had been set up and guards posted, the Elros moved on to the mud baths.

Wilson, Sparling, and Bonnel went to see Donavan and Esposito to re-assign the troopers to equalize the units. Then Sparling inquired, "Sir, there's a name we need to discuss."

"That would be?"

"Rear Admiral Jonathan Flynn."

Donavan reminded him. "All we have is an insinuation from a tainted Tweeb commander. If your reports are read, how much creditability would command give to anything they contained?"

Esposito remarked, "Those reports wouldn't be believed? Talking Elros, Trirobs, and Orebs working as our allies. The things we did would get us court-martialed."

Wilson was thinking about Kevin Zack and his girlfriend, Wendy Axer. "I'd really like to know who blew up the *Resolute Bay*. Pay back for Axer and the rest of the crew."

Donavan spoke almost in a hushed tone. "Sadly, the realities of us being on this planet, the harder it'll be to keep everyone together. Memories and thoughts of home, family and friends will breed frustration and discontent. A tough reality you'll have to deal with."

"You make it sound like you wouldn't be with us."

"I doubt I'll ever go back. If I did, Rear Admiral Flynn would die and I'd be executed."

"Those are ominous statements."

As Donavan regretted voicing his feelings, Bonnel said, "If there's any chance of us going home, we'll all be going back together. They couldn't say we all were lying. Right, sir?"

"If and when the time comes, it'll be a choice each of you will have to make."

Wilson gazed at Donavan, "If not home, then where?"

"Ganter told me of a green valley with people who are friendly."

"You're serious?"

Esposito interjected, "I thought Donavan was going to suggest something crazy like he'd go find Matagam Pagwa's people."

Donavan smiled. "The man had a beautiful dream to find an uninhabited planet and start a peaceful society. After what we've seen here, I think the man was an idealist but he had the right ideas."

"Matagam and his refugees from war-ravaged planets. It's a myth handed down from generations of romantic idealists." Wilson said.

Esposito defended his belief. "They were real and the descendants of those refugees are somewhere. Hopefully, they found an uninhabited planet where they could live peacefully."

Wilson snapped. "And where would Donavan get a ship to travel through worm holes and vast distances of the universe?"

"All I'm saying is the man was real and he had the right ideas."

Donavan interrupted to end the debate. "Matagam Pagwa was real. Ask Taunt-Toe when he gets back. Now check on your people and get some rest. Wood should be here tomorrow by mid afternoon.”

“How would Taunt-Toe know? Wilson retorted.

“He met a couple of them on Dulque Zoowang in an aid station during the battle. The medic told Taunt-Toe they each had the M-Marker in their blood.”

“And what’s that?”

“All of Matagams refugees were given an injection against streamer’s disease and space sickness. It’s said to be passed down from generation to generation.”

# Chapter 9 Terry Horton

After Taunt and the others got to the deserted Tweeb fort, Yaugur had to convince the Elros pulling the half-clam shells to go into the compound. The Elros' instincts were to fear any human-made enclosures. When they resisted, Yaugur asked Taunt to untie one of the clam shells and tie it to him. Then he and Taunt walked inside the fort's compound to a building Taunt had selected pulling the clam shell.

Taunt had two troopers go upstairs and bring a bed down to the ground floor. Then Al Frizz and Wayne Phoss, with Roy Glenn and another trooper, carefully picked up Trooper Terry Horton's body and took it inside to put her on the bed.

When Pam and Amie Longbow told Taunt they would stay with Horton, Roy Glenn asked, "Master Sergeant, may I have permission to stay with Trooper Horton?"

"Take shifts with the Longbows."

Yaugur reminded Taunt, "Miss Horton will be weak and thirsty when she wakes. Give her fluids and remember no stairs."

"How much longer, Yaugur?"

"Hours, maybe not until morning. At times, the jungle can be a home."

Yaugur turned and lumbered out of the compound and looked at the other Elros with the clam shells, "If I have to, I'll tow each of those things inside myself, and you'll answer to Ganter and Mosey."

The youngest female Elros nodded her head and dragged her clam shell and walked past Yaugur into the fort's compound. Out of total embarrassment, the older and larger male Elros soon followed the younger female's lead. As the members of Taunt's group helped the injured up the stairs and into rooms with beds, the Elros quickly headed out of the compound.

Yaugur tilted his head toward Taunt and said, "You

understand their hesitation. To them, these walls represent enclosures and enclosures represent pain."

When Yaugur left to be outside the walls of the fort, Taunt went into the building to see that Horton was being cared for. He told Glenn, "Before you eat, have a bed brought down here. Then bring the Longbow girls some supper. Pam and Amie, you take shifts through the night. I'll be on the wall. If Horton even twitches, send Glenn to get me."

"Taunt-Toe, may we send Phoss and Frizz to stay the night with you."

"They'll help pass the time."

It was 0230 hours when Pam noticed Horton's left-hand twitch. She immediately woke Amie and Glenn, and sent Glenn to notify Taunt.

Pam took Horton's hand and rubbed it gently to see if her hand would react. Horton's hand responded by pulling back as her dry, hoarse voice mumbled, "Water, water, I'm thirsty."

Amie opened her canteen, poured some water into a cup, and handed it to Pam for her to help Horton take small sips. By the time Glenn returned with Taunt, Horton with Amie's and Pam's help, was sitting up on the bed resting her back against the wall.

Taunt asked, "Has she spoken yet?"

Horton answered his question. "I'll tell you a secret. The whole time I could hear you all talking. I couldn't speak, but I could hear you."

"Even when we're putting those hot leaves on you?"

"Yes, Amie. Thank you and I want to thank Yaugur and Phoss."

Taunt questioned, "You can do that in the morning. Are you hungry?"

"I would like to try to eat something."

Pam saw the depth of concern and hope in Glenn's eyes and told him, "Amie and I will find something easy for Horton to eat. Taunt-Toe, I'm certain Glenn will stay with her until we get back."

"I'll check with Frizz and Phoss."

After they got outside, Taunt told Pam to find Horton

something easy to digest. Then he asked Amie to come with him to see Yaugur.

As they approached the big Elros, he turned and watched them. Then he said, "I take it Miss Horton is improving."

"We have her sitting up in bed and she's talking."

"Very promising events, but Miss Terry's joints will be stiff. I suggest you use warm water and give the lady's legs and arms a gentle massage. Miss Amie, I'd appreciate having a word with Taunt."

After Amie left, Taunt asked. "What's on your mind, Yaugur?"

"Your Med. Tech. Peter Defoy. I don't like him and Clare's instincts are not to trust him."

"I can understand you not liking Defoy, but do you always trust Clare's instincts?"

"She is my mate and Mosey's sister. Seldom are Clare and Mosey wrong."

"I'll consider what you've said. See you in the morning, Yaugur."

When Taunt got up to the catwalks, Glenn was there talking with Phoss and Frizz. He explained Amie and Pam were giving Horton a sponge bath and he needed to make himself scarce. Taunt told him, "Make some fresh coffee and bring two cups out here. Wayne, you and Al get some sleep. Glenn and I will finish standing watch the rest of night duty."

* * *

In the morning, Amie and Pam helped Horton exercise her legs by being on each side of her as she got out of bed and walked around the room, then outside. The first question Horton asked was, "Where are the Elros?"

"Terry, they have an aversion of being confined. They're outside the walls."

"I want to thank Yaugur. Please walk me out to him."

As they passed through the gate, Yaugur with Clare, and Enza were there. The three Elros knelt on their front knees. Then Yaugur spoke. "Miss Terry, please sit and rest while we talk."

After Horton sat down, she said, "All the time I was paralyzed, I could hear what was being said. I owe each of you my life."

"Ganter gave us the responsibility of bringing everyone back."

Clare added, "That's only partly true. Mosey and the rest of our females owe your friends a debt of gratitude for defending our young against the Mongrels."

Amie detailed to Horton the history of meeting the Elros and the battle with the Mongrels on the open grasslands. When she finished, Horton asked, "I've missed so much. What about our Tweeb objective?"

Amie avoided telling Horton about the experiments done in the Citadel. She only stated, "Taken and by now, it should be razed to the ground."

Yaugur interjected, "Miss Terry, when you eat, please limit your intake and allow your system to re-adjust. If you don't, your system won't be able to handle it.

Enza offered her advice. "Amie and Pam take Terry back inside and get her a light breakfast. Then allow her a couple hour's rest before we start for the Wishbone River."

Yaugur stated, "Miss Terry shall ride on Kinya. She's young and strong. It will be less stressful for you getting on and off her."

It was late morning when Taunt and his troopers left the deserted Tweeb fort. When they got to the Wishbone River, Yaugur stopped the herd. With their trunks up and their ears out, they stood nearly motionless with Taunt quietly asking Yaugur, "What is it?"

"A plane. Your people should dismount and hide in the bushes. I'll have the Elros throw branches over the clam shells to hide them."

Once everyone was in the bushes, Taunt used his binoculars to watch the plane fly passed high and far on the other side of the river. With an unwelcoming feeling, he told his people to mount up. As they crossed the river, some severed body parts and bits of torn tweed uniforms floated by them.

Yaugur stated, "The Mongrels must be filling their bellies. It's a good sign for us."

* * *

It was near nightfall before they reached the warm spring pools. Donavan and others watched as the injured were helped off the Elros.

Taunt went over to Donavan and Wood and said he wanted to talk privately. He explained Defoy's attitude and unwillingness in not listening to Yaugur.

When Wood asked where Horton was, Taunt took him and Donavan over to see her. After the introductions, Wood asked her how she was feeling and asked if he could examine her.

Horton replied by asking, "Yaugur said I should spend time in the warm spring's pool to exercise my joints and muscles. Could we do it after that?"

Donavan stated, "Sorry, I'm sure you're sore from the trip. I'll have the Longbow sisters stay with you."

"Sir, Trooper Roy Glenn said he'd accompany me."

Donavan glanced at Glenn and nodded the affirmative. Then he took Wood and Taunt and went to confront Defoy. When they got there, Donavan stated, "Horton owes her life to Yaugur's knowledge and Amie and Phoss' actions. What the hell were you thinking?"

"If it's not in my medical books, would you expect me to follow the instructions of some jungle beast?"

"The Elros are the main reason any of us are still alive," Wood retorted.

"Some of the troopers have told me what was done to the laboratory. Do you realize the Tweebs are years ahead of us in numerous areas of research? Your actions have jeopardized any co-operation we might have gotten from Tweebs. Have you thought about that, Lieutenant?"

As Wood reached for his sidearm, Taunt gripped his hand, "He's not worth it."

"Think about it, Lieutenant. When we get back, my report will clearly state that the actions taken at the Tweeb research facility should be considered genocide. You and the other senior officers will be up on charges."

Donavan intervened. "Defoy, I wouldn't tell too many people your plans. When the Citadel was taken, everyone got a tour of the lab and saw the living specimens and how they were suffering. Someone might take exception to your views."

"Is that a threat?"

"I'd call it a warning but you can take it any way you like."

Esposito was close enough to hear the heated discussion and came over to diffuse the situation. "Donavan, we have bigger issues. That plane that went over earlier? At some point a Tweeb ship will come to investigate and that could cause us problems."

Ganter reminded Donavan, "The valley past our birthing canyon would be the safest place for you and your people."

"At least it would give us a safe place to make plans," Taunt suggested.

Wood added "At some point, the Tweebs will register a diplomatic grievance about what happened at the Citadel with our government. They'll have to send people to document the facts. It could be our way off this planet."

Esposito stated, "Our diplomats will view it as genocide. Especially with Defoy's attitude. The real questions are: when will a ship come and how do we commandeer it? Then we'll have to decide where to go."

"For now, there's only one question. Do we go with the Elros to their calving canyon?" Donavan pointed out.

With the affirmative nod of heads, it was decided they would go there.

In the morning, Donavan and the four senior officers held a question-and-answer time with the troopers. The idea of going with the Elros was explained. Without any alternative in mind, the members of the Black Sentry accepted the facts and agreed with the plan.

Donavan had Ganter explain the route and the only obstacle which could be a problem. "The crossing at the Wishbone River is the shallowest and narrowest. It's the place where the Mongrels wait and attack as we cross."

Amie piped up, "If we snipers stay on our side, we can pick off those cross-breed mutts."

Phoss stated, "Our grenade launchers will keep them scattered."

Esposito asked, "Ganter, one more day to give our wounded rest, then if you agree, we head out with you and your Elros?"

"It will be making things tight but Mosey has given me the sign to agree."

That evening after dinner, Wood unintentionally heard the Canz sisters talking.

Tracy was asking Brie, "What's bothering you?"

"Emerson's death is like an invisible fence between Donavan and me."

"Sis, he knows you well enough. It's not like he suspects you."

"I wasn't implying that. For his sake, I wish it hadn't happened."

"It did and he'll get over it. He's in love and that's all that matters."

Quietly Wood walked away to find Donavan. He found him sitting alone looking up at the night sky. With some reluctance, Wood asked Donavan, "What's weighing so heavily on your mind, son?"

"Everything, Fred. Being stuck on this planet with no optimistic or tangible way of getting my people off it."

"How's Brie taking it?"

"She's a trooper and accepts the reality of the situation."

"The situation? Is there a problem between the two of you?"

"She knows Emerson's killing is getting to me. When we were talking about it, she had the notion I figured she was involved."

"Son, I know for a fact Brie had nothing to do with it. I took that shot and I'd do it again."

"Fred, why would you?"

"Kevin Craggs. Emerson froze and that's when Craggs bought it. It would've been a shot anyone could've taken, but Emerson froze. She cost him his life and could've cost more people their lives. I saw too many inept officers at Zoowang. Ones who cost too many people their lives. Now write up your report, I'll sign it and if we ever get back, submit it. Or you will have enough senior officers here to charge me and I'll face the firing squad without any regrets."

"Why, Fred? Why are you telling me now?"

"Brie's a good woman. Emerson's death shouldn't be an invisible fence between the two of you."

"Even if I believed you, there's no evidence."

"The word of an officer and friend isn't enough for you?"

"You, Grant, and Gwen Hoi pretty much raised me after my parents were killed. The official report of Emerson's death as friendly fire shall stand as is."

"At least let Brie know the truth. And do it tonight."

* * *

In the morning, Brie and Donavan were awoken in their tent by Victoria Wilson kicking their feet. "Wake up, you two. Horton and Glenn are AWOL. I'll be waiting outside."

When they got outside, Brie asked, "Have you checked the warm pool?"

"That was the first place I looked."

Donavan asked, "Did either of them leave a note?"

"It was addressed to you and Brie saying they were eloping. What kind of question was that?" Wilson replied sarcastically.

"If you had been near death and lived, what would you and Vince be doing?"

Brie stated, "I'd be at the grotto at the far end of the pool."

Donavan spoke quietly. "Wilson, check it out subtly. If they're not there, let Taunt-Toe and Wood know. If not, have them get everyone up and organized into search parties."

After Wilson left, Brie questioned, "Last night you were really restless, is Emerson's death still bothering you?"

"If I tell you, promise me it'll be kept between us. No telling your sister."

"I don't tell her everything, especially not what's between us."

Donavan spoke softly and with a hint of remorse in his voice, "Last night Wood told me he was the shooter."

Brie stared wide eyed in disbelief. "Is he that good of a shot?"

"He used to practice with Taunt-Toe. So yeah, he's that good."

"Why? Why would he do it?"

After Donavan recounted what Wood had said, she asked skeptically, "Do you really believe Wood did it?"

"Honestly, I'm of two minds. He has the ability and watching Emerson freeze and seeing Craggs killed has upset him.

"After my parents were killed at Zoowang, Wood, Taunt, and Gwen Hoi raise me while they were on leave. When I said I was going to enlist, they sat me down and explicitly detailed the bleak realities of a grunt's life. Part of it was that friendly fire executions were done as a last resort. They told me at Zoowang dimwitted single-minded officers had cost thousands of troopers their lives. My parents were among the troopers who were killed. Brie, what do I do?"

"Nothing. Do nothing, Jason, and forget about it. Officially it's listed as a friendly fire incident. Let it stand as is."

# Chapter 10 The Crossing

At 0800 hours, Terry Horton and Roy Glenn were found at the Grotto. After that, Ganter and Mosey reported to Donavan and Brie Canz. Mosey suggested she and Brie should take a short ride. She bent her front knees and with her trunk, very gently hoisted Brie onto her back. When they got out of earshot of Donavan and Ganter, Mosey set Brie on the ground to explain in a kind-hearted tone of voice, "Female Elros can sense when another is with calf."

"With calf?"

"I'm talking about Capt. Wilson and Trooper Kim Choi."

"They haven't said anything."

"With their physical life in the military, I'm not surprised. Wilson and Kim might not realize their conditions. Are you going to tell them or would you like me do it? I want the two of them to take care of the gifts they're carrying."

"I'll find a way to tell them."

"We'd better get back before Ganter says too much."

On their way back, they met with Donavan and Ganter. Mosey set Brie on the ground before Ganter could say anything. Donavan told Brie, "Ganter said there's something we need to talk about."

"We'll talk later, Jason."

Donavan looked up at Ganter, "Should I be asking you?"

Brie deliberated before bluntly stating, "It seems Wilson and Trooper Kim Choi are pregnant."

"What next?"

"Mosey says in seven months. I don't think Wilson and Choi know and I'll find a way to tell them. Now you and Ganter make sure everyone else is getting ready to leave and explain things to Wood and Taunt-Toe."

"Brie, when you tell Wilson, have her put Luangwa in charge of Charlie Unit."

For Brie, talking with a subordinate Choi, things went smoothly. Kim was excited and anxious to tell the father.

When Brie spoke to her superior, Capt. Victoria Wilson, the difference in ranks made things dicey. Wilson's reaction was almost defiant, "Not here, not now. Some other place and time I'd deal with it."

Brie braced herself, and responded "Donavan wants you to put Sergeant Vince Luangwa in charge of your unit."

"Talk about being done over twice. Luangwa, the father of my child, taking over my command. There has to be some warped humor in this."

The Black Sentry loaded up and headed out on their trek to the Elros' calving canyon. On the second afternoon, Mosey halted the herd so the females could form a circle with a younger female and a male in the center.

Ganter stated with admiration. "It's her first. The females are providing her with privacy." Then he raised his trunk giving quiet instructions for the males to form a circle with their backs to the females.

Donavan asked, "Do they always form a circle when delivering a calf?"

"It provides the mother privacy and protection."

"Good point. I take it the male is the father."

"Hugo is Lilly's mate."

The female members of the Black Sentry stayed on their Elros until Lilly squatted to give birth. When the calf was on the ground, Brie asked Mosey, "Would I be permitted to get closer?"

"I'll let you down, but wait until Lilly has finished cleaning him and has him steady on his feet. And he takes his first nourishment from her."

All the females watched as Lilly used her head to move the calf while curling her trunk around its tiny body. Lilly so gently picked him up that his feet barely touched the ground. She slowly lowered him to the ground and held him as his legs began to get used to holding his weight. The first time Lilly loosened her trunk's grip, the calf lost its balance and fell face first to the ground. The mother picked up her calf and set it on its feet. Then she grunted her encouragement to him and let go with her trunk. As the calf struggled to keep his balance, Hugo grunted a father's encouragement. Lilly stood so the calf could take its first nourishment. Hugo used his trunk to move the calf in the right direction.

When Hugo turned and looked at Mosey, she gave Brie a nudge with her trunk. "Now you can go over to congratulate the parents and welcome the calf into our herd."

Brie approached the parents speaking respectfully to congratulate them. When the calf finished suckling, it turned its head to look at the woman. Hugo invited Brie to rub the calf's forehead as a sign of affection. Brie stroked him with great gentleness.

After Lilly got to her feet, she invited the women of the Black Sentry to welcome the calf into the herd. One by one they went over and congratulated the parents and rubbed the calf's forehead. Brie asked Lilly what she would name the newborn?

Lilly told her, "Fathers name the sons and mothers name the daughters."

Hugo answered with the pride of a father, "Primo, because he came early and is the first calf of the season."

"A good strong name for our son."

Donavan asked, "How long before Primo will be strong enough to walk?"

Ganter replied, "Two hours at most. Calves have to be able to move with the herd or be left behind with the parents."

"That's harsh."

"Would you risk jeopardizing the safety of your people because of one misfit?"

Without answering, Donavan thought of Emerson and the needless death of Trooper Kevin Craggs.

Brie suggested to Mosey, "We could camp here for the night and get an early start in the morning."

Mosey talked the idea over with Ganter and he knew better not to disagree.

* * *

In the morning, the members of the Black Sentry were up early and ready to leave at 0730. At noon, Ganter stopped the progression a thousand yards short of the Anguish River. As the troopers ate their cold lunches, Donavan with Esposito and Ganter surveyed the far shore. Esposito threw a stick into the water and watched as it drifted in the current. Then he asked Ganter, "Three hundred yards across. How deep is it?"

"Belt high on you. The river is only my first concern. The Mongrels don't attack while we're in water. They'll be waiting downwind between the trees for us to step ashore. It's where our trail begins and there's no room for us to maneuver."

"Donavan, the opening needs to be widened to make a defensive position." Esposito offered.

After a lengthy discussion, they went back to the others to lay out the plan. Donavan explained, "The trees and underbrush are as thick as maple syrup. The sniper teams except for Brie Canz will spread out on our shoreline left of the opening.

"Sparling, your job is to widen the opening on the far shore. Hopefully, the Mongrels hiding there will be killed or scatter. Snipers, Ganter says the rest of the Mongrels will be between the trees to the left of the opening. Your job is to eliminate as many as possible.

"Then Esposito will use the clamshells to take his unit across to establish a beachhead. When they're ashore, I'll send some of Ganter's male Elros to help clear the area of the debris."

Bonnel asked, "Where do you want my people?"

"With the Elros Ganter selects to assist us."

"Once we're on the other side, how far to the canyon?"

"Miss Wilson, all going well, a day and a half."

After Ganter answered, Donavan continued, "I'm sending Taunt-Toe with Hoi with two troopers and Esposito's people."

Donovan turned to Esposito and said, "Drake, let them do their own thing."

As Esposito's and Bonnel's units pushed offshore, Sparling had his unit firing grenades deeper and wider into the trees and pounding the beachhead. As soon as the units got close to the far shore, Sparling's unit fired far left of the opening. The snipers fired their rifles between the trees at the scattering Mongrels. After some of Ganter's male Elros got to shore, they started to clear the debris.

Once Donavan got the word from Bonnel that the area was secured, he had Brie get into a clamshell and had Hugo place Primo in with her. Lilly explained to her calf, "You lie down with your head by Brie's feet. Your father will pull you across while I secure the back of the clamshell."

As the parents crossed the river, Ganter and Donavan watched as Brie stroked Primo's forehead to keep him calm. Once they were safely on shore, the rest of the Black Sentry mounted up on the Elros and headed to the beachhead.

When they got to the clearing, Donavan smiled at Brie. "I'm sure Lilly and Hugo appreciated you taking care of Primo.

"They did and I'm glad the river is behind us."

# Chapter 11 The Trail Down

When the Elros and the members of the Black Sentry were across the Anguish River, Donavan met with Esposito, Bonnel, Paul Sparling and Vince Luangwa with Ganter and Mosey. Ganter explained that the trail from the beach to the valley was narrow. He fully expected the Mongrels would try attacking in smaller packs. Donavan called Taunt and Fred Wood over to ask them what they'd suggest.

Taunt looked over to the snipers, then outlined his plan. "The Longbow sisters with Wayne Phoss and Al Frizz take the left flank on foot while Tian and Jing Zhang with Wood and I take the right. Keep the Canz and Lawson sisters on the Elros. Keep Victoria Wilson, Kim Choi, and Terry Horton on foot."

Sparling questioned, "Who's got our six?"

"Seeing as you asked, Able Unit."

"Taunt-Toe, someday I'll learn to keep quiet and just listen."

"I suggest you do that while you're following us. It could keep you alive."

After the orders were passed down the line, everyone took their positions. As Ganter had said, the trail was narrow with branches brushing close to or against the Elros. For the troopers on the ground and the sniper teams on the flanks, there was a lot of brush slashing to do. Every so often, shots were heard from either flank or from the rear.

After three hours of slow traveling, Ganter stopped the progression at the edge of a down slope. He pointed at the five-mile-long grade. "Donavan, soon it'll be too dark to venture down there."

"It's too dangerous to make camp here. I'll have Esposito take his people down to see if the path is slippery and what's at the bottom."

"Have it your way. Tell your people to mount up and we'll take it slowly. Yaugur with Taunt will bring up the rear. You and I shall go first and when we're at the bottom, you may ask Miss Brie to have Mosey lead the others down."

* * *

When Donavan and Ganter reached the bottom of the slope, he asked, "That was easy, so why were you so hesitant?"

"Bats, they come this far from the calving canyon at night."

"Bats, you're afraid of bats?"

"Not me, your people. Especially your females with long hair. If a bat gets tangled in their long hair and she starts to try untangling it or swatting at it, the others will swarm her. Donavan, a few thousand bats swarming is a dangerous thing. Now tell Miss Brie to have everyone mount up and have Mosey start down. Two miles along the trail is a place where we can make camp."

Donavan contacted Brie with Ganter's instructions and added, "Brie, make sure all heads are covered and long hair tucked into uniforms. Ganter says bats might be flying."

After Brie passed the order, Mosey explained, "Brie, there are two species of bats that live in the canyon: the brown ones and the gray ones. At night, they do a flyby to harvest the insects that bother us. It's like a symbiotic relationship, both parties' benefit."

"How many bats are there?"

"I'd say about five thousand of each species. They enjoy swarming the Mongrels to put them on the run. Brie, they make good allies against the brutes."

After Mosey and Brie led the Elros to the foot of the decline, Ganter told Mosey to lead the Elros to the clearing further along the trail. Ganter with Donavan stood at the bottom of the hill watching to be sure all the Elros made it down without any of them stumbling.

Donavan watched with special interest how Lilly and Hugo cared for Primo as he slowly and carefully took each step. As Yaugur and Taunt passed by, Ganter stated with a tone of relief, "That's all of them."

When they got to the first clearing, Ganter explained, "Your

176

people camp here, we'll be a mile down trail. Tell your people not to bother the Beavpines."

"Beavpines?"

"A manipulated cross breed between beavers and porcupines. Instead of fur, they have sharp pointed quills. When they slap their large round, flat tails, they can use the quills as projectiles. They're extremely painful."

"Thanks for the warning. Do the Beavpines talk?"

"Several languages. Now tell your people to heed my warning."

"How much further to your canyon?"

"If we leave by first light, we'll make it to the mouth of the canyon by mid-afternoon. Now have your people rest."

After Ganter let Donavan down, Ganter ambled away to check on his herd. Donavan went over to his senior officers to inform them of the Beavpines and have them pass the warning.

When the bivouac area was set up and the evening meal was eaten, Donavan had Taunt organize pairs of sentries around the encampment.

As was Taunt's habit, he checked with the sentries periodically through the night. At one point, he heard some rustling in the bush and stealthily trailed it to the river. When he got in sight of what he had heard, he saw Amie Longbow sitting on the ground with a Beavpine beside her.

At first, Taunt watched from a safe distance, not wanting to startle Amie or the Beavpine. Then he heard, "Taunt-Toe, we know you're watching. Join us and I'll introduce you to Stump."

With the thought of getting a quill shot into him, Taunt approached slowly.

Amie made the introductions and said, "Stump would be more at ease if you were to sit down."

Taunt sat down. "You've got some gift when it comes to making friends with different species."

"And we have a gift in knowing who we may trust. Amie assures me you are trustworthy," Stump said.

"Amie, may I ask what are you doing out here?"

"Listening to the water. Taunt-Toe, if you're very quiet, you can hear the sound of the waterfall we passed at the top of the decline. It helps me to re-evaluate."

"Who or what are you re-evaluating?"

"Love and this place. If we ever to get off this planet, there are a few species I'll miss."

Taunt knew Amie was thinking of her relationship with Phoss. "Love has many faces. I love all my female snipers but I'm not in love with one of them."

"Taunt-Toe is that some kind of military double-talk?"

Taunt had to think of his wording before replying. "I love my mother and sister but I wasn't in love with either of them. Amie, do you understand the difference?"

"The man loves his snipers like a father, not in an intimate way," Stump commented

Taunt looked at the Beavpine, "You're perceptive."

"Does it surprise you I have a mate that I'm in love with and we have offspring we love but are not in love with?"

Amie interjected, "So how do I tell which face of love Phoss is showing me?"

Again, Taunt had to think before he could answer honestly. "It's difficult. Start by putting the passionate stuff like how he holds you and kisses you aside. Focus on the compassionate stuff, like how he converses with you. Does he listen, even when the two of you have opposing positions? Does he concede the point when you're correct and he's wrong? Amie, intimacy is only a small part of a lasting relationship. Respecting each other is the basis of lasting love."

Stump concurred. "The man speaks from experience."

Amie asked, "Were you in love?"

"She was killed at Zoowang. If Phoss is in love with you and doesn't realize it, Amie, shove the toe of your boot where it will hurt him most. Then tell him you're not waiting any longer."

"That's harsh, Taunt-Toe."

"I love my snipers and I don't want any of you hurt physically or emotionally. If you want, I'll speak to Phoss in a way that will wake him up."

Amie almost smiled as she spoke. "It's all right, Taunt-Toe. I'll talk to him."

"Miss Amie, if you tell me which tent this Phoss is in, I can get him to see the point."

"Stump, please don't. He needs both of his eyes to be my spotter."

"If he can't spot and you're in love with him, he couldn't be much of a spotter."

"You've both been sweet. I think it's time for Phoss and I to have a conversation."

After she walked away, Stump commented, "Taunt-Toe, that's a different name. But you're a different type of man, a good difference. Watch over Miss Amie, she's special."

"And you watch over your mate and young ones."

* * *

In the morning while the members of the Black Sentry were getting ready to leave, Phoss asked, "Taunt-Toe, could we speak off the record?"

"What is it?"

"Shove the toe of your boot where it will hurt him the most?"

"Phoss, I guarantee you the toe of Amie's boot would hurt a lot less than the toe of mine and a lot less than a Beavpine quill in the eye."

"And that's supposed to reassure me?"

"If we end up spending the rest of our lives on this Tweeb-infested planet, Amie needs to be sure that you love her."

"No wonder the snipers think of you as a father figure. I suppose you'd expect me to ask your permission before I propose?"

"That would be expected. Now get finished packing up and ready to leave."

Once the members of the Black Sentry were mounted on their Elros, Ganter told Donavan, "There's one more river we need to cross before we reach the calving canyon. It runs from the eastern mountains and flows into the Anguish at a very fast-moving rate. Tell your people to stay on their Elros. We don't want to be plucking any of them out of the water."

Ganter stopped before crossing the eastern river to gauge the flow and the best place cross it. Then he and Yaugur took up their positions on each side of the river, slightly down stream. Ganter gave Mosey the nod to lead the herd across.

After the river, it was an easy trip to the calving canyon. Ganter stopped and told Donavan, "Have your people glass the ridge lines to see if anyone is watching us."

"Do you think some Tweebs got here before us?"

"No, they are indigenous Bec who live here. They know when our calving time is and they're usually here to make sure the Tweebs aren't following. Now, please have your people glass the ridge lines."

Donavan gave the order to the snipers and their spotters.

After a few minutes, Tian reported, "Donavan, there are people scattered along both ridges for as far as we can see."

Zhang stated, "There are two rows of what appears to be hundreds of portals on both walls of the canyon."

Ganter clarified, "Those portals are where the Bec lived before they revolted against the Tweebs. We'll continue in for ten miles, then your people will dismount and stand by their Elros. You and Brie stay mounted while Mosey and I take you five miles further in. Then you'll both dismount and walk beside us."

"And the reason for this is?"

"It will show the Bec that we travel as equals. Donavan, from those ridges, your people make very good targets."

"You didn't tell me the Bec have weapons."

"There are many things I haven't told you. If the Bec accept you, they'll teach you many things on how to survive."

After five more miles, Ganter and Mosey stopped and knelt so Donavan and Brie could dismount. Then side by side, they continued on for another mile and stopped again.

Ganter stated, "We'll wait here for Harlan, the Bec leader. Keep your eyes on the mouth of the cave at the end of the canyon. He and his wife Julia will come out to find out who you and your people are. Donavan, keep quiet and please let Mosey do the talking."

"Why Mosey, not you?"

"Mosey plucked Harlan's son Tyler out of the river before he drowned. Harlan and Julia remember such things."

Donavan glanced to his left at the two-mile-wide swift-running water of the river, "I'd owe a debt of gratitude as well."

After seven minutes, Harlan and Julia exited from the mouth of the cave and walked up to Mosey. Julia asked "Riders? That's not your style."

"Julia, this is Brie Canz. Brie and the others with us are members of the Black Sentry. The group who destroyed the Tweeb Citadel."

"Bitcher, Slayer, and especially young Trasher told us of them. Any enemy of the Tweebs is welcomed here."

"Ganter and I are hoping they would be welcomed on your side of the mountain. They need a safe place to live."

"Harlan and I shall discuss that over the next few days. You'd better have Brie use her comm to tell Yaugur's rider he can bring the herd in. Then tell me about the new calf our observers have reported."

As the herd moved deeper into the canyon, the Black Sentry spotters kept watch on the figures on the ridgeline.

Taunt commented to Yaugur, "You've got everything you need here. On both sides of the river, there's at least twenty miles of tall grass and trees where you can pick leaves. Why would you ever want to leave?"

"The walls, Taunt. The walls would seem as confining as cages."

"Got it."

"Under the mountain and on the other side, there's lush, green fertile valleys. Your people will be safe and happy there."

"Yaugur, do you ever go there?"

"Only in times of severe drought. We prefer the jungle with the vegetation it offers. It's home to us."

While Yaugur and Taunt were talking, Mara, Tracy Canz's Elros, suggested, "Tracy, take note of the bottom two rows of the portals in the walls of each side of the canyon. At night, sleep in them until you move into the valley. You and the rest of your females don't want any bats getting tangled in your hair."

"Are there really that many of them?"

"Use your binoculars and count the cave opening near the top of the walls on each side of the canyon. The brown bats sleep in the ones on the right wall and the gray ones sleep in the openings on the left. We've estimated there are about five to seven thousand brown bats and approximately the same number of gray ones."

"Do they ever fight with each other?"

"That would be a sight to see. No, they have their own separate territories to hunt. Both groups come out at the last glow of the setting sun. Now that's a sight you should see. Five to seven thousand bats on each side of the canyon swarming and heading off on their night's hunt."

As the herd got closer to Ganter and Mosey, the Elros who were not carrying riders or pulling clamshells wandered into the grassy areas and in between the trees by the river. When Taunt and the others got to Brie and Donavan, Harlan and Julia had already left for the mouth of the cave leading under the mountain. Donavan gave orders for his senior officers to bivouac their people inside the caves on the right side of the canyon.

Just before dusk, Tracy talked to some of the female members of the Black Sentry standing outside watching the two groups of bats exit their caves and swarm before flying off in the night. It was an unbelievable sight to behold. After the bats had performed their aerobatics, Jill Lawson suggested, "Now we can let our hair down and have a campfire."

As the women were gathering wood, Phoss was talking with Wood, "You and Taunt-Toe were at Zoowang, so you've known each other for years. Could you explain his preoccupation with snipers to me?"

"Phoss, what do you see when you look at our snipers?"

He answered with a perplexed expression. "What do I see? Women, good looking but very dangerous women. Give them a rifle or a knife and they can take care of themselves."

"Is that all you see?"

"I'm not sure what you mean. What else is there?"

"Taunt-Toe and I picked our snipers. All eight of them are

minorities from different walks of life, color, or beliefs. They have no social standing on our planet."

Phoss thought about what Wood had said, then questioned, "The Lawson sisters aren't from a minority?"

"Joan and Jill Lawson are of mixed blood which makes them part of the minority."

"What blood? What do you mean?"

"Have you ever heard of Matagam Pagwa or ghost ships?"

"Ghost ships? But that's only a story or a myth."

"I'd tend to believe they are as real as Matagam Pagwa was. And that's where the question of blood comes into play."

"Meaning?"

"His people were all injected with antibodies to protect them from space sickness and something called streamer's disease. The thing that helps prove the story is that the marker in the blood is passed down from generation to generation."

"And you're saying the Lawson sisters have it?"

"I've checked. Both of their blood tests show the marker. Now for me to answer your question of Taunt-Toe's preoccupation with snipers. Obviously, he's of a minority group in our population. Some people categorize him as not having any social standing. It is a bleak reality that Taunt-Toe has to face and find ways to dealing with. Phoss, it's even harder for minority females. That's where Taunt-Toe's preoccupation stems. Hopefully I've answered your questions."

"You know what's ironic, sir?"

"What's that?"

"On this planet, we're all part of a minority without any social standing."

Wood smiled at Phoss' evaluation. "Walk with me, Phoss. The ladies are having a bonfire. I promised Farmane and Valgoski I'd sit with them."

# Chapter 12 Esposito's Idea

The morning after the ladies held their bonfire, the members of the Black Sentry were standing at ease in front of Donavan. He explained it would be several days before Harlan, the Bec leader, and his wife, Julia, would make their decision on whether to let the troopers live on their side of the mountain.

After numerous remarks and some questions, Donavan explained what Ganter had told him the night before. "This canyon is where the Bec stone cutters lived. The majority of them live on the other side of the mountain. Their society runs the full spectrum from farmers to manufacturers. After they revolted against the Tweebs, weapons became their number one industry. Hundreds of Bec lost their lives during that war. Understandably, they are concerned that if we move into their area, the Tweebs will try to take revenge on them. Ganter and Mosey assure me that the Bec have a secret weapon. Your commanding officers have the duty rosters and I fully expect those duties to be carried out. Dismissed."

After the troopers were given their duties, Esposito and Wilson spoke privately with Donavan. Wilson spoke with firmness as she stated, "You twit, Choi and I are pregnant. We're not incapacitated. I'm in command of Charlie Unit so you can shove your male chauvinist attitude."

"Why not tell Donavan how you really feel?" Esposito asked with a smirk.

"How would you like—"

Donavan cut Wilson off mid-sentence, "Capt. Wilson. Don't confuse my caring with chauvinistic attitude. As long as you and Choi promise not to endanger yourselves recklessly and have Wood or Defoy do weekly medicals, I'll do my best to respect your sensitivity."

"Monthly."

"Biweekly."

"Agreed."

Donavan stared at Esposito, "And what's your complaint?"

"The beds are too short."

Donavan smirked, "The beds are too short and that's your biggest complaint? Tell me you've got a practical idea for getting off this planet."

"Bats, thousands of them."

Wilson quipped, "Yeah, we'll stick them together and have them fly us to Izbax."

"Izbax is a shit-hole planet."

"Then what's your brilliant idea?"

Esposito turned his attention from Wilson to Donavan. "If Ganter can talk with the bats, we can use them to confuse and blind whatever aircraft the Tweebs send to recon what is left of the Citadel. When they land, we commandeer the craft and get off this planet."

Wilson asked with limited relevance. "I'll give you that much, the bats could blind the pilot visually. How do you expect them to confuse the navigation system?"

"Bats use echo location to fly and hunt at night. Thousands of bats pointed at one aircraft would temporarily disrupt normal system operations and force it to make an emergency landing or risk crashing."

"One aircraft?"

"Does being negative come naturally with you being pregnant? We could use it to ferry our people off this planet."

Wilson shot Esposito a strong look of frustration. "Did your parents have any kids born without brain damage?"

Donavan interjected, "It might work until some other Tweeb ship shoots it down. The fact is whatever they send will be headed to the Citadel. Now how do you propose diverting them to the canyon?"

"I don't have all the answers, Donavan, ask our four-legged tactician."

Wilson glanced at Esposito. "The Bec might have another idea."

"I'll talk it over with Ganter, and when I see Harlan and

Julia, I'll ask them. Wilson, find Choi and make appointments with Wood. Esposito, you see if you can do anything about lengthening the beds."

When Wilson left with Esposito, Donavan also left and found Ganter by the river. After he told him Esposito's idea, the big Elros commented, "Bat language is not one I have mastered, but Harlan and Julia have. Actually, I think the idea is not workable. Your best bet is to go back to the Citadel and try commandeering a craft there. Donavan, I thought you'd resigned yourself to stay."

"Given the chance some of my people will want to leave, I owe it to them to do what I can to make it happen."

"Tomorrow we'll talk with Harlan and Julia when they get here."

When Wilson left Donavan and Esposito, she went to tell Choi about her conversation with Donavan. The two of them had a good laugh at what Wilson had said and Donavan's response.

Esposito had gotten together with Sparling and Bonnel to ask, "If we came up with a plan to get off this planet, would you be in?"

"And go where? We can't very well go home; we'd be seen as criminals. As things stand, I'd like to see what's on the other side of the mountain."

"Only if the Bec agree to let us live there. What if they don't?"

"Donavan will come up with something. Esposito, if you really want a way off, I suggest you talk with Wood and Taunt-Toe."

"They'd back Donavan."

"But if there was a way, they'd be the ones to convince Donavan to take it."

* * *

That night in bed, Donavan made the mistake of saying, "Esposito was right."

Brie asked, "About what?"

"These beds are too short."

"We can manage."

She started to laugh, "I wasn't suggesting you should. Donavan, after your parents, were there any women involved in your upbringing?"

"Gwen Hoi. Why do you ask?"

"Wilson was right about you. I think Gwen failed to teach you certain things about women."

"You haven't complained."

"Not about that, about women being pregnant. It doesn't make them incapacitated."

"I was trying to be considerate and cautious."

"Check with Wood in the morning. He'll tell you exercise is good for the mother and baby. Then have Gwen finish your education. Now roll over and go to sleep."

* * *

By mid-morning, Harlan and Julia had spoken with Donavan and Ganter. They informed them they had met with Ryan and Shue, the leaders of the closest Bec village. Donavan was invited to choose three others to meet with Ryan and Shue and see the area that had been selected for the Black Sentry to settle. He pondered who to take and then used his comm link to have Brie, Wilson, and Choi join him.

After he explained where they would be going, Choi asked, "Why us?"

"Because you two are pregnant and you should see the place where your children may be growing up. Last night Brie informed me that exercise is healthy for you."

Wilson asked, "Did you ask if they had any ideas for getting off this planet?"

"First things first. I'll bring that up as we're looking at the area they want to show us. Wilson, it's another reason for you to come."

"When do we leave?"

"As soon as you pack what you need."

When the women were ready, Harlan and Julia led them into the tunnel under the mountain. As the four of them were scanning the immense size of the cavern, Harlan was by the shore of the large underground lake talking with his men who were with the canoes.

Julia explained the plan to men in canoes doing the paddling. "It will take forty-five minutes for us to reach the area where your people will be allowed to live. After you've seen it, we'll cross the river to the city where Ryan and Shue live. They'll be able to answer any questions you have."

Choi asked, "How deep is the water? What I mean, is the water that flows out of the lake a lot slower than the river flowing in."

Julia answered with respect. "Good observation and good question. At places, the lake is over three hundred feet deep and it drains out in two directions. The one you see and one that drains underground five miles east of the river. Harlan and the men are ready. Please select a canoe and we'll head out."

When they exited from under the mountain, Choi turned her head to look back at the side of the two-thousand-foot-high mountain. In Choi's eyes, it stood as a fortress wall dividing the canyon from the fertile valley she was entering.

Donavan was pondering the two-hundred-foot-tall trees with the lush undergrowth and the fertile ground with the vegetation present.

Wilson's eyes were peering between the trees scanning to see what sort of wildlife inhabited the area. All the time, she was hoping to catch a glimpse of a troop of Borven baboons.

Brie was watching the flow of the water, the sky and the clouds, and the canoe in front of her with Donavan.

When the canoes tied up on the west side of the river, Harlan pointed. "A mile up the path are the remnants of a village our people abandoned twelve years ago. We'll hike up so you can see if it would meet your needs."

Wilson immediately asked, "Why was it abandoned?"

Julia responded, "Ryan and Shue felt the place on the other side of the river offered a more defendable position. Plus, the population had outgrown it"

"I haven't seen any Borven baboons yet."

"That's not surprising. Their coats change with the

surroundings. Part of chameleon lizards' DNA and stem cells that were integrated into the Borvens' ancestors.

"Wilson, if you look very carefully, you may see their eyes watching. Their eyes have been on you since we started downriver."

Choi commented, "It's like being on the wrong end of a sniper's scope."

Harlan put Choi's mind at ease. "Kim, Borvens don't carry rifles. Now if you're ready, let's head up trail to the village called Old Town."

When they got there and had looked around, Donavan stated, "The place looks better than I expected."

Harlan explained, "Some people still use it as a camp when they're hunting on this side of the river."

"What do they hunt?"

"Rabbits, pigeons, and wild boars. The boars are particularly vicious and I advised you to shoot them in the head. Their meat is good eating."

"What about the rabbits and the pigeons?"

"Kim, the rabbits are good eating. As for the pigeons, they make a mess wherever they deposit their droppings. The foxes will clean up the dead pigeons. They need to eat as well."

As Choi and Wilson continued asking Harlan about the village, Brie was asking Julia, "Is there a hospital or clinic?"

"Follow me."

Julia took Brie three streets over and showed her the two-story clinic. "It hasn't been used for anything more than superficial hunting wounds. The place needs a good cleaning and the instruments need sterilizing, but I believe your medical people can make use of it."

"Wood will be very impressed. He's our senior med. tech.—doctor."

"You had a special interest in asking me this, are you ..."

"Wilson and Kim are. That's why Jason—Donavan—had them come with us to see what you and Harlan were offering."

Julia's expression changed to a look of being pleased. "How far along are they?"

"Close to three months now."

"Brie, there's a school with a nursery on the next street. Shall we?"

"Please."

While Wilson and Choi were talking with Harlan, Brie was with Julia, Donavan did his own walk about. As he turned a corner, he came almost face to face with a Borven baboon and froze. Then his mind asked, "Do they talk?"

The Borven baboon smiled as he saw Donavan's hesitation. "Are you one of the Black Sentry who destroyed the Citadel?"

"Yeah—you can talk? Sorry, no one told me you could talk."

"Trasher told us Borven many good things about your people, especially one female named Amie Longbow. Is she one of the females with you?"

"No, but if you'd like to meet her, I'll make sure she comes with us the next time."

"Please do, my mate would like to meet her."

"My name is Jason Donavan and yours is?"

"Moore. I was born bigger than most and as my father watched my delivery, he kept saying Moore?"

"Do you have any more growing to do?"

"I've reached my expected size. When are the rest of your people coming?"

"I'm not sure. Some of them are looking for a way to get off this planet. The rest of us have faced the fact we'll probably be staying."

Moore shrugged. "Getting off would be easy. You should get back to your people, Donavan."

He turned and took long strides walking away. As Donavan watched, his mind questioned, "What would a baboon named Moore know about getting off Vulzar?"

As Donavan left purposely in the opposite direction, he met up with Brie and Julia coming out of the school. After he told them of his meeting Moore, Julia stated, "Moore is the patriarch of the local troop. Donavan, you should be honored that he talked to you."

"He said Trasher had told the Borven's about Amie Longbow and he said his mate wants to meet her."

"Moore's mate's name is Tabla, meaning drummer. She

beats on a hollow log to signal a meeting. Tabla has a great deal of influence in the troop. Donavan, you should bring Amie to meet her as soon as possible."

Donavan questioned, "Julia, Moore said getting off this planet would be easy. Do you know what he meant?"

"There are ways if you put your mind to it and are willing to risk all it takes. When you bring Amie to meet Tabla, ask Moore to explain."

Brie interjected, "Some of our people want to leave. Donavan, as their commanding officer, needs to try to help them find a way."

Donavan added, "It's not like they can ever go home again. After what we did at the Citadel, we'd all be up on charges."

"Then why do they want to leave?"

"After what they saw in the basement of the Zavtar Building, I think they want to put as much distance between themselves and this planet as possible."

"I don't blame them."

"Julia, some of us are really hoping that your people will welcome us and help us to adjust to life on your side of the mountain."

"Then Brie, it's time we find Harlan and the others, and paddle across the river so you and Donavan can meet Ryan and Shue."

# Chapter 13 Ryan and Shue

When Donavan and his people along with Harlan and Julia got out of the canoes on the other side of the river, Ryan and Shue were there to greet them. After the introductions, they got into open trailers pulled by ground transport vehicles called Altervs.

Shue told them, "Alterv is short for all-terrain vehicles. I apologize for the ride in these trailers, but you understand the Altervs weren't built for people of your size." It took twenty-five minutes to get from the river to the city called Candale.

When they got to the city, the Altervs stopped and they all got out so Shue could describe one of the defenses of the city. "There are four-foot-high walls that completely encompass the city."

Choi asked, "Where did they get stone blocks from? You can't float them down the river in a canoe."

"Most of them came from the canyon. We'd drill and blast slabs off the walls. Then cut them into blocks and float them on rafts under the mountain to our side. The Borvens would tie vine ropes to the rafts and pull them down to where you came ashore. Then we'd use the Altervs to pull them here. Of course, the Borvens did the heavy lifting. The first blocks came from the cavern under the mountain. We had to make it larger so our plan would work. The Borvens are helpful when they see you as friends. Let's load up and we'll give you a short tour of the city."

As they drove the wide streets and looked at the stick-frame buildings, Shue continued to answer questions.

Kim thought of the size of the trees in the forest and the fact the buildings were made of lumber. "I suppose the Borvens helped cut down the trees for your lumber mills?"

"You supposed correctly."

"What's the population of Candale?" Wilson questioned.

"At the last census, twenty-five hundred and twelve. But that was three years ago."

"What do your people do for a living?

"A variety of things, Victoria. Civic government, trades, loggers, educators, and doctors. We have the people doing what people do in any city."

"Doctors?"

"Quite good ones. Even the Borven allow them to operate. And considering the procedures some of the Borven have experienced in the past, they speak well of our doctors."

Ryan finally spoke, "Next stop, the mess hall. I don't know about the rest of you but I'm hungry."

When Ryan pulled up to the two-story building, everyone got out of the Alterv. The members of the Black Sentry looked at the doorway and knew they would have to bend a little to go through. Inside, they were relieved to stand and see the walls were eight feet tall.

Ryan pointed to the long short-legged table and the cushions on the floor on either side. "When we were told you'd be coming, the chairs were replaced with cushions. Tradition dictates women on both sides at one end facing each other, with the men at the opposite end."

Shue explained, "That's so we can talk without the men interrupting or dominating the whole conversation."

Wilson happily stated, "I'm in agreement."

As the group was eating the dinner of rabbit stew, they talked and asked each other a myriad of questions. Because Julia and Shue knew Kim and Victoria were pregnant, they kept the conversation mainly on the medical and social aspects of the village being close to the Bec city of Candale.

Harlan and Ryan discussed with Donavan how fertile the land by the village was and how the Black Sentry could be mainly self-sufficient.

At the end of the evening, Ryan and Shue took the four members of the Black Sentry upstairs where Shue explained, "Beside each bed is a full-length cushion with pillows and sheets. Those bed frames in the caves of the canyon must be far too short for you to be comfortable."

Wilson replied, "Major Esposito made that point to Donavan and he ignored it."

Brie cut in by saying, "Thank you both. I'm sure we'll be comfortable tonight."

Wilson stated, "Donavan, you didn't ask about a way of getting off this planet?"

"When I come back with Amie, I'll ask Moore what his idea is."

"Moore, the over-sized Borven? Why ask him?"

"Simply because he hinted there would be an easy way?"

* * *

In the morning after breakfast, Ryan and Harlan took Donavan to see the municipal office to show him maps of the area. At the same time, Shue and Julia took Brie, Choi, and Wilson to the children's hospital. Shue introduced the three of them to Doctor Bonnie Imbue who considerately walked them through the maternity ward. During the tour, Wilson commented to Doctor Imbue, "It would be nice to have a woman doctor."

"Male and female doctors are available for medical care. Patient choice is important. It's a tradition within the Bec society."

Choi asked, "What about the delivery room? Will our size be a problem?"

Doctor Imbue smiled reassuringly, "Before any of you are due, we'll have larger faculties ready. Once you get situated in Old Town, I'd like to schedule each of you for regular exams. I'll show you the rooftop patio, it's one of the favorite places where nursing mothers like to relax."

When they got up to the roof, there were two mothers with their newborns. Brie and Choi talked to them as Wilson spent her time looking out at the city.

Shue spoke caringly, "Victoria, Vulzar may not be home to you now. If you give it a chance, you'll find it could be."

"Julia, don't take me wrong, you're nice and the valley is beautiful. It's just I want the freedom of being able to leave."

"Is it being pregnant that bothers you?"

"I apologize, Julia, your people have been great in welcoming us."

"In our culture, children are counted as a gift of life. Having them is a marvelous thing our female bodies are able to do. Creating life, nurturing the embryo, then teaching the child the values we hold most dear.

"Once you've settled into Old Town, we'll organize social events like playing cards and hunting or fishing outings. Bec women are fond of having socials without their husbands. It gives us time to talk."

Brie, Kim, and Julia walked over with Brie reminding, "We should be going back for lunch. After that, we're due to head back to the canyon."

Julia informed them, "Harlan's had two of our river boats brought up to take you back."

"No canoes?"

"Kim, we'll be towing four of them behind each boat to leave in the cavern. They'll be left for you to use to bring your people downriver to Old Town. Now, like Brie said, we'd better get back for lunch."

After lunch, they loaded up in the Alterv trailers and went to the river. Harlan and Donavan were in the first river boat. Julia had Brie, Victoria, and Choi in the second one. The boat engines ran quietly as they pushed the boats up stream with power to spare.

When they got under the mountain and inside the cavern, Donavan and Harlan began to tie the canoes to the hitches hanging off the east wall. Before they were finished, Esposito, Sparling, and Bonnel were there to help.

Sparling explained, "The Lawson sisters are on the wall and saw you coming up stream."

After Donavan introduced Harlan and Julia, he told the men, "Tomorrow at 0700, I want everyone assembled."

"When are you going to brief the senior officers?"

"Right after chow tonight."

After they said goodbye to Harlan and Julia, and the others had left the cavern, Donavan sat with Brie to ask, "Yesterday and today you've been quiet, what is it?"

She smiled a smile that was easy to respond to. "Just letting the idea of staying here sink in. I know the reality is we don't have any place to go."

"Hopefully, you realize how much I love you."

"Kiss me then. We'd better go and start answering questions."

When Donavan and Brie exited the cavern, they met Wood. Immediately, Brie told him about the small hospital in Old Town, then about the larger one in Candale.

As they were talking, Sparling walked up to them and waited patiently. Donavan asked, "What is it?"

"Everyone wants to hear what the Bec had to say."

"What? They can't wait until later?"

"Sir, they're anxious to know. Well, I'm anxious to know."

"Okay, get them assembled by that dead tree lying across the river. And get the Longbow sisters down here. Tell Amie I want to talk with her afterwards."

After Sparling left, Wood told Donavan, "From what Brie says, the valley sounds promising and the Bec come across as being accommodating."

"They are a lot more advanced than I thought they'd be."

"That surprises you?"

"I had the preconceived notion they'd be stone cutters and farmers, but there's a lot more to them."

"Okay, son, what's bothering you?"

Brie answered before Donavan could. "He's not sure how I feel about us living on this planet."

"Well. I'm not."

Wood interjected, "Brie, we'll all make do for the time being. Right, Jason?"

"I wish I could offer Brie a normal life."

She gave him a smile as she spoke. "Let's go explain things."

When the three of them got to the dead tree, everyone was gathered around with Ganter and Mosley standing off to one side.

Donavan thought about the best way to say all the things that needed to be said. First, he asked Wilson to give her impressions of the Bec people and the city of Candale. As Donavan expected, Wilson gave a sterilized commentary.

Next, he had Choi give her overall opinions of the people, the valley, and Old Town. Choi's voice and her hand gestures gave a totally optimistic outlook of moving into the valley and Old Town.

When it was Brie's turn, she spoke honestly from her heart. "The medical facilities at Candale have made me feel secure that Wood will have everything he will need. Even the clinic in Old Town was impressive."

When Donavan spoke, he was optimistic. "Your futures are important to me. We can live in Old Town comfortably while considering ways of getting those who want to leave off this planet. Tonight, think of the questions you have. In the morning, approach myself, Choi, Wilson, or Brie. We'll do our best to answer you. A list will be posted of the names of the first group to relocate. At noon in groups of twenty-four, we'll begin relocating to Old Town. Amie Longbow and Wood, I want to see you. The rest of you are dismissed."

When they stood with Donavan, he explained. "Wood, I want you and Brie to talk with Farmane and Valgoski. I want them in the first group to get the clinic in Old Town cleaned up."

"What about Defoy?"

"He'll be among the last I want there. The Bec have a good relationship with the Borven baboons and I won't have Defoy's attitude compromising our chances of having a working relationship. Amie, that's where you'll be an important part. Your little friend, Trasher, has spoken well of you to Moore, the patriarch of the Borven. His mate, Tabla, wants to meet you. Amie, we'll need their help, so work your magic with her."

"Magic?"

"You got Trasher to trust you. We need Tabla to trust us as well."

"May I bring Pam and our spotters?"

"If you need them to make this happen, bring them."

* * *

After Donavan had dismissed the troops, Luangwa spoke privately with Wilson. "Victoria, ever since you told me you were pregnant, you've been different. We haven't talked about us and our future."

"It was a careless night, Vince. I'll deal with it."

"We'll deal with the baby together."

Luangwa was getting frustrated but kept his temper in check, "Think of the horrors we saw in the Tweeb lab, then think of the natural wonders your body is performing in growing our baby inside of you. If our baby has your looks and intelligence, then we'll be blessed."

"Vince, you're romanticizing. Life doesn't always have happy endings."

"After what we've seen on this planet and being stuck here, you're telling me that. I think it's wonderful you're pregnant and we're going to be parents."

"You sound like you honestly believe that."

"I do and I know you'll be a great mother and wife, if you'll have mc?"

Wilson thought about Luangwa's tone of commitment, then said, "What's the unit been doing while I was down river?"

* * *

After the troops were dismissed, Choi with Trooper Steve Colsrud found a secluded place under a tree by the river to talk. He grinned at her. "I'm glad you're happy. Are thing as good as you made them sound?"

"Steve, are you happy, honestly happy?"

Colsrud took Choi's hand. "How do I prove it to you?"

"By staying with me."

"Of course, I'll stay with you. You're carrying our child."

# Chapter 14 Old Town

First thing in the morning, Donavan and Brie, Choi and Wilson answered the troopers' questions. After that, Donavan and his selected people left in the canoes for Old Town. When they reached there, they beached the canoes and made their way up the trail for a mile. Donavan had Wood with Farmane and Valgoski start cleaning up the clinic while most of the others started cleaning houses.

Taunt with Joan and Jill Lawson set up observation posts at three points. Donavan asked them to keep watch for an oversized Borven named Moore with his mate, Tabla.

* * *

By the end of the first week, all of the members of the Black Sentry had relocated to Old Town. Wood with Farmane, Valgoski, and Defoy prepared the clinic for service.

The following day, Ryan and Shue, the leaders of Candale, paid Donavan and Brie a visit. Donavan had the troopers stand to as he introduced Ryan and Shue. After the formal introduction, Shue asked to meet First Lt. Longbow. Donavan arranged for them to meet in the town hall cafeteria.

When they were seated, Shue asked Amie, "Are you ready to meet Moore and Tabla?"

"Yes, but I don't fully understand why she would want to meet me?"

"If you're ready, you can ask her."

"When?"

"Now. Tabla and Moore have been watching you all week long."

Donavan interjected, "None of our people have noticed them."

"Borvens blend in while watching before being seen. If you want to see them, look for their eyes. Now, if you're ready?"

"We're ready."

"Just Amie and I. It's a matter of showing trust. We'll take no weapons."

Amie laid her rifle, sidearms, and her ankle knives on the table, then stated, "I'm ready."

"Shue, at least tell me where you're taking Amie?"

"For a long walk in the forest. Tabla will pick the place."

"Let her take someone with her."

"I'll be fine, Donavan."

"Take your sister."

Amie looked at Shue.

"Bring your sister, but no weapons."

Amie called her sister Pam on her comm and explained they would be going to meet the Borvens, Tabla, and Moore. Then she told her, "No weapons, sis. Not even your ankle knives."

"Al's saying no way."

"Then Shue and I will be going without you and without any weapons."

"Give me five minutes to get there."

After Amie left with Pam and Shue, Ryan took Donavan outside and asked him to call Taunt to meet them at the edge of town. When the three of them were together, Ryan asked Taunt, "What do you see when you look out there?"

The Master Sgt. looked toward the forest questioningly before answering, "Trees. Big tall trees."

"What else?"

Taunt glanced at Ryan, then looked out between the trees, "Shrubs, grass, and shorter trees. What am I supposed to be looking for?"

"Daylight."

"Yeah. I can see it?"

Ryan pointed as he talked, "There between the trees—daylight. Then a thicket of trees and to the right—daylight."

"Okay?"

"Focus on the thicket of trees and over the shortest one. What do you see?"

"Daylight, what's the point?"

"Now keep your eyes on a spot about eight inches down from the daylight."

Taunt watched not knowing what he was supposed to be looking for. After about two minutes, he spoke hesitantly. "There's something shining—two of them? It's like eyes watching us."

Ryan grinned. "The eyes of a Borven looking back at you."

"They weren't there a minute ago."

"He knew you were looking and kept his eyes shut to avoid being seen. Now wave to him so he knows you've spotted him."

Taunt and Donavan both waved in the direction of the eyes. Then a Borven walked out from between the trees and straight to them. When he got to them, Donavan started to make the introductions.

The Borven spoke before Donavan could finish. "You're Donavan, the leader. You're the one the females call Taunt-Toe. Ryan, you gave away my position."

"Sorry, Monty. I was teaching them how to spot Borvens."

Monty spoke to Taunt, "Your people respect you—especially the females. You leave your weapons and come with me and I'll educate you in our ways."

"Now?"

"Do you want to learn or not?"

Taunt handed his weapons to Donavan and said, "School's about to begin. See you when I get back."

Donavan asked Monty, "When will you bring Taunt-Toe back?"

"Tomorrow afternoon, the same as the Longbow ladies."

"Hold on, Monty. No one said anything about Amie and Pam staying out all night."

"They will learn our ways. One day a week, they shall be taught our ways the same as I shall teach Taunt-Toe. Each week, they can teach others what they've learned."

"Why not take more than Taunt-Toe with you?"

"One other. Gwen Hoi."

"Why Gwen?" Taunt asked.

"As you did not see me, you do not see Gwen Hoi. You'll be

taught to see a tree's aura as a reflection of its soul. Then you'll see the soul of Gwen Hoi."

Taunt was intrigued. "How are you going to teach me to see one's soul?"

"Have you ever looked at a tree then looked slightly to the right or left and for a second you see a ghostly form of the tree?"

"It's just the image fading before the eyes refocus."

"That image is the aura of the tree's soul. Everything and all things have a soul. Even us who had their natural biology tampered with by the Tweebs. Now call Gwen Hoi and we shall leave to begin your lessons."

When Hoi arrived, she and Taunt left with Monty. Donavan asked Ryan, "Why didn't you tell me about this?"

"It wasn't my call. When the Borvens decide to befriend someone, it's their call. Donavan, only a few of us Bec ever have been educated in the Borven's ways. Accept it as the highest compliment your people can be given."

"Fine. Where's Moore?"

"He'll be around tomorrow to see you."

* * *

Amie and Pam walked with Shue for five miles before coming to a small lake where they sat down to rest and survey the area. Pam asked, "Shue, are you sure Tabla really wants to meet Amie? Or are we being tested somehow?"

"She's had her eyes on us since we left Old Town. Now focus between the trees and tell me what you see."

After a few minutes, Amie pointed. "The tree in that thicket isn't a tree. It's shorter and its branches don't move in the breeze like the rest."

Shue shouted in the direction Amie had pointed, "Tabla, you've been spotted. You might as well come over and introduce yourself."

Tabla walked slowly toward them saying, "It took you long enough. Pam, at one point on the trail, you turned and looked right at me when I rustled some branches. I was sure you would have seen me."

"Tabla, I thought it was my imagination when I saw two branches move in opposite directions."

"Trasher spoke very highly of each of you. Amie, he considers you an honorary member of their Trirob pack. Shue, you might as well head back. I'll begin teaching the girls what they need to know."

After Shue left, Tabla began by teaching them about the vegetation: what could be eaten, how to prepare it, and which leaves and roots could be used for medicinal purposes.

Amie stated to Tabla, "We should have brought Wood and Defoy, our med. techs. They're the ones who should be learning this more than us."

"Two at a time, fewer questions, more learning, and med. techs. aren't always there when you need them. Defoy wouldn't accept anything I'd say. He wouldn't listen to Yaugur when Terry Horton needed his help."

"You know about that?"

"Word travels fast between the species living on both sides of the mountain. Defoy has a superiority complex, not an easy attitude to work with."

* * *

In the morning, Moore was sitting on a log at the treeline outside of Old Town. Wood notified Donavan of his presence and the two men walked out to speak with him.

When they stood in front of Moore, he stated, "I don't blend in so well while sitting out in the open like this. I figured it would make it easier for you to see me."

Wood smiled and responded with a respectful tone. "Moore, it's some kind of contradiction of logic how a guy your size can disappear into the forest."

"How many contradictions are there in your medical practice? At times you have to re-break a bone to set it properly."

Donavan interjected. "Moore, the first time we met, you gave me the impression you had a way for our people to get off this planet."

"It does seem evident that some of your people are less than content in their current circumstances."

"There's always the probability of the Tweebs hunting us down for revenge," Wood stated.

"The Tweebs know better than to cross the mountains."

"So what's stopping them?"

"The Bec were pacifists when they stopped working as stone masons for the Tweebs. A large number of ships had landed and the Bec befriended them. So in return, the people on one of the ships built a shield over this side of the mountain. Any ship flying higher than the mountains will experience electronic failure. After our friends left, the Tweebs attacked. Their ships and troopers were destroyed. They tried it one more time with the same results. As long as each group stays on their own side of the mountain, it's like a non-aggression pact exists."

Wood asked, "Who were your friends?"

"The descendants of Matagam Pagwa."

"I've heard of him and his descendants."

Donavan questioned. "So what are you suggesting, Moore?"

"The Tweebs would like to take some of us to experiment on. A few of us could cross into the canyon as bait."

"You could be killed. We can't ask you to sacrifice any of your kind."

"Donavan, if the bats help and with your people, theoretically you could take one or two Tweeb ships."

Wood stared at Moore and then at Donavan. "With ten thousand bats using their echo location to disrupt their systems, plus flying around blinding their visuals, it could work."

"Who's going to talk the bats into it?"

Moore stated, "Ryan has a good rapport with the leaders of the bats."

"I'll think about it."

"What's to think about?"

"Fred, hundreds of bats could die as well as some Borvens. Moore, when will my people be back?"

Moore stood up and looked down at Donavan. "Have it your way. They'll be back later this afternoon." With that, Moore walked away.

Wood asked Donavan, "Do you have a better idea?"

"Call Esposito, Bonnel, Sparling, and Wilson to join us in the town hall meeting room. We'll talk about Moore's idea."

* * *

When the six of them were together, Donavan explained the idea.

Esposito questioned. "We use a couple of Borvens as bait?"

Wilson commented, "You sound uncertain."

"Victoria, there's the moral factor to consider."

"After what we saw and did at the Citadel, now you're hung up on morals?"

"I want off this planet as much as you and Luangwa. Watching them risk their lives—yeah, there's a moral issue."

Sparling intervened. "We can protect them. Have the snipers camouflaged on the canyon walls with the rest of us hiding in the caves. We'd have them covered."

"And who's covering Taunt-Toe's snipers?" Wood questioned.

"Now it becomes a moral issue."

"Esposito, it's the moral issue of having the snipers covered. We've already lost too many of our people on this planet."

Sparling stated, "Donavan, you haven't said much."

"I'm thinking how to cover Taunt-Toes snipers."

Taunt called Donavan on the comm link. "Donavan, the Longbow sisters, Gwen and I have returned. We should sit down to talk."

"You have Brie with you? I'll be along as soon as I can."

Esposito stated, "The moral issue is friendship. The Borvens are teaching our people while we're debating using them as bait."

Donavan responded, "I'll think about this tonight. By morning, I'll have made my decision. I want to hear what the girls and Taunt-Toe have learned."

When Donavan got to the town hall cafeteria, he sat beside Brie. Taunt had Amie and Pam detail what they learned about the local vegetation as food and for medicinal purposes. Then Taunt had Hoi explain how to see a tree's aura as a reflection of its soul.

When she finished, Taunt explained, "This week each of

us are to teach two people what we've learned. Then they'll each teach two people. Next week, Gwen and I go back into the forests with Monty while Amie and Pam go with Tabla. Donavan, the Borvens are towers of knowledge. Wood, Monty says next week you come with us. What we've learned of the medicinal uses of the vegetation so far is only the beginning."

Donavan waited for Taunt to stop talking before he stated, "We may have more pressing issues."

"Like what?"

Donavan explained Moore's idea of using some Borvens as bait with Spalding's plan to use the snipers on the wall and the rest of the troops in the caves.

Brie stated very firmly. "Two things. First, if anyone is being used as bait, it will be us. Second thing, we wait until the Elros calving is done and they've moved out of the canyon. Have I made myself clear?"

Hoi stated, "I'm with Brie."

Amie and Pam agreed with Gwen. Then Taunt piped up. "Brie makes sense. You have to agree. It's some of our people who want to get off this planet and we're the ones that should be taking the risks."

Wood grinned. "Some of our people? You've decided to stay?"

"Where have we got to go? Anyway, Gwen wants to stay."

Donavan glanced at Gwen. "I didn't see that happening."

Gwen spoke softly, "Monty helped Grant see the obvious."

Donavan stated questioningly, "I haven't heard anyone call Taunt-Toe, Grant—not that I can remember."

Amie smiled, "Mrs. Gwen Taunt, sounds good."

Pam asked, "Mrs. Gwen Taunt-Toe sounds better. Gwen, are we invited to the wedding?"

"Grant and I would like the whole complement to be there. Right, Grant?"

Taunt looked at Wood, "Fred, I expect you to stand up with me."

"Don't you mean hold you up?"

"Donavan, as the commanding officer, would you do the honors?"

"It'll be my privilege."

Gwen looked at the Longbow sisters and Brie. "I'd like all the first lieutenant snipers as my maids of honor, just in case someone gets cold feet."

Brie cracked, "That'll make some wedding picture, the eight of us with our rifles slung over our shoulders."

Wood asked, "Gwen, who's going to be standing with you?"

"If you girls don't mind, I'm planning on asking Terry."

Amie nodded affirmatively, "Good choice. So when's the big day?"

"Grant and I want to have it in the canyon before the Elros leave. We want them there as our guests."

"Terry Horton will appreciate having Yaugur there. He saved her life."

"That's the way Grant and I see it."

Wood stated, "It's going take time for me to get used to hearing Gwen calling Taunt-Toe, Grant."

"Only Gwen, everyone else will still call me Taunt or Taunt-Toe. Donavan?"

"I'll pass the order, Grant. Now let's have dinner. In the morning, I'll talk things over with Wilson, Esposito and Sparling."

# Chapter 15 Getting Organized

In the morning, Donavan met with Wilson, Esposito, and Sparling to explain Brie's concerns for the Borvens and the Elros. When Donavan finished, he handed out the assignments. "Wilson, find out when the Elros' calving will be finished and when they'll be leaving. Sparling, take a poll and see who plays musical instruments. Esposito, you'll be in charge while I'm in Candale."

Esposito asked, "Why are you going to Candale?"

"To see what instruments Ryan and Shue can provide and invite them to the wedding."

"What wedding? Who's getting married?"

"Taunt-Toe and Gwen Hoi."

Sparling asked, "Why do we need to know when the Elros are leaving?"

"The three of you listen up. Taunt-Toe and Gwen want the wedding and party in the canyon so Yaugur, Pippa, Mosey, and Ganter will be there. We'll use the whole thing to our advantage. The wedding will be right out in the open. That night we'll have bonfires with music and dancing."

"Do you want the Tweebs to crash the wedding?"

"Sparling, we know the Tweebs have spotter ships looking for us. They'll radio our position and it will take the Tweebs a day or two to put together a strike force to get to the canyon. We'll set it up for after the majority of the Elros have left."

"What about the Borvens? Are they in on the plan?"

"No. We'll be the bait. Any more questions?"

"Have you told Moore?"

"No, Wilson, I haven't."

"You should, you know."

"Any more questions other than from Wilson? Okay, then get to it."

After the meeting, Esposito and Sparling headed off to find

Taunt and Gwen to congratulate them. Donavan met up with Brie, and together with Wilson and Luangwa, the four of them walked to the river.

Wilson and Luangwa took a canoe and paddled to the cavern in the mountain. Then they walked through the canyon to find Ganter and Mosey.

Donavan and Brie paddled across the river with the intention of walking to Candale to talk with Ryan and Shue. When they beached the canoe, Moore walked out from between the trees.

Donavan asked, "What are you doing here?"

"When you declined my offer of help, I knew your next step would be to talk with Ryan and Shue. So what's your plan?"

"We'll explain it when we get to Candale."

"Planning on walking there, are you?"

"Unless you're offering to carry us."

"I would politely offer to carry the lady. Your feet will have to carry your own weight."

"Thank you for your generous offer, Moore."

"You are most welcome, Miss Brie. The reality is I notified Ryan and Shue and they shall be arriving shortly. Now what shall we talk about? Maybe you could tell me why your man Donavan declined my help?"

"Moore, we can't ask your Borvens to risk their lives. If some of our people want off of Vulzar, then it's our responsibility to help them—not yours."

"Donavan didn't refuse the help of the Elros, the Trirobs, or the Orebs. Why refuse the help of my Borvens?"

Brie continued to explain. "The Trirobs and Orebs suffered losses when we attacked the Citadel. We don't want any of your Borvens to suffer the same fate."

"Very considerate, Miss Brie, but has Donavan considered how many of his people will suffer the same fate without our help?"

Donavan interrupted, "Moore, we're here simply to ask Ryan and Shue if they have any musical instruments they'd be willing to loan us."

"Sounds like a party. Are we invited?"

"Master Sergeant Taunt and Capt. Gwen Hoi are getting

married, so we'd like to have a party for them. Of course, you and Tabla are invited. We're inviting Ryan and Shue as well."

"Most gracious of you, Miss Brie. Tabla and I would be honored to attend."

"Moore, the wedding and the party is going to be held in the canyon so Ganter, Mosley, Yaugur, and Pippa can attend. Are you sure you'd be comfortable being there?"

"Donavan, Tabla would insist on our attending."

"I thought you said Ryan and Shue were on the way?"

"I lied so we'd have time to talk. Shall we walk on to give Ryan and Shue the happy news?"

Brie started laughing and Donavan gave Moore a questioning look.

When the trio got to Candale, they explained things to Ryan and Shue.

Ryan stated, "You'll need more than canoes to move your people. I'll let Harlan and Julia know to bring up some river boats."

"Brie, when's the big day?"

"We're not sure, Julia. Wilson's gone to check with Ganter and Mosey to find out when the calving will be completed."

Julia took a minute to consider. "Based on previous years, I'd guess seven to ten days before they'd be leaving."

* * *

When Victoria Wilson and Vince Luangwa got to the calving canyon, they were met by Ganter. With great concern, the big Elros explained, "It's Pippa. She's having problems delivering her calf. Mosey and Yaugur are with her."

Wilson immediately responded. "Vince, tell Wood to bring Farmane and Valgoski. And make it fast, Vince."

Luangwa went through the cavern to the west side of the mountain and called Wood on his comm link to explained things. When he got back in the canyon, Ganter was waiting for him and took him to where Wilson was with Mosey and Pippa. Yaugur and Ganter stood back while Luangwa slowly walked close enough to mildly ask, "Is there anything I can do?"

"Where's Wood?"

"He's contacting Donavan to let him know there's a problem."

"The calf is in the wrong position and I'm guessing Wood will have to try and move the calf."

As they all waited for Wood, Pippa was resting on her side grunting and moaning. Mosey and Wilson tried to comfort and reassure her that Wood was on his way and would know what to do.

When Wood arrived with Farmane and Valgoski, they talked with Mosey and Wilson. Then Farmane spoke calmly to Pippa, explaining that Wood was going to examine the unborn calf's position by sliding his arm inside the birth canal.

Wood examined Pippa's unborn calf carefully. When the exam was completed, he explained to Pippa that one of the calf's legs was bent the wrong way. He and Laura would try to carefully reposition it using a small cord around the hoof.

"Pippa, it is important that you remain calm and relaxed. We brought sedatives that will help you and relieve the pain."

Mosey listened carefully and asked Zaivour, "Will Pippa be able to have another calf after this?"

"Wood says he's done this with horses. Laura and I have done a few procedures on Elros in the past. It is the least invasive way to give Pippa's calf a chance to be born healthy."

# Chapter 16 The Big Ruse Owl

When Donavan and Wood returned to Old Town, they were met by Esposito who asked, "What was the emergency?"

Donavan left it to Wood to explain that Pippa needed assistance birthing her calf. "I left Valgoski and Farmane to make sure there aren't any unforeseen complications."

"I'd better find Taunt-Toe and Gwen and let them know their wedding is on hold for a while."

"Hang on, Wood. How long is awhile?"

"Two weeks at most. I want to make sure Pippa and her new calf have no complications. "What do Wilson and Luangwa say about all this?"

Donavan told Wood to go find Taunt-Toe and Gwen and leave him and Esposito to discuss things. After Wood left, Donavan spoke plainly. "We either wait until Wood says Pippa's well enough to travel or we come up with a new plan."

"We could always go back to the Citadel and wait for the Tweebs. They'll most likely want to rebuild the place."

"On foot with the Mongrels roaming around, we'd end up as dog food. Come up with a better idea and we'll come back and talk about it."

After Esposito left to find Wilson and Luangwa, Donavan sat alone thinking of Pippa's birth experience and hoping Wilson's and Choi's pregnancies would be easier.

Sparling arrived and said, "That big Ruse Owl, Gus, is outside sitting in the middle of the road and wants to see you."

"Did he say why?"

"He said if you're serious about getting some of your people off this planet to get your pompous ass outside to talk. He has a way with words."

"Gus talks like that and he calls me pompous. We'd better hear what that overgrown nightingale has to say."

"Donavan, it would be nice to have the option of staying or going."

"And where would you go, Sparling?"

"Definitely not to Yenna. Just having the option of leaving for somewhere would make me feel less stranded."

When Donavan and Sparling got outside, Gus complimented them, "That was nice what your people did for Pippa."

"I'm glad you approve. Now what did you want to see me about?"

"You turned down Moore's suggestion for getting off this planet. Are you ready to listen to me now?"

"Let's hear what you have to say."

"About time, Donavan. The Tweeb's scout ship has seen the rubble left of the Citadel. No doubt they've reported it back to their naval base on the north coast. It'll take that ship two days to return to base. Then three more days for the Tweeb command to decide what they'll do. Then three more days to send troops from their army base on their home world."

"What do you mean, home world?" Donavan said.

"You do realize Vulzar is only a dwarf planet?"

"Why would size matter?"

"Size and distance does matter to the Tweebs. Vulzar is not their home world. It's a planet they colonized to carry out their research. Whoever sent you, they sent you blind. If your people were doing what was done at the Citadel, I doubt they'd do it in the open. People demonstrate against research on moral and ethical grounds. On the Tweeb home world, Vulzar is known as a wilderness planet where people go to hunt big game animals."

"Ganter said we were misled, but he didn't tell us that," Donavan said.

"Maybe, he knew you wouldn't believe him. Think about it, Donavan, are there any Tweeb big cities, aircraft constantly going overhead or anything else you'd expect on a home-world planet? The answer is no. Now that I've educated you, I'll continue. It will be two more days before they start looking for your people. So we have about ten days to take action. Are you with me so far, Donavan?"

"You mind telling us why you think it'll take the Tweebs so long to react?"

"Your people aren't the first aliens to take arms against the Tweebs. They're cowards and like to devise a way of having an advantage before they commit their troops."

"If we aren't the first, then why was the Citadel still standing?"

"Simply because you were the first to be wise enough to listen to Ganter and accept the help of his friends."

Sparling asked Gus, "Why would you say the Tweebs are cowards?"

"Think about that wooden fort and that deserted village you came across. The fort was empty because of the Orebs' and the Trirobs' attacks. With the Tweeb's weapons, it should have been easily defended. That deserted village was one of the Tweeb's outposts where they billeted off-world hunters."

Donavan asked mildly, "So what's your plan, Gus?"

"I'll send word to my cousins, the Orebs. Then I'll talk with Moore while you talk with Ryan and Shue. Ganter and Mosey will supply your people with Elros to carry them. They like and respect you and your people. Even more now after what you've done for Pippa and her calf. We will all rendezvous behind the mountain near the quarry to make a plan to commandeer whatever ships come."

"Gus, I'll think about what you've said and discuss it with my senior officers."

"Donavan, your only other option is to wait until Pippa's well enough to make the trek, and by then, it will be too late. The Tweebs will have troops and construction people at the Citadel. Too many for you to challenge."

"Gus makes a good point. Maybe we can't afford to wait."

"And maybe the Bec, the Borven, and the Orebs will say no."

"You won't know until you ask Ryan."

"All right, Gus, I'll ask."

"And I'll ask Moore and George and have an answer tomorrow. And you?"

"Tomorrow at noon."

With Donavan's response, Gus spread his broad wings and flew off.

Sparling noted, "If Ryan says yes, we'll have allies and a good shot at getting a ship."

"And how many shots will be fired and how many of our allies will fall?"

"You are going to talk with Ryan?"

"I said I would."

When Donavan and Sparling got across the river, Ryan was waiting for them. "Gus said you'd be coming."

"I suppose he said why?"

"He did. Donavan, it's been years since my people have gone head-to-head with the Tweeb. We've had skirmishes with them but nothing like what Gus is suggesting," Ryan said.

"Ryan, I said I'd ask and I understand. Your people have taken enough risk letting us stay in the valley and I'm grateful. We'll get a ship on our own."

"Odds are the Tweebs suspect your people are on our side of the mountain. Yet they haven't done anything about it. In the past, due to our lack of vertical height, they underestimated us. I understand some of your people want to stay while some are set on leaving. Donavan, this could work to our advantage. If you're successful in getting a ship, the Tweebs might think you've all left."

Sparling questioned, "Ryan, are you hinting you might be helping?"

"If things are done properly."

"Meaning?"

"No Tweeb survivors. It has to be done in a way the Tweebs think your people did it. That way when the ship leaves, they'll think their problem has left with it."

"It sounds as if you have a plan."

"A partial. Remember the camouflaged pits in front of the Citadel, the ones dug to snare Elros. I'll have some of my people in them with thermal blankets. You'll need to create a diversion to draw the main group of Tweebs away from their ships. That will leave fewer for you to contend with."

Sparling recommended, "Thirteen-mile Camp. We could have a unit there to draw the Tweebs out of the way."

"Ryan, how many ships and troops do you think they'll send?"

"Two ships. A smaller command ship and a troop carrier with about one hundred Tweebs.

Donavan asked, "Next question is where do you think they'll land?"

"After they do a fly over, they'll land close to the remains of the Citadel on the road leading to the quarry. It's the best place. No Elros pits to fall into and no cover for your people to hide behind."

"Ryan, it's going to put your people and the Elros at risk."

"Donavan, do you want to get your people off this planet or not?

After a long pause, Ryan repeated the question "Do you want to get your people off this planet?"

"Of course I do. I want to put this place behind me so Brie and I can try having a life."

"Now you're making sense. You'll leave at zero-eight-hundred tomorrow morning."

"I'll have to talk with Ganter before setting a time."

"He'll agree. So have your people ready to go."

"Where do we meet you?"

"My people will use our Altervs and meet you behind the mountain back of the quarry in three days."

Sparling asked, "Why don't we just come with you?"

"Sparling, Altervs leave tracks and things need to be seen as your people did it all on their own. Now I have things to arrange. Donavan, I suggest you leave. Do the same with Ganter."

After Ryan walked away, Sparling began to state, "He's one bossy little—"

"Little opinionated man. Sparling, as far as Sara Taku goes, remember she's of the same blood as the Longbow sisters." Donavan said.

"Meaning what, sir?"

"If you're in love her, ask her. And if she's in love with you, she'll tell you."

Donavan used his comm to inform Esposito where he and Sparling were going. Then they headed up river into the cavern where Ganter was waiting for them. He pointed to the ridge as he stated, "Abriil, Gus' mate. So what have you decided?"

"Ganter, do you really want to risk some of your herd?"

"You wouldn't make it to the Citadel otherwise, not all of you anyway with the Mongrels around. We're not fast but we're quicker in the long haul. How many people are we talking about?"

"I haven't decided yet. How's Pippa?"

"A question better answered by Miss Valgoski and Miss Farmane. Shall we?"

When they got to Pippa and her calf, Donavan smiled at Brie, "How's Pippa doing?"

"Laura has her sedated and the calf is doing well. Jason, what's on your mind?"

"Tomorrow morning, some of us are going back to the Citadel in hopes of commandeering a way off this planet."

"Some?"

"Maybe two units. I'll discuss it with Esposito tonight."

"And when did you decide all this?"

Donavan detailed what Gus and Ryan had told him. "I'll leave Laura and Zaivour here to take care of Pippa with a unit to protect them."

"Jason, I want to be at that meeting with Esposito and I strongly suggest Wilson be there."

Mosey stated, "Donavan, you don't to need to leave people here. You'll need them."

"Those who want off Vulzar will be coming. I'll ask for volunteers from the others. Mosey, I'm not prepared to risk everyone on this. When Pippa is healed, Laura and Zaivour can go back to Old Town to be safe with whoever is left there."

"If we're leaving in the morning, we'd better get back to find out who's coming with us."

Donavan told Ganter and Mosey he'd be back at 2000. They asked how many Elros he thought he would need and they agreed to have them ready.

When Donavan, Brie and Sparling got back to Old Town, Donavan had Sparling get the troopers together. Then he announced, "Everyone who wants to leave this planet take five paces forward. The rest of you take five paces back." Then Donavan looked at Esposito and Sparling, "That includes you two. I need to know where you stand."

After Esposito and Sparling took their chosen stances, Donavan continued. "Those of you who wish to leave, pack your kits and get some rest. We'll be heading out at zero-seven-hundred to meet with Ganter's Elros. You're headed back to the Citadel to wait for the Tweebs and commandeer their ships. As for the rest of you, I need volunteers to come with us. Please step to the right. The remaining group will be split in two. Half staying here and the other half will be posted in the canyon to protect Laura and Zaivour. Now get to it."

Wood and Taunt walked up to Donavan. Wood said, "With that tone of voice, don't ever run for politics, son. Now what's got you so agitated?"

After Donavan told them what Gus, the Ruse Owl, had said about Vulzar not being the Tweeb home planet, Wood stated, "Rear Admiral Flynn should be hung. So have you decided who you're taking?"

"You, Taunt, and the snipers with their spotters. Plus a handful of others."

"Detail the plan for us."

When Donavan finished, Taunt said, "Using a diversion fire at Thirteen-mile Camp would catch their attention. They'll send out a sizable force to investigate. Say eighty of them. I'll need at least twenty with me to have a fighting chance. My ladies with their spotters and three others. I'll pick the ones I want."

"We'll need to be close enough to their ships to surprise them when the Bec come out of their holes," Wood stated.

"Any ideas?"

"Foxholes with fresh Elros dung over them to disguise our heat signatures. A little Borven dung wouldn't hurt."

"You two, find those you want to take and are willing. Right now, I want to talk Brie."

# Chapter 17 Return to the Citadel

It took three days for Donavan's group riding on the Elros to reach Thirteen-mile Camp. Taunt with his snipers and their spotters along with Master Sgt. Hanyu Peng, Trooper Terry Horton, and Capt. Gwen Hoi were lowered to the ground. Donavan looked at Horton and told Roy Glenn, "Stay here and keep Horton alive."

"I'm supposed to continue on with you, sir."

"You have your orders. Sparling, did you ever ask Sara Taku what I told you to ask her?"

"No, sir."

"Sparling, you and Taku dismount. Ask Taku about her bloodline."

"Now make your defenses. Plan your tactics. Keep them alive."

Ganter wrapped his trunk around Donavan's waist and lowered him to the ground. "You go over and kiss Miss Brie and promise her you'll be back."

Mosey nudged Brie with her trunk. "Kiss him in a way he'll be sure to return."

After Brie did as Mosey told her, Donavan replied, "I should have ordered you to stay at Old Town. Don't take any chances."

"You do the same. Let Esposito and Wilson take the chances."

When Donavan got hoisted back onto Ganter, he called Wood over. "Pick nine. You'll stay here with them."

"Think about it, son."

"Make sure you pick Kim Choi and Steve Colsrud."

Then Donavan and the rest of the troop he had brought continued to the mountains on the far side of the quarry. He met up with Ryan and the Bec at the opening of a box canyon.

As Ryan looked at Donavan's troops, he asked, "So few?"

"I left twenty-seven at Thirteen-mile Camp to create the diversion. And you? How many did you bring?"

"Sixty. Now let's finalize our plans."

"There are six camouflaged pits in front of the Citadel. The twenty-seven Elros without riders can take my men to them to dig in. Your people will dig trenches one hundred yards off both sides of the road. They'll camouflage them and then the Elros will defecate on them to hide your heat signatures. It's rather crude but effective.

"Donavan, I brought enough thermal blankets for your people. The Elros dropping will certainly help. The Borven are on the far side of the river where the Orebs dropped the bodies from the Citadel. When they're given the word, they'll get into the river with rotting Tweeb corpses floating around as camouflage. I have four teams of women on the mountain a hundred miles apart to glass for the Tweeb ship. It should give everyone time to hide."

Donavan stated, "First thing in the morning, we get started."

"Tonight, everyone camps on the far side of the mountain. Ganter, that includes you and your Elros."

Over the next two days, the pits in front of the Citadel were readied. At the same time, Donavan had Esposito and Wilson and their people dig trenches on each side of the road. At night, they returned through the narrow corridor through the mountains to bivouac. They all knew once they took up their positions, hot meals and sleep would be put on hold. On the morning of the third day, the Elros took the Bec and Donavan's people to their hiding places. Then they returned to the far side of the mountains.

On the morning of the fourth day, the teams of Bec women on the mountains used their comm sets to pass the word that a *Tide Hornet* command ship and a *Granby* troop carrier had been spotted. The Bec got into the six pits. Esposito's people got into the trenches on the left of the road and Wilson got her people into the trenches on the right.

* * *

On board the *Tide Hornet*, Fleet Admiral Wavell was issuing his orders. "I want a full and thorough scan of the area around the Citadel. And tell the Captain on the Granby when I say it's time to set down, his ship will be first with his troops searching the area before my Hornet lands."

When the Tweeb ships got close to the Citadel, the Tide Hornet did two passes scanning the area. After Wavell was told of the negative results, he contacted the Granby directly. "Captain, tell your pilot to set down. Then get your men off their asses to search the area. You make sure it's safe before I land."

"Understood, sir."

An hour later, the *Granby* was on the ground with the troops offloading. The pilot of the *Tide Hornet* informed Wavell, "Sir, we've spotted what appears to be a camp thirteen miles north of the Citadel."

"Tell that idiot Captain on the ground to have his people check it out."

"Should I remain in a holding pattern while his men search that area?"

"Do the scans show any reason not to land?"

"None, sir."

"Then land this damn thing. Our guest wants to scrutinize the carnage."

As Wavell and his guest walked towards the rubble of the Citadel, the loud sounds of a fire fight could be heard closer than thirteen miles away. As they turned to look in that direction, the Bec were out of the pits. At the same time, Esposito's and Wilson's people emerged from their trenches.

Most of the Tweebs were killed by the Bec. The troops guarding the ships were neutralized by Esposito's and Wilson's people. Wilson and two others rushed into the *Tide Hornet* and shot the pilot so he couldn't radio for help or take off.

Esposito took the same actions on the Granby troop carrier. After the Tweebs had been neutralized, Wilson and Esposito stood with Donavan beside the ships wondering how things were going at Thirteen-mile Camp. He looked skyward and gave the orders, "Wilson, take your people to mount a rear action and relieve the pressure on Taunt-Toe's people. Esposito, have your people drag the Tweeb bodies out in the open for the Ruse Owls."

After Wilson had left, Ryan walked over to Donavan and Esposito. "I've sent some of my men to check on the Borven."

"Any idea how many Tweebs headed to the river?"

"At least a dozen, maybe more. You and Esposito might want to see the body of one of the dead?"

"Why?"

"He's not a Tweeb. He's wearing a uniform very similar to yours."

When they stood staring down at the body of Rear Admiral Jonathan Flynn, Donavan stated, "It would've been nice if you'd taken him alive."

Esposito snapped. "Yeah, then we could've questioned him to see who else was involved. Then killed the bastard slowly by tying his wrists and ankles to four Elros and have them stretch him slowly before ripping him apart. A true threshold study of his pain tolerance."

Donavan glanced around and asked, "Where's Defoy?"

Ryan pointed. "On the other side of what's left of the walls of the front gate. Nice paint job. 'Death comes from above in the night skies on the silent wings. Woe to those who stand the night watch. They come from underground quietly at night while you sleep, not making a sound. Woe to those who sleep with both eyes closed.' The Tweebs should've heeded the warnings."

When the three men walked between the remaining portions of the front wall, they found Defoy documenting the rubble that was pushed into piles.

Esposito demanded, "What the shit are you doing, Defoy?"

"I'm finishing what I think the Rear Admiral came to do."

"And what's that?"

"Cataloging the destruction and carnage that has taken place."

"Donavan, listen—it's quiet."

"Defoy, get out there and tend to the wounded.

Then Donavan got on his comm, "Taunt-Toe, come in, Taunt. Answer me, Master Sergeant."

"Donavan, Wood, and Taunt-Toe are busy with our casualties."

"Peng, how's Brie?"

"Hoi and Brie are helping Taunt-Toe and Wood. We could use Defoy's help."

"How many, Peng?"

"I'm needed. Get back to you when I can. Out."

"Donavan, it's Wilson. Bring every med kit you can with the Elros. Out."

Donavan looked at Defoy, "You heard her. Get all the med kits you can find and be ready to when the Elros get here."

Ryan stated, "I've passed the word and the Elros are on the way. When they get here, take Esposito and his team to help them. We'll handle things here."

After Ganter and the Elros arrived, Donavan, Esposito and his people mounted up to get to Wilson and the others. When they got close to Thirteen-mile Camp, Esposito and his people dismounted to neutralize the remaining Tweeb troops. Donavan stayed seated on Ganter while looking at the dead and wounded and scanning for Brie. Luangwa caught Donavan's attention and told him, "Taunt-Toe and the others are about three miles farther."

When Donavan got down the trail, he found Taunt-Toe bandaging up a trooper. He dismounted and asked, "How many?"

"So far twelve dead, eight wounded. Brie's with Horton two thousand yards in that direction."

"And Wood?"

Taunt pointed without answering and put his head down to continue bandaging the trooper.

Two thousand yards does not sound like a great distance but to Donavan on foot, it was miles. He stopped twice to talk with some of the wounded and the people caring for them. When he finally got to Brie, she was with Horton and Glenn.

She left them, walked over to Donavan and shook her head. "Jason, he's not going to make it. Have you seen Taunt-Toe?"

Donavan nodded slowly, then meekly asked, "Wood?"

"Somewhere."

"Gwen Hoi?"

"She's over there with Sara Taku. They're caring the best as they can for the wounded."

"Where's Phoss and Frizz?"

"I'm not sure. Call them on your comm."

"Phoss, what shape are you and Frizz in?"

"We're pissed, sir."

"And Amie and Pam?"

"More pissed than we are. What do you need, sir?"

"The four of you get on your Elros and go back to the Citadel. There's a *Tide Hornet* command ship and a *Granby* troop carrier. I want you to see if you can fly them."

"Frizz and I will wind those engines up."

"I want you to use them to get the wounded back to the canyon. Laura and Zaivour are there and I'll ask Ryan to have some of his doctor's help."

"We're on it, sir."

Next Donavan called Wilson, Esposito, Sparling, and Bonnel to pass the orders to make stretchers to load the wounded and the dead. "Have the Elros pull them back to the ships." Then he looked at Brie, "I haven't asked, how you are?"

"Pissed—just like Phoss. Sparling and Bonnel didn't answer because they can't. This wasn't worth it, Jason."

Ryan called Donavan over his comm set, "Gus and ten of his Ruse Owls are here. He wants to talk with you."

"Put him on, Ryan."

"Donavan, we'll meet you in the canyon. I hope this was worth it to your people."

"It wasn't to me, Gus. See you back at the canyon."

As the Elros pulled their stretchers to the troop carrier, the Bec loaded them on board. When Donavan and Brie got there, Amie Longbow told them, "Phoss and Frizz ran up the engines, then shut them down. Fuel gauges show both ships are at eighty five percent. They're ready to go when you say."

"Esposito, Wilson, take the wounded and dead to the calving canyon."

As the Tweeb ships lifted off, Ryan told Donavan, "I'll have doctors and nurses in the canyon to meet them. See you when you get back."

"Thanks, Ryan. I really appreciate your help."

After the Bec left on some of the Elros for the mountains behind the quarry, Donavan asked, "Nothing to say, Ganter?"

"First, we stop at the warm springs for your people to bathe. When we get back to the calving canyon, Taunt-Toe and Gwen Hoi should have their wedding after your people leave this planet. A party would be good for morale."

When Ganter's Elros returned from taking the Bec to the canyon, everyone was hoisted on Elros' backs to wait. Donavan sat on Ganter's back and watched the Ruse Owls pick up the Tweeb bodies and fly off to drop them on the far side of the river. Finally, he said, "Lieutenant Tracy Canz take the lead."

"Sir?"

"Lead our people to the warm springs for a bath. I'll be bringing up the rear. Ganter, would you mind?"

The big Elros turned to face the front walls of the Citadel so Donavan could quietly read the warnings.

Death comes from above in the night skies
on the silent wings.
Woe to those who stand the night watch.
They come from underground quietly at night
while you sleep not making a sound.
Woe to those who sleep with both eyes closed.

Mosey, with Brie on her back, walked up beside Ganter and Donavan who quietly commented in a remorseful and respectful tone, "Too many good people dead and for what?"

Brie waited a few minutes before suggesting in the same respectful tone, "Jason, we should stop at Thirteen-mile Camp to pay our respects to the eight we buried there."

By the time Donavan and Brie got to the warm springs, the others were in the water bathing and washing the dung off their uniforms. After Ganter and Mosey trekked off to the mud baths, Brie smiled and pointed to the warm spring pool. Donavan took the hint and stood up and went to wash up. When he came out of the pool, Taunt-Toe had the Black Sentry troops assembled on the grass.

Donavan stood at ease before them explaining, "You are the people who have chosen to stay on Vulzar. Sadly, some who chose to stay, like Lts. Bob Bonnel, Paul Sparling, and Roy Glenn have paid the ultimate price.

"Once I get all the after-action reports, other names will be added to that honorable list. We'll head out at zero-seven-hundred for the canyon and see where the others stand. That's all for now. You're dismissed."

# Chapter 18 Decision Time

It took three days to get back to the calving canyon. Donavan waited until the morning of the fourth day to have the troops assembled. Then he asked each member to confirm their choice to stay or to leave.

"Most of my unit will be going to Tilszum," Esposito said.

Luangwa spoke next, "Capt. Wilson and our group has decided on Tilszum as well. It's where my grandparents came from and some others have agreed it would be a safe place to start over."

Donavan quietly stated, "Tilszum's known as the dark planet run by Bald Brad Zakalar. He has quite the reputation for being ruthless."

"My family still has political ties with the Zakalars."

"You'll be on the *Tide Hornet*. I honestly hope things bode well for you."

Aime spoke up next. "Phoss, Frizz, Pam and I plan to settle on Izbax.

"Sir, if I may ask where are you going?"

Donavan looked to Brie to answer. She walked up and stood beside him. "We'll be staying here and living on the west side of the mountain."

Next to speak was Troy Gross. "Most of Able Unit is looking forward to a peaceful life in Old Town. You wouldn't mind some company, would you?"

"Donavan and I will be honored to have you as our neighbors."

Taunt spoke, "Lieutenant Wood with Farmane and Valgoski will be staying as well."

Wood added, "On Zoo Wang before Donavan's mother died, Taunt-Toe, Gwen Hoi, and I promised her we'd watch over her son and we intend to continue."

Snipers Jing Zhang and Lin Tian walked over to Taunt's

group with Tian explaining, "We'll be staying to have Brie's back."

Donavan looked at Zhang and Tian, "There are no guarantees. You might want to rethink your choice."

"It'll be nice to have a town to live in. Not always moving from one military camp or deployment to another." Tian stated.

Gross shrugged, then walked over and stood with Zhang.

After Donavan had listened to each of the group's spoke persons, he looked at Brie's sister and waited for her response.

"Where the hell do you think I'll be? Here."

# Epilogue

Over a period of years, the disbanded members of the Black Sentry began to put their new lives together.

Phoss, Frizz, Amie, and Pam Longbow spent three years on Izbax. They bought a low-class bar and pool hall called the Eight Ball Bar. It's rumored that after three years, they sold the bar and left Izbax with a group called the Salvage Crew. The legend of Matagam Pagwa descendants and the ghost ships had caught their interest.

Through a source in the Advocate's General Office, it was learned that the members of the Black Sentry who had returned to Yenna had been arrested and convicted on charges of taking part in the murders during the attack on the Tweeb Citadel. Most were sentenced to fifteen years hard labor in a military prison. Defoy had been the prosecutions only witness. For his co-operation, he was let off with a military reprimand and a letter from the Yenna Medical Licensing Board barring him from ever having a license for a private practice.

Out of the seventy-five surviving members of the Black Sentry, twenty-four of them stayed on Vulzar and lived in Old Town.

Taunt-Toe and Hoi were married late that spring before the Elros left the calving canyon.

# About the Author

Author Colin F. Carter was born in Toronto, Ontario, Canada. His early years were spent in Toronto. His curiosity took him traveling around the world. He spent time visiting Southeast Asia, the Middle East, and Europe, until finally returning home to Canada. Colin settled in the Canadian North and worked for a variety of businesses in both the Yukon Territory and the small town of Atlin in Northwestern British Columbia.

Colin had a passion for writing and shared his stories with many friends in town, always looking for feedback. During one such discussion, a suggestion was tossed out that it would be interesting to find out what happened to Matagam Pagwa, one of Colin's characters. Colin was off and writing, which led to a series of short novels beginning with *Defender Down*.

In the winter of 2023, he finished writing the final story in the series and submitted the books to Connie Taylor with Fathom Publishing. Colin was gravely ill and knew he would not be able to finish the final edits nor would he live to see the finished product. He gave all of his writings to his friends, Jerry and Susan Kuelbs, with instructions that when the books were published, proceeds after expenses were to go to Atlin Supportive Living Society.

Colin passed away on May 23, 2023, and he was laid to rest surrounded by the mountains he loved and his community of friends. The following winter, Connie and Susan began preparing the series for publication.

As Brenda Cowan, one of Colin's friends, wrote "Colin, you our friend, will be sorely missed and not soon forgotten. You were such a character in Our Book of Life."

www.ingramcontent.com/pod-product-compliance
Lightning Source LLC
Chambersburg PA
CBHW061246210726
48293CB00003B/879